Luca's Magic Embrace

Immortals of New Orleans, Book 2

Kym Grosso

Copyright © 2012 by Kym Grosso
All rights reserved. No part of this publication may be reproduced, distributed, or transmitted in any form or by any means, including photocopying, recording, or other electronic or mechanical methods, without the prior written permission of the publisher, except in the case of brief quotations embodied in critical reviews and certain other noncommercial uses permitted by copyright law.

MT Carvin Publishing, LLC
West Chester, Pennsylvania

Edited by Julie Roberts
Formatting by Polgarus Studio
Cover design by Cheeky Covers

DISCLAIMER

This book is a work of fiction. The names, characters, locations and events portrayed in this book are a work of fiction or are used fictitiously. Any similarity to actual events, locales, or real persons, living or dead, is coincidental and not intended by the author.

NOTICE

This is an adult erotic paranormal romance book with love scenes and mature situations. It is only intended for adult readers over the age of 18.

ACKNOWLEDGMENTS

I am very thankful to those who helped me create this book:

~My husband, for encouraging me to write, editing my articles and supporting me in everything I do. Also for listening to me read the love scenes out loud to him, which he thinks are the best parts of the book. Ooh la la. Keith definitely provides me with ideas on how to make them even better.

~ Tyler and Madison, for being so patient with me, while I spend time working on the book. You are the best kids ever!

~Mom & Dad, for giving me a loving family and guiding me along my way. Dad is my biggest supporter and I am so grateful. My brother Kevyn, who is the very best sibling a sister, could have.

~Julie Roberts, editor, who spent hours reading, editing and proofreading Luca's Magic Embrace. I really could not have done this without you!

~My beta readers, Sandra and Diantha, for volunteering to read novel and provide me with valuable and honest feedback.

~Carrie Spencer, CheekyCovers, who helped me to create a sexy novel cover and my new website.

Chapter One

Naked. Bound. Luca strained his wrists and ankles upward, seeking a release from the silver cuffs and chains that burned his flesh deeper with every movement. The sound of sizzling skin echoed in the room with the slightest movement. Luca lay imprisoned flat on a stone altar, his battered body racked with pain. His arms were spread to each side, the chains on his wrists wound around the hard pedestal legs. His feet were tightly bound together, effectively immobilizing him.

Where the fuck am I? Scanning his surroundings, Luca realized he was in an abandoned building, a Catholic church. He could see the Stations of the Cross painted on the faded, chipped walls. Streams of light shone through a broken, stained glass window. The church smelled of mold, urine and blood. His blood. Used surgical syringes littered the floor. A rubber band was loosely tied to his arm. Because there were no marks on his arm, he reasoned he must have healed himself. *Shit. Someone had been syphoning his blood.*

The last thing he remembered, he had been escorting the witches to their coven. An attack, a blinding silver spray flashed in his mind. Luca couldn't remember how long he'd been unconscious. *Weak, so weak.* It took everything he had to wriggle his arms. The silver burned and drained his energy as uncontrollable thirst enveloped his thoughts.

He screamed into the desolate cathedral, hoping someone would hear him. "Help me!" No answer. His eyes burned with fury, knowing it was unlikely help would come. How long had he been shackled without blood? Would his captors return to torture him? In his diminished state, he was surprised that they hadn't staked him. Why was he still alive and not dead? Crying out in agony, he was again met with silence. It was useless.

Lying on the altar in his stink and dried blood, he felt like an animal. Glancing around the dilapidated structure, he could not assess a feasible means of escape. He closed his eyes and concentrated, praying he could establish a connection with his maker, Kade. Kade would not rest knowing something had happened to him, his best friend and confidant. Luca prayed to the goddess that he could link with him soon. Feeling his life slip away like air leaking from a balloon, there wasn't much time left. If he wasn't rescued soon, he'd die.

Kade's eyes flashed open, sensing Luca's consciousness. *He's alive.*

Sydney stirred in Kade's arms and placed a kiss on his bare chest. She felt him tense beneath her; something was amiss. "Kade, what's wrong?"

"It's Luca. He's alive. I can sense him. I need to concentrate and see if we can make contact."

"Oh my God, Kade. Where is he?" she asked excitedly. Luca had been missing for over a week. Attempts to find him had been fruitless.

"Shhhh, love. Just give me a minute to focus on him. Lay still." Kade closed his eyes, letting his mind wander. Settling his thoughts on Luca, he mentally reached out across New Orleans. Since Luca had disappeared, Kade had been unable to establish contact with his progeny.

While in Philadelphia with Sydney, Ilsbeth, a local ally and powerful witch, had contacted him with the news that they'd been attacked while returning to the coven. Both Ilsbeth and newly transformed witch Samantha, had made it safely home; Luca, however, had been taken. Kade, the leader of New Orleans vampires, and his fiancée, Sydney, a police detective, had searched the area of the attack for days on end and had turned up no clues to his abduction. Immediately after the fight ensued, the coven had been set to lock down, so none of the witches could describe Luca's abductors or provide assistance in finding him. Kade had tried numerous times to reach out to Luca psychically.

Throughout time, they'd always shared a connection. But since the attack, only a silent hum remained of Luca's existence. Kade could not sense Luca's death, but neither could he sense Luca's location. It was as if he'd dropped off the face of the Earth.

Kade surmised that the lack of communication meant one of two things: either Luca was incapacitated to the point of death, perhaps silvered, or he had purposefully left the area, refusing to contact Kade. Luca had been a loyal friend since Kade had turned him at the start of the nineteenth century, so Kade knew for a fact that Luca would not take off without notice. Because of this, the former conclusion concerned him greatly. If Luca was hurt, it would be nearly impossible to find him.

As Kade meditated on Luca, a flicker of vibration resonated back to him, alerting him again to Luca's presence. It felt as if Luca was far from the Garden District but still within the city limits. *Luca, can you hear me? Where are you?*

Drifting into unconsciousness, Luca perceived the sensation that Kade was there with him. He wasn't sure if he was hallucinating or dying, but he moved his lips, trying to speak into the darkness. No matter how he strained to talk, no more words could be spoken aloud; he was too weak. His thoughts raced. *Please let this be real. Help me. An abandoned church. Mold. I can't...I can't last much longer.*

Kade swore, "Goddammit. I felt him, but he's lost to me again. He must be unconscious or badly hurt. I heard something…something about an abandoned church. And mold. But shit, that could be just about anywhere down here. The only thing is that I can feel he's within the city limits; not in our district, but he's not far." He raked his fingers through his hair in frustration. "Shit. I should've sent someone else with him to escort the witches so soon after that clusterfuck with Simone and Asgear. This could be related to them, or maybe someone's trying to get to me," he speculated.

Sydney scrambled out of bed, pulling on a pair of faded jeans and a t-shirt. "Don't blame yourself. This is not your fault. We don't know that this is related to Asgear or Simone. We'll get him back," she said determinedly. "Where could the church be? There were hundreds of abandoned buildings after Katrina. But there has been lots of cleanup. Where could there still be a church? Lower ninth ward?"

"No, he feels closer. We need to get the car and go for a drive." Kade quickly got dressed, pulling on a pair of black denim pants and a black polo shirt. He pushed his feet into his leather boots and began to pace, anxiously wanting to resume the search. "This isn't good, Sydney. If he hasn't fed, he could be dangerous. I'm just warning you in case we find him. He'll need human blood immediately. You'll have to do what I say, no questions, okay? It feels like he's almost gone…not yet dead to us, though."

Sydney wanted to comfort Kade. A lot of shit had gone down over the past few weeks; she was determined to help find Luca. Kade felt helpless not being able to locate Luca and blamed himself for not anticipating the attack. She wasn't sure how to make him feel better except by comforting him in the one way she knew how. Wrapping her arms around Kade's neck, she kissed him lightly, letting him know she was there for him. "Kade, I will do whatever you need me to do. I promise we'll find Luca. I love you."

"But Sydney..."He wasn't convinced. In the nearly two hundred years since he'd turned Luca, they'd never gone without speaking for so long. Kade felt Luca dying; they needed to work fast.

"But nothing. I mean it. I would do anything for you. No exceptions. You felt Luca. Maybe it was just a slight sense, but he's here somewhere. Now, let's go get him."

Kade zipped through the streets of the Garden District, driving feverishly towards the French Quarter. "It's getting stronger. He's not far away."

"Is he in the French Quarter?" Sydney asked.

"No, a little farther. Maybe Foubourg Marigny?" Kade guessed.

"Hmmm...along the water? Well, that would explain the odor Luca described," she replied.

"Sydney, we don't know who took him or if there will be danger where we're headed. Please. For the love of God, let me go in first. We can't take any chances." He knew Sydney had a tendency to act first and think later.

"Really? Are we doing this again? I have my guns with me. And do I need to remind you that you are the one who's weakened during the day, not me? How about this...we go in together, I stay behind you." She smiled coyly at Kade, knowing he could not refuse her during the daytime. She swore to him that she'd do what he said but that didn't mean she couldn't hold her own.

"All right. But no heroics and as promised, you do as I ask. We go in, get Luca, put him in the back of the SUV and get the hell out of there. Luca will most likely need emergency attention. Étienne, Dominique and Xavier are procuring donors to feed him when we return."

Sydney cringed at the term 'donors'. She knew there were plenty of humans out there who would willingly donate their blood in exchange for the pleasurable bite of a vampire. Given that most humans climaxed during the experience, she couldn't understand how someone would let a strange vamp bite them, regardless of the high it guaranteed. She sighed. "I promise I'll behave myself. Let me know if you sense any vampires or witches, though. I hate surprises."

Kade reached across the seat and ran the back of his hand across Sydney's cheek. He loved her so much. She was brave and beautiful. And she'd agreed to be his wife.

Sydney felt chills run throughout her body straight to her womb. God, how she loved that man. She didn't want to worry him, and after the mess with Asgear and Simone, she'd learned her lesson. Vampires were seriously dangerous creatures, and she worried about how Luca would react to the smell of a human after being injured. Luca was formidable on a good day, let alone when he was hurt.

As they approached the riverfront neighborhood, Kade slowed the car. "There!" he shouted, pointing over to a church.

Sydney noticed the heavy broken padlocks lying on the concrete sidewalk. "Looks like someone has been goin' to church. The locks have been broken," she observed.

The enormous stone building must have been beautiful in its heyday. Three large arches adorned the front of the building, giving way to large, wooden double doors. Ornately carved gargoyles perched along the top of the structure guarded its entrance, providing a gothic warning to evil ne'er-do-wells. Remnants of stained glass mosaic windows accentuated the church in broken shades of indigo and evergreen.

Kade parked the car but left it running. "Sydney, you stay behind me. Remember what I told you. It's possible that Luca hasn't eaten in days. If he's injured, he won't be himself."

"What do you mean? Luca's always just so pleasant and friendly with us humans. Warm and fuzzy comes to mind," Sydney joked sarcastically, knowing that Luca wasn't crazy about humans. She made a face.

Kade frowned. "It's more than not winning the mister congeniality contest. I expect that he'll want to see you, but not because he necessarily wants to have a chat. It's more than possible that the man hasn't eaten since he was taken. You're food. Need I explain more?" He shook his head, knowing his friend would not be in good shape. "You can follow me in and assist me if…and this is a big if, I need help. Otherwise, just stay back. I will get Luca. Please Sydney. I need you to obey me on this."

Sydney nodded. She'd been in more than a few scuffles with vampires lately and did not want to become Luca's dinner. She was as tough as they came, but she knew with certainty that Luca would not be the cool and collected vampire she knew. People were warned never to touch injured wild animals, because they might attack due to fear or pain, and you could get injured in the process of trying to help. A starved and injured Luca could be like a large and dangerous lion. And a lion tamer she was not. As much as she wanted to help, she needed to be cautious. *The road to hell is paved with good intentions and all that business.* She decided to follow Kade's directions to the letter.

Kade exited the car. The warm summer breeze blew against his face; his nostrils flared, concentrating on finding Luca inside the church. "I can smell him. Something's wrong."

Sydney placed a comforting hand on his shoulder. "Kade, he'll be okay. Luca is tough. Come on…let's go. I promise to stay back." She reached for her Sig Sauger and clicked the safety off.

With a great shove against the decrepit, weather-worn doors, Kade stumbled into the open vestibule. Rank, moldy air choked their lungs and dust danced throughout light beams, pulsating through the cracked stained glass windows. Sensing no one but Luca, Kade cautiously proceeded into the antechamber. Glancing back at Sydney, he held up his hand to her, reminding her to stay behind. She nodded in agreement as Kade entered the church.

With preternatural velocity, Kade rushed to the stone altar and hissed at the sight of Luca chained to the slab. "Sydney, come quickly. He's silvered. I need you now."

Sydney sprinted up the aisle, aghast at seeing Luca's handsome face now crusted over with dried blood. His once muscular body looked emaciated, with burns oozing from the silver chains. "Oh my God. What did they do to him? Luca...we're here. We've got you." She reached over and began unraveling the heavy chains from his limbs. Sydney expected Luca to wince but he remained unnervingly still, unresponsive to the pain. The chains clanged onto the floor, dispersing the dirty needles and dried leaves that had blown in through the broken windows. "Kade. Look at all the needles. What the hell? Why would they do this?"

Kade showed no emotion while circling the altar, scanning the mess around them. He waited patiently for Sydney to remove all the silver. "Fucking assholes. They probably took blood from Luca to be sold on the black market." Anger surged as he kicked the needles aside, silently vowing revenge on the perpetrators.

Since the vampires had become known to the public, both pharmaceutical companies and entrepreneurs had been looking to capitalize on the immortality of vampires. Try as they might, no progress had been made towards perpetual life without incurring that nasty little side effect of becoming a vampire. While plenty of vampires were willing to sell their blood for profit, it didn't stop the gangs from kidnapping and draining vamps to sell their blood on the black market at a discounted price.

Kade lovingly swept his hand across his old friend's face, trying to clear the dried blood off of him. "Luca," he whispered. "You are safe now. We've got you."

Luca and Kade had been friends for over two centuries, meeting during the early eighteen hundreds. While Luca had been born in Britain, he had been raised in Australia. He'd come over to America during the War of 1812. When he'd been badly injured and lay dying on the battlefield, Kade had turned him. He was indebted to Kade; they were partners, best friends.

Kade was infuriated; whoever had done this would pay dearly. "Sydney, you drive. I'm going to lie in the back of the SUV and feed him. Don't get near us. When he wakes, he could be dangerous." Kade frowned. "Look at what they did to him. He's starved."

"Will he be okay?" Sydney didn't know that much about vampire medicine except that they had healing properties in their blood. Said properties were most effective on humans and werewolves but held minimum benefit for other vampires. She knew he needed a mortal donor.

"Yes, he'll heal, but we've got to get him human blood. Call Dominique and tell her to bring the donors into the house and get them ready now. She knows what to do." Kade gingerly slid his hand underneath Luca's head and knees, bringing him close to his body. Swiftly, he lifted him and carried him out of the church.

"Put the back seat down," he ordered.

Sydney clicked the release on the seats, pushing them until they were flat. Kade laid Luca in the trunk and climbed into the back. With his hands underneath Luca's arms, he gently pulled him all the way into the car. Thank God they'd brought the Escalade. It would be a tight fit with two large males lying in the back, but they'd fit.

Kade sighed as he leaned up onto his side, and reached over to Luca's mouth. Placing one hand on Luca's chin and cupping his cheeks with the other hand, he slowly opened Luca's cracked lips.

Sydney started the engine and stole a glimpse of Kade biting into his wrist. No matter how many times she'd witnessed a vampire feeding someone or feeding from someone, she was always fascinated by the intimacy of the act. It felt almost intrusive to watch them together. Anxious to get home, she pulled her eyes back to the road and drove.

Kade cradled Luca's head as he pressed his wrist downward. The crimson droplets trickled down the sides of Luca's face; he wasn't swallowing. Kade reached with his mind, willing Luca to drink. *Please Goddess, let me through to him. Drink Luca, drink.*

Luca jerked in Kade's arms as a single drop of the life-giving blood was absorbed into his body. Yet he didn't wake. He could not move. Immobilized within his friend's arms, Luca's consciousness awakened. *Safe. Kade. Friend.* He tried to move, but couldn't manage more than a swallow.

"That's it, Luca. Drink," Kade ordered. Relief flooded his mind; he'd been worried about Luca's ability to recover. While vampires only needed to drink a few pints every couple of days, they needed to feed regularly. Going without feeding could send them into a frenzy, which could cause them to lose control and kill a human. Going several days without feeding could cause their demise.

Pulling into Kade's compound, Sydney saw Dominique waiting impatiently near the mansion's entrance. Dominique, another vampire, was a longtime loyal employee and friend of Kade's. Sydney described her as a badass fashionista. She and Dominique had initially clashed when they'd first met over a month ago. Since then, they'd forged a friendship based on mutual respect and a love of leather.

Parking the car, Sydney ran around the SUV and slowly pulled open the hatch. She understood that Luca could be dangerous, so she moved slowly with no sudden movements. Yet looking at his frail, battered torso, she couldn't fathom what harm he could do in his weakened state. While typically well-composed, her breath caught in her throat at the sight of him. She could not resist the need to provide both Luca and Kade with comfort. As she reached to touch Luca, his eyes flew open; he strained to break free of Kade's hold. *Human blood.*

"Don't touch him! Get away now, Sydney!" Kade hissed at her.

Sydney jumped back, startled at the bloodlust in Luca's eyes. He was dangerous. Hungry. She thought she must look like water in the desert to him. Heeding Kade's order, she ran inside to see what she could do to help.

Dominique intervened, helping Kade to restrain Luca. "Fuck, what the hell happened to him?" Dominique questioned.

"He was silvered, starved. Possibly tortured. Not sure what all they did yet. But I know they got his blood. There were needles all over the damn place," he spat out. So many years had passed since he'd been turned. At times, he was astonished by how little progress humanity had achieved. Evil, hate and torture still beat strong within the hearts of so many. *How could they have done this to him?*

He sighed wearily. "Sydney's blood is making him crazy. We need to get him inside. Where are Xavier and

Étienne? Do we have donors?" Kade held tight onto Luca while trying to move him slowly out of the SUV. Luca was still in no condition to walk and he'd be damned if he'd chance letting him loose.

"They're on their way. I have a room prepared upstairs. I can help carry him," she said, looking around to make sure Sydney was gone. Like Kade, she could not trust Luca not to attack her. They had human donors waiting upstairs, and they would monitor the feeding closely so Luca didn't end up draining them.

"Where's Sydney?" Kade asked.

Dominique looked around. "It seems your woman had enough sense to make herself scarce when he looked at her like she was lobster dinner. Don't worry, she'll be fine. It isn't her first time at the vamp rodeo."

"I know. It's just that she's not used to seeing Luca like this. Neither am I." He shook his head. Seeing Luca in such an animalistic state would serve as a reminder to Sydney that she was marrying into this lifestyle. He needed to find her and make sure that she was all right.

Kade easily lifted Luca, with his arms under Luca's neck and the crook under his knees. Luca's eyes were wide open, yet he wasn't speaking. Kade wasn't sure if Luca understood what was happening as he took him upstairs to the guest bedroom. Dominique motioned Kade into the bathroom, where she had a bath filled with warm water. "Kade, over here. The warm water will help get his body temp back up."

Kade placed Luca's emaciated naked body into the warm, soapy water. "Shit," he said as water sloshed over the sides of the tub and all over the floor. Without even taking the time to undress, Kade carefully climbed into the tub and lay next to Luca so he could hold him still while he fed. Deeply concerned about Luca's state, he waved over at Dominique. "Where's the donor? We need him now!" he commanded.

She pointed at a shirtless, twenty-something male who was waiting in the bedroom. "You, over here, on your knees by the tub."

"Yes ma'am," said the donor as he willingly and quickly complied with her demand, and held out his arm. Donors were easy to come by these days. They signed up at blood clubs, hoping to experience a sexual encounter with a vampire. At the very least, they hoped to be chosen for a bite, knowing the orgasmic properties that could be granted by the vampire.

Issacson Securities, Kade's company, had contracted with Sanguine Services to procure donors when needed. Dominique had called in advance to procure a couple of strong males who would be able to provide enough blood for Luca. She just hoped the blood would be enough to bring Luca back from his atrophied state. She had never seen a vampire so far gone and wasn't convinced they could save him. But she didn't want to cause Kade further worry, so she kept her reservations to herself.

Dominique gently took the donor's wrist and flashed him a quick smile. "Hey there, what's your name?" she asked.

"Milo," he obediently replied.

"Okay, listen, Milo. This person here; he's a good friend of mine. His name is Luca. He hasn't eaten in days, so this might be a little rough at first but I promise you will be safe." She hoped he would, anyway.

Kade tried reaching out mentally to Sydney to tell her to stay away. Their telepathic connection was in its infancy, but short of yelling for her, he needed to send some kind of warning to stay away from Luca. Sensing she was in the house but not near, he breathed a sigh of relief. It was time to get started. He nodded at Dominique to begin.

Dominique brought Milo's wrist to her finely-painted, coral-colored lips. Her tongue darted out, licking his sensitive inner wrist. She resisted the urge to play with her food, knowing that Luca needed blood as soon as possible. Expeditiously, her razor-sharp fangs pierced his flesh; he moaned aloud, sexually excited by her bite.

Leaning over to Luca's lips, with the donor's wrist in her mouth, she seamlessly transferred Milo's bleeding wrist from her mouth to Luca's. Another loud groan of excitement resounded along the granite-tiled walls as Luca began to voraciously feed.

Kade had his arms locked around Luca's upper body, preventing him from making any violent attack on the donor. "That's it my friend. Drink. You'll be fine, and we'll find out who did this to you," he said, looking directly into Luca's eyes. He could tell Luca was starting to become fully conscious, but he still couldn't tell if Luca's cognition was stable. Their mental connection was still severed.

A loud groan emanated from Milo, indicating sexual release. Dominique had already readied the second donor as Kade pulled Milo away from Luca. They were very careful to ensure that Luca did not kill the donors. Luca latched onto the second donor and was starting to regain color, warmth. Despite being close to getting enough blood, something wasn't right with Luca.

Kade released Luca as he pushed the second donor away. Luca again closed his eyes as his physique appeared to regenerate before their eyes. Kade climbed out of the tub and grabbed a towel as Xavier and Étienne entered the bathroom. "Nice of you to join us. Please attend to the donors and make sure they get safely home," he said as he rubbed his hair vigorously with the towel, annoyed that they'd just arrived at the mansion.

"Sorry we're late, Kade. Downtown traffic is a bitch this time of night," Étienne explained. "He's looking well, no?"

"Looks can be deceiving. Something's not right. Our mental connection's shut down. He isn't verbally responding either. But he's had quite enough vampire and human blood to bring him back physically." Kade was worried about Luca.

Xavier leaned down and touched Luca's head. "Mon ami, what happened to you?" Xavier tried reaching for him mentally and also failed to contact him. "I see what you mean. Do you know what's going on? He's here but not here."

"Not sure. Perhaps he needs time to rest. For now, let's get moving, people. Get the donors out of here." He looked over at Dominique. She had a single, blood-red tear running down her beautiful face.

"Dominique, look at me," he ordered. She complied, meeting his eyes. "Luca will heal. Finish bathing him, and get him to bed. Watch over him until I return. I'm going to call a doctor, and I need to find Sydney. She may be able to help him…"

"But how, Kade? Look at him…he's not responding to us," she cried.

"Trust me. I've been around a very long time. I know what needs to be done, even if I'm not happy about it."

Sydney could not stop thinking about what had just happened outside of the car. Luca and Sydney had had a rough start. Because she was human, which equated to weak and vulnerable in his eyes, he hadn't been happy about her working with them on the Voodoo murder case. But they had forged a deep friendship during battle. Sydney was a hardened detective from Philadelphia, so she'd seen most of the worst the world could dish out. But it didn't stop the pain in her heart from seeing a friend injured. Nor did it stop the surprise she felt seeing the look in his eyes. She could feel the pull of him mentally, wanting to feed from her.

She was confused about how this could be possible. Sydney had been regularly drinking small amounts of Kade's blood since they'd got engaged. Blood sharing was an incredibly intimate and sexual experience. As a result of their bonding, she was starting to be able to feel a mental connection to Kade. Right now, she could sense single words or feelings from him, but he told her that soon she'd be able to send messages back and forth. She had thought that connection would only be with Kade.

However, today at the car, Luca's eyes had bored into her soul, calling to her to help him. It was if she could hear him speaking to her. Frightened, she obediently ran into the house at Kade's command. She wasn't afraid of Luca attacking her. No, she was afraid of the message she sensed from him. He needed her blood.

CHAPTER TWO

Dr. Sweeney, Kade's personal physician, had assessed Luca's health. Even though he'd received human blood, there was the possibility he might not return to who he had been. The doctor estimated he'd gone without blood for at least seven days, which would have been long enough to easily kill a younger vampire. She said there was a chance he would recover fully after several feedings, but they might have to wait over a month before they knew for sure. Devastated by the news, Kade went to search for comfort in Sydney.

Sydney was hunched over, with her face in her hands, sitting in the master bedroom when Kade found her. He would never get used to the feel of his heart squeezing in his chest when he was around her. Detective Sydney Willows was his woman, his fiancée: strong, sexy, loving. She was all he would ever need in this life, but would he risk her to save his friend?

"Sydney, love. You okay? What's wrong?" he questioned, kneeling before her.

Sydney silently shook her head.

"You cannot hide from me. We need to talk about what happened back in the car...Luca," he whispered. Kade removed and discarded his wet shirt and pants. He then knelt before Sydney and slid his hands up her calves. He would never get enough of her, feeling the strength of his woman's body.

Sydney snapped her head upward to gaze into Kade's eyes; her mane of long, curly blonde locks spilled over her shoulders. A chill of sexual excitement shot into Sydney's body, but she tried to quell the feelings in the wake of what had just happened to Luca. "How is he?" she asked, knowing Kade would remain stoic in the face of crisis. That was just the kind of man he was: authoritative, confident and courageous. He'd be strong for Luca, for Sydney.

"Dr. Sweeney came over and checked him out. She says he'll most likely recover. But it could be a month before we know for sure. But you know Luca; he's strong. He's fine...physically," he answered.

She cupped his face in her hands and leaned into him for a brief kiss. She needed Kade's warmth, to bring him comfort.

"What do you mean, baby? Did he tell you what happened, who did this to him?" She realized she had shifted into detective mode. Stopping herself, she changed her approach. "Kade...in the car...he..." *How could she tell Kade?*

"What happened in the car, love, was that Luca smelled your blood and was simply ravenous for human blood; he was starved. He wouldn't have hurt you. I'd swear my life on it. But he may still need you..." *How could he ask Sydney for her help?*

Sydney got up out of the chair, raked her fingers through her long hair and began to pace. She was confused, scared. She was afraid for herself and how Kade might react. "Kade, something happened in the car. Luca. I don't know how to explain it. Our mental connection. Somehow, Luca...when he looked at me. He needs me." She stood still, waiting for Kade to respond.

Kade loved her so much. He hated having to tell her what might help Luca heal. But somehow, Luca had communicated with her instead of him. Rushing over to embrace Sydney, Kade let himself briefly enjoy the feel of her soft breasts against his bare chest, the smell of her strawberry-scented hair. Pulling back, he kissed her, a soft loving kiss. "Sydney, I don't know how he communicated with you. Maybe the blood connection. He is mine...of my making. Please don't be afraid."

Sydney held her chin high, feigning courage. "Me? Afraid? Seriously?" Then she giggled nervously, knowing that she was very much afraid. But she didn't want Kade to have to worry about her in addition to Luca. It was too much.

He smiled, letting her save face. "My brave detective, I know you're as tough as they come. And I love you for it.

But we need to be honest with each other. This is serious, understand?"

"Okay. I'm a little afraid," she whispered.

"He needs you. More specifically, he needs you to feed him. Your blood...it's special. You have my vampiric blood in you, and your own very special, sweet mortal essence." Kade was confident in their relationship. He loved her unconditionally, and she him. Yet he wanted Sydney to feel safe. Sure, she knew the dangers and realities of his world, but she was still a novice. He knew that she was just starting to become comfortable around the other vampires.

"Yes," she quietly responded, unsure where he was going with his explanation.

"You know how it is when I bite you, correct?" He needed to make sure she was clear about what could happen and had no regrets. "Sydney, if you do this, I will be there with you. You'll be safe. But I want to be clear, it very well could be...well, you know, sexual in nature. You know how it is..." his words trailed off.

Before he met Sydney, Kade and Luca had often shared women. He had even shared a brief dance with Sydney and Luca, at Sangre Dulce, a local bondage club, where they'd been investigating a crime. But he'd had no intentions of sharing Sydney with Luca, ever. It hadn't been an option...until now.

Kade watched Sydney as she pulled away from him and resumed pacing. He could see her thoughts spinning in her head. She'd been attracted to Luca that night in the club but that didn't mean she'd wanted anything further to happen. Added to the fact that she wasn't a big fan of vampires; would she agree to let another man bite her?

Kade blew out a breath. He hated to rush her, but he felt as though they were running out of time. "Sydney, you don't have to do this if you don't want to. But if you do agree, I want to be crystal clear that I am not asking you to have sex with Luca. You should be aware by now that I have grown quite possessive of you." He smiled and approached her, seeking her touch. "But you need to know that Luca may, indeed, touch you, and you, in return, may feel the need to touch him. And I don't want you feeling guilty or uncomfortable with it. It is our nature."

Sydney closed the gap between them and wrapped her arms around Kade's neck. "I love you, Kade. I love you so much it hurts sometimes. I would do anything for you, or to save Luca. And I want you to know that I'm not afraid, because I know you will protect me. I'm nothing but secure in our relationship. I know you and I are meant to be. So if I do this for him, whatever sexual feelings bubble up during this…this feeding…it's just a feeling that happens. Like that night in the club…" She blushed, remembering how she had felt, sandwiched between both Luca and Kade's hard, sexy maleness.

Kade nodded knowingly, "Yes, I remember." He knew his reserved detective had been inordinately aroused by dancing with two men.

"It was overwhelming that night…dancing so intimately with both you and Luca. I never thought I would enjoy my little walk on the kinky side, but I did. But I also know that I love you...You and you alone. So I don't plan on making love to Luca when we do this...no matter how good he bites," she joked.

Kade tightened his hold around Sydney's waist. "As if I would let you make love to another man, love. You are mine," he growled. Kade captured Sydney's lips, his tongue swept over hers, drinking in her sweet nectar. She was the most amazing, sexy woman. He wanted to make love to her right then, right there, but Luca was waiting. He reluctantly drew back from their kiss. "Okay, this is how it's going to happen. I will be directing this show, understand?"

Sydney nodded in agreement, eagerly anticipating helping Luca.

Kade and Sydney stood at the entrance to Luca's room watching Dominique busy herself. She was placing the dirty towels in a laundry bin and straightening the sheets on the bed as if they somehow affected Luca. Sydney knew that Dominique was simply struggling to keep her mind off of the fact that Luca was unresponsive. Despite her typical flippant comments and hard exterior, Dominique cared deeply for Luca.

Luca was resting quietly in the bed with only a white cotton sheet covering his legs and groin. His broad, muscled chest, now restored, quietly rose and fell as he slept peacefully. His dark, shoulder-length hair was tousled across the white pillow case. He looked peaceful, rested and healthy. Yet they all knew he wasn't.

Kade, still shirtless, wore loose-fitted, faded blue jeans; he wanted to be comfortable when they did this. Sydney had nervously changed into a casual, spaghetti-strapped, black sundress that could easily be mistaken for a nightgown, deciding that she needed to be in comfortable clothing. She wasn't exactly sure of the logistics but since Luca was still in bed, she figured she would at least be on a chair or kneeling beside the bed.

She was about to ask a question when Kade interrupted her thoughts. "Dominique, leave us. We'll watch him," he ordered.

Understanding his meaning, Dominique quickly left the room and shut the door.

"Sydney, you ready?" he asked.

"Yes. Where do you want me?" she responded.

"Remember Sydney, I am in charge here. Luca will not be dangerous. You are safe with us. But you must listen to me, no questions. I am in control," he said matter of factly.

Sydney had to admit that was one of the things she loved about Kade. He was one hundred percent alpha male. He gave orders, didn't take them. And Sydney always felt safe giving him control sexually. She was under a lot of pressure most days to lead teams and investigations. Sexually, she desired to submit to him occasionally. It wasn't in her nature to submit, but Goddess, this man brought out things in her personality she never even knew existed.

"Sydney?" His voice brought her thoughts back to Luca.

"Sorry. Yes, I'm ready." She listened intently for her instructions.

Kade grabbed her hand and kissed her palm. "Luca's resting, so we need to get his senses awakened enough to feed…to bite you. The best place to let him bite you would be your neck." He traced his fingers around the side of her face, down her neck. "Come."

Sydney felt her body shake in anticipation of what would happen. She trusted Kade, but damn, she was nervous. *What the fuck was I thinking, telling Kade I'd let Luca feed from me?* But she'd promised to help Luca. For both their sakes, they needed him back.

"Lay on your side, next to Luca. I will be right here behind you, love," he directed. "Get in." He patted the bed.

Sydney got into bed; her breasts struggled to stay in her dress as she pressed up next to Luca's arm. "Is this okay?"

"Move closer, Sydney. Put your arm across his chest. Press closely up against him without getting on top of him. He will sense you. Concentrate. Reach out mentally for him. He's there." Kade spooned Sydney and put his strong arms protectively around her waist. "There you go, love. That's it…I feel him. He knows we're here. Why we are here. Don't struggle, Sydney. Just let yourself go.

Don't worry about losing control, okay? Remember that I'm here. You'll be fine."

In Luca's mind, he could hear her calling him. *Sydney.* But how could that be? Then Luca heard another voice. *Kade.* He struggled to listen. He knew he was at Kade's home but he couldn't talk, move. What was happening to him? The scent of strawberries teased his nose. Soft, warm hands on his chest. Female hands. *Samantha?*

No, not Samantha, Sydney. He sensed Kade, too. The scent of Sydney's sweet blood called to him. Not just human blood. No, mortal blood infused with the blood of his maker. He needed it to survive. The desire to live was strong.

Tendrils of awareness fingered throughout his body awakening his senses. *Feed.* The command coming from Kade was strong. Yet, it didn't make sense that he would share Sydney. No, he wouldn't do that to his friend. Sydney belonged to Kade. *Feed.* Luca started shaking his head; his eyes opened. "No," he pleaded. His first words since the attack.

Feed. This time from Sydney. He could hear her speaking to him telepathically. She was offering herself to him. No, that couldn't be. He couldn't understand why this was happening. Confused, he looked down to see her stroking his chest, cuddled up next to him, staring into his eyes.

"Yes, Luca. It's me, Sydney. We know what you need. It's okay. Kade and I are both here." She reached up and caressed his face, placing her finger on his lips.

"Luca, feed. Listen to Sydney. Her blood's special. She offers her blood to you freely as do I. Now feed," Kade ordered again. He knew Luca would resist, but he'd force him if necessary. Sydney's blood would restore him.

Luca's fangs descended on hearing Kade's command. He rolled over onto his side, to gaze into Sydney's eyes, wanting to be assured of her permission. Luca glanced at Kade who nodded. *Feed.*

Luca had always found Sydney incredibly sexy but never wanted to infringe on his friend's woman. Yet, here she was in bed with him, offering herself to him. He slid his hand around her waist, feeling the back of Kade's hand holding her gently in place. Luca whispered to Sydney, "Thank you." With those words, he let his lips fall onto hers, kissing her softly, pressing his chest to hers.

He pulled his head back slightly. "I promise to be gentle, Sydney."

She gasped as she felt the slice of Luca's fangs at her throat. "Kade..." It was all she could manage as moisture flooded her core. She ached for release as Luca held her closer still, draining her blood. Sydney felt strangely at peace having two strong male bodies surround her in such an intimate way. *Kade. Luca.* She embraced his bite, realizing she'd lost control.

Luca moaned as her nourishing blood swept into his throat. A magical mixture of human blood infused with his maker's awoke his consciousness. Memories of the past two weeks flashed before his eyes. The killing of Simone and Asgear. Touching Samantha's soft hair, comforting her in Kade's basement. Traveling to the coven. An attack. Silvered. Drained of blood. Tormented. Malnourished. Dying. A rushing vortex of energy propelled throughout his entire being as he voraciously drank her gift to him, her blood. Exhilaration rose within Luca as his emotional connections regenerated.

Kade watched intently as Luca suckled Sydney's neck, careful to make sure Luca kept himself under control. He disliked the thought of sharing her with any man, but he was desperate to save Luca. Watching his friend feed from his fiancée, he sensed Sydney's growing arousal from the bite. Luca's dark kiss could send her into erotic bliss or agony, depending on his intentions. He cared for her, so of course, Luca tried to make it pleasurable. Sensing Sydney's desire, Kade reluctantly grew aroused as well. Lost in the moment, Kade pushed up Sydney's dress, and slid his hands along her flat stomach to cup her bare breasts. He found himself grinding his hardness into her ass, and yearned to make love to her while Luca drank.

"Oh, yes, Kade. Please, I need..." Sydney found herself begging, writhing between Kade's aching erection at her back and Luca's bare hardness on her belly. She needed something but couldn't articulate her thoughts. She struggled for control in an effort to relieve the ache.

"Sydney, love. You're safe. Remember who's in control. I'll take care of you," he reminded her. Kade unzipped his jeans and made short work of undressing himself. Pulling Sydney's thong aside, his fingers slipped into her wet folds and found her most sensitive area. He began to rub her clitoris firmly but gently in circles.

"Yes, Kade," she cried out as he touched her. She knew in her mind that she shouldn't be doing this with two men, but she also understood that vampires were sexual at their core. At the very essence of their nature, they were capable of inflicting extraordinary pleasure or pain. Under the best of circumstances, they could restrain their need to climax and simply feed. Depleted of all nourishment, Luca had suffered tremendously; he wasn't capable of holding back. They needed to restore him by tending to his every physical and emotional need.

Kade understood that she'd feel conflicted. She was still very much human, not accustomed to the ways of vampires. "That's right, Sydney. Don't fight how you feel, just go with it," he coaxed. "Take Luca in your hand. It's okay."

Sensing Luca had drunk enough of Sydney's blood, Kade directed him to stop feeding. She'd be too weak if he didn't stop now. "Luca, release Sydney. Enough."

Luca did as told, licking over the holes in her neck. He hissed as Sydney reached to stroke his velvety steel hardness. His forehead fell against her shoulder as she cared for him. Luca caressed her breast with one hand as Kade paid attention to the other one.

Sydney was completely overwhelmed. It was so wrong, but so right. She'd never done anything like this in her life. She wanted to save Luca but how had she gotten herself into something like this? Worse, she admitted to herself that she didn't want to stop. She just needed release. "Kade!" she screamed as he entered her from behind in one thrust. She felt full with him, yet needing more.

"Sydney, so tight, warm. I won't last like this," he whispered into her ear. Kade began pumping in and out of her moist heat. He felt so connected to both Sydney and Luca in this single moment. The love of his life. His best friend. Kade felt Luca speak to him; "*Thank you, friend.*"

Sydney couldn't keep her orgasm at bay much longer. She was grabbing the back of Luca's head, pulling him into her shoulder while taking Kade into her from behind and stroking Luca. *Too much. Can't hold on.*

Hearing her urgency, Kade reached around with his thumb to press her sensitive nub. "That's it love. Come for me. So good. Let go."

At his words, Sydney began to convulse against Luca and Kade, riding the waves of her climax. Kade slid one last long stroke into Sydney, holding her tightly against him and releasing his seed deep within her.

As Luca came along with them, a single thought escaped his lips as he cried, "Samantha!"

Kade quickly slipped out of Sydney and turned her around to him to hold her. He looked her directly in the eyes, realizing the gravity of what they'd just done. He was concerned about how she'd feel now that it was over.

"I love you so very much...more than life itself." He feathered her closed eyes with kisses. "This thing between us, here, will never happen again. But make no mistake, we helped Luca come back to us, and I will be forever grateful for what you did today."

"No regrets, okay. We helped him, didn't we? Is he okay?" she asked quietly. *Yeah, we helped him all right.* She rolled her eyes thinking about what they had just done. She hoped Luca was healed after all that.

"Yes, love, he's healed," Kade replied.

Sydney felt embarrassed, but didn't want to show it. She wanted to leave and give them space. She sat up, turned around and looked at the two very naked vampires lying in bed. "Okay, so who's hungry? I get that you vamps only need blood, but a girl like me has got to get some real food," she joked, desperately needing the levity.

Kade and Luca looked at each other and laughed. Kade made a move to sit up, and Luca reached out to put a hand on his arm. "Kade. Sydney. I don't know what to say, so I will just say 'thank you'. Thank you for rescuing me. Thank you for this, now. I am not sure what to say. After I had the donor blood today, I still couldn't function. It was like I was there but not there. I know you both took a risk feeding me," he looked around at the sheets. "And a risk knowing it might turn out to be a little more than just feeding." He smiled knowingly.

Luca felt refreshed but angry as he recalled every detail of his attack and capture. Remembering the look on Samantha's face as they'd attacked, he needed to know she was safe. From the minute he'd met Samantha, he'd felt protective of her.

"Listen, I know I have been out of it, but what of Samantha? I blacked out right before her and Ilsbeth..." Luca questioned.

"Ummm...she must be on your mind, huh, Luca?" Sydney grinned, interrupting his train of thought. "I know you aren't crazy about us human women, but perhaps this one has gotten under your skin? You did call her name instead of mine. I'm crushed," she teased and hopped off the bed towards the door, knowing that Luca had feelings toward Samantha. She smiled, thinking that her friend could actually be attracted to a mortal. *Could it be that Luca was actually growing a heart?*

Kade got up out of bed, leaving Luca leaning against the headrest. He watched Sydney leave the room, pulled on his jeans and turned to his friend. A serious expression washed across his face. "Luca, let's be clear. You are my best friend. But know that I will not be sharing Sydney with you in the future. What we did today..." He looked to the bed and then met Luca's eyes. "We did it to heal you, to bring you back. And while I am grateful you appear well, you need to stay out of trouble. I am not sure I could do this again."

Luca smiled. It was unusual for him do to so, given his serious nature. "Understood, Kade. Sydney is beautiful, indeed. But I have always known she was yours and yours alone. It was very hard for me to accept her blood knowing she belonged to you. Thank you again for finding me. Healing me." Luca stood up. Realizing he was naked, he wrapped the sheet around his waist. "I need to know though. Are Samantha and Ilsbeth safe?"

"Yes, it was Ilsbeth who called me to tell me you'd been attacked. Since your absence, she's called me a few times to let me know that Samantha was cleansed and continuing her training. She's at the coven still."

"Kade." He paused, thinking through the events of his kidnapping. "Whoever did this to me weren't after me. I mean, they could have killed me, but they didn't. Whoever attacked us knew better than to kill me lest you would rain hell down upon them in this city. They knew who I was and left me alive. It wasn't me they wanted. No, they were after the witches."

"Perhaps," Kade pondered. Was Asgear working with someone else besides Simone? "I don't know, Luca. Why would they want Samantha? She doesn't know what she is. Ilsbeth holds a lot of power, but I can't imagine who would be foolish enough to try and capture her at her home. Besides the magical wards she's set, she could literally transport herself away from the captor."

"Kade, there's something about Samantha. I don't know..." Luca was troubled. Something wasn't right. Why hadn't they killed him? "Talk to Sydney. Get her take on what happened. I plan to rest today while the sun is up, but tonight I'm going to the coven to see Ilsbeth and the girl."

"Luca, my friend. You refer to Samantha as a girl, yet you cannot deny she is a woman. Perhaps there is another reason why you feel compelled to see her?" Kade asked.

"A human? No way, Kade. You know I'm not into mortal women. Give me a break. I was just drained and starved for over a fucking week. I'm pissed as hell and there's got to be a goddamn good reason why this happened. Who the hell even knew I was transporting the witches? Who else knew about Asgear and Simone's plans to take over the city? What if there's more to Samantha than we really know? Ilsbeth should know by now what the hell kind of magic the girl has. Is it even real? Over a week has passed and I need to know what the hell is going on over there. Something isn't right with what happened." Luca was steaming mad.

Luca sighed, *Samantha*. Remembering the first time he'd met her, he wondered why she dominated his thoughts. Something about the human woman stirred his emotions, yet he could not fathom why he would care. The pixie-sized, fair-skinned beauty had barely been holding onto reality the last time he'd seen her. After she'd been bespelled by the evil mage, Asgear, who'd turned her into a submissive and beaten her to a pulp as a prisoner, she learned that the magic had infused itself into her very being. She was now a witch. Yet, she was technically still very much a mere mortal who knew nothing about witchcraft.

The last time he saw her she'd been in 'protection' at Kade's estate. *Protection.* Hell, who was he kidding? After they'd rescued her from her shackled existence, they imprisoned her once again, albeit in a gilded cage. Tainted by the evil, infused by magic, she could not return home.

Instead, Ilsbeth, a close confidant of Kade's and a well-respected witch, insisted Samantha go with her to the coven to be cleansed and learn her new path in life.

The very first time he'd met Samantha, she was working at Sangre Dulce. He and Kade were working a case that night. As she had stood naked before them, serving drinks to his group of vampires, Luca was instantly attracted to the submissive, red-haired beauty. Samantha, who'd been introduced to him under the false name of Rhea, had offered herself for 'play'. Luca had turned her down. He'd been there to work the case, find clues to a killer, not fuck. And then there was the undeniable fact that she was human. Not his first choice for playing. Humans were good for feeding, but way too emotional and breakable. No, when it came to sex, he preferred a supernatural with no attachments. As for love, it simply was not an option.

The next time he'd seen Samantha, she'd been bruised and battered, a shell of the woman he'd met at the club. He wondered how such a fragile woman had survived life locked in that desolate, filthy prison cell. When he'd broken the locked metal cuffs off her naked body, Luca had cursed the monster that had injured her. Later at Kade's house, his heart had constricted as he'd watched her come to terms with what had happened to her. With no memory of the club or her actions, she had learned of her fate as a witch.

She was shocked on discovering that she'd never return to her work, her friends, her life. Vulnerable and shaken, she'd agreed to go with Ilsbeth to the coven...as if she'd been given a choice. Her soul was tainted; Kade would have never let her return without cleansing her soul.

Luca stared at himself in the bathroom mirror; the hard planes of his muscles looked as if he'd just returned from the gym. There was no indication that he had been on the brink of death. Luca touched his hardened abs, slick from sweat. He reveled in being vampire, in being indestructible. *Almost.* True, he was pure alpha male, perhaps even tougher than Kade, yet not as old. And despite being vampire, his time on Earth had almost ended. He didn't have time to dwell on how he'd almost died. Rather, he contemplated why he was attacked. *Why the fuck am I still here? Who wanted Samantha?*

His thoughts raced as he stepped into the shower. He needed to see Samantha just one more time. This time, no crying...just talking. She would be calm. She'd had a week to adjust. Perhaps not much time for a human but it would be better than the last time when she couldn't stop 'leaking'. Humans, such weak creatures. Luca had no time or patience for their outbursts. The only human he'd tolerated was Sydney, and clearly that was due to Kade's influence. She had proven her warrior abilities, fought alongside him, earned his respect.

One human woman in his life was enough. He decided that he would go to the coven, investigate what had happened and sate his curiosity. He'd question the little lovely human and find out who exactly was behind the kidnapping attempt.

As he rinsed the soap from his body, his cock jerked at the thought of seeing her again. *Shit.* He admonished himself for the thought. Yet as he stroked his hardness, he could not circumvent the vision of her. *Samantha.*

CHAPTER THREE

Samantha pushed open the cabin door, thankful to be back in Pennsylvania. She tried thinking of something else, anything else but what had happened to her in New Orleans. She felt dirty. Violated. A loss of identity.

She should have listened to those who'd told her not to go to New Orleans. Her family had warned her that the city was dangerous. Ignoring their concerns, she'd gone anyway. At the time, going to the computer conference had seemed like a great way to go on a 'working vacation'. After a day of lectures and workshops, her co-workers had talked her into going to a local bdsm club in New Orleans. She had heard that supernaturals supposedly went there. Samantha had expected maybe to meet a vampire or a werewolf. She'd thought they'd dance, maybe get to watch some interesting scenes and have some fun. That was all it was supposed to be. A night of fun.

Now her life was destroyed. No friends who she could talk to about what happened. No job. No life. No Samantha. The man she'd met at the club, James, had turned out to be a mage. His real name was Asgear. She vaguely remembered the beating he'd given her after she dared to escape his lair. A beating that she could barely remember was something she could get over. She'd trained in karate when she was younger and had earned and given her fair share of fighting bruises.

No, this was far worse. Memories locked away, stolen. She couldn't remember anything of what had happened or what she'd done. Being taken to a vampire's mansion, Kade Issacson had shown her the disgusting evidence of her violation. Naked. Submissive. She'd been under the control of Asgear and had done his bidding. Her body was used. Her mind was taken over as well, but the memories refused to surface. Despite being told she'd been bespelled and seeing the photographic proof, she could not accept that what she'd done was real.

Was she raped? Did she willingly have sex with others? Did she hurt anyone? She had no recollection. They told her that she may have hurt a female vampire. But that wasn't her. It was a nightmare; one she could only escape by running.

Witch. She despised the word. While Ilsbeth had been nothing but kind to her, she refused to believe she was a witch. She didn't want to be a witch. This was not happening. She would take the medical leave she'd requested from work and take a long rest in the mountains, and then try to get her life back. Maybe remember what had happened. Maybe not. Regardless, she was determined to heal.

No one was guaranteed an easy life, she knew that. You worked hard, and reaped what you sowed. Working in a sea of men in her technology company hadn't been a walk in the park when she'd first started. A female programmer worked twice as hard and long to prove herself worthy. And she'd done just that, earning her rank as one of the very best engineers. The phrase, 'giving up', wasn't in her vocabulary. She preferred to fight the good fight in the face of adversity. Samantha steeled herself; she resolved that nothing would break her spirit.

The cabin she rented in the mountains was a welcome reprieve from the intense training sessions she'd experienced over the past week. The weather was lovely, as was the foliage. Towards the end of August, evenings were beginning to cool off, beckoning fall to approach. After being in the humid, hot air of New Orleans, Samantha welcomed the change in temperature.

Samantha opened the sliding glass door to check for firewood. The rental agency had assured her that the cabin was fully stocked, which meant she could have a fire on a cold night. Drinking in the tranquil setting, she sat on the Adirondack chair and breathed in the fresh, mountain air. She stared out at the large lake situated on the property. Aside from the small clearing leading to the lake, the house was surrounded by woods. Samantha was pleased the property was isolated, as had been promised.

Alone at last. No vampires. No werewolves. And no freakin' witches. While Ilsbeth was friendly, she'd not received such a warm welcome from all the others. They'd glared at her, resenting her newfound gift. Most witches were born with magic, not accidentally infused with it. To the other witches, she was an unnatural freak who was tainted not blessed.

Ilsbeth had sat with Samantha and gently cleansed the evil then explained how Samantha could draw power from within. Out of respect for Ilsbeth, she did try. Unsuccessfully. Night after night, she sat in the calming room, meditating and chanting, yet nothing stirred.

Fed up with the insulting comments from the other witches, and her lack of apparent powers, Samantha resolved to get her old life back. She was very grateful to Kade, Luca, Sydney and Ilsbeth for rescuing her. She didn't want to seem unappreciative, but she'd had enough of the mystical side of life. She yearned for normalcy. It was like a hardened nightmare from which she could not awake. Finally, yes, finally, she was feeling like her old self, relaxing into the forested wilderness.

Samantha reached across the table and lit a small citronella candle. She laughed to herself; the only bloodsuckers out here were the damn mosquitos. *No way are you getting me tonight.* The crickets and cicadas sang her a soothing lullaby. Convinced she was finally finding peace in her rustic sanctuary, Samantha let out a breath, closed her eyes and fell asleep, breathing in the crisp air.

"She what?" Luca could hardly believe it as he stood before the always ethereal Ilsbeth. "She left? Where the hell did she go?"

Ilsbeth's golden hair shone in the candlelight that illuminated the coven's foyer. While well over a hundred years old, she looked like she was in her twenties. But there was no mistaking the power that flowed within the beautiful witch. She was like a graceful swan; gorgeous and generally calm, but would kill in an instant if provoked.

"Luca," she spoke in an unemotional even-toned voice. "Please come in and have some tea."

Ilsbeth motioned him into the parlor. The room was comfortably airy, almost spa-like, decorated in hues of tan and blue. A large, four-foot tall pillar candle stood in front of the fireplace; its flame appeared to dance to the new age music softly playing in the background.

Luca strode into the room and turned to face Ilsbeth. He was enraged that the coven had misplaced Samantha. "Over a week ago I brought her here to remain in your charge. Did you fail to see or understand the seriousness of my attack? She's in danger."

"Luca, please sit." She gestured for him to have a seat. Power rolled off of her, filling the room with a gentle, soothing hum.

Luca reluctantly sat on a large, linen covered chair. Ilsbeth elegantly walked across the room and sat on the matching sofa across from him.

"Luca, I understand your concern, but you must consider two factors. While the attack could have been intended for Samantha, it could equally have been meant for you or me. As you are aware, I'm not without my fair share of enemies, nor are you." Ilsbeth closed her eyes, took a deep cleansing breath and then opened them again. "Second and perhaps most importantly, I cannot keep Samantha against her will. After purifying her, I was required by the Goddess to let her go her own way. She asked to leave, knowing the dangers, and I had no choice but to let her go."

Luca could have cared less about what the Goddess wanted. "They could have killed me, Ilsbeth. Yet they did not. No, they wanted her. She's special. There's something…something I cannot put my finger on." Luca raked his fingers through his raven hair. He wore it loose tonight and it fell into his eyes.

"I don't disagree, Luca. She is, indeed, special. Goddess knows we don't see a human turned witch very often. It is extremely rare. But she should have had more powers. The magic should've shown itself by now. Magic is drawn to its witch, knowing where to go, wanting to be utilized. But she couldn't concentrate; there was simply nothing. She was frustrated with her progress. Now it may have been caused by stress. You know, even though her physical injuries have subsided, she's quite vulnerable emotionally. What that awful man did to her…" Ilsbeth gritted her teeth in anger, her eyes lit with fire. She quickly composed herself; her face transformed back into its normally placid expression.

"And you should also be aware that she doesn't fully accept her gift yet. She does not wish to be magical. I'm sorry we couldn't do more for her, but she's a grown woman. She knows she can return anytime. Perhaps her leaving the state will keep her from danger," Ilsbeth speculated.

Luca's thoughts raced. Was it possible that she'd be safe away from New Orleans? It was true that she'd be away from the heart of magic, after all. But then he remembered that Asgear was able to extend his reach to Philadelphia. He might not have physically been there, but he was able to funnel his magic to others in the area, making them do things, awful things. No, she needed to come back to the safety of the coven where the magical wards would protect her. She'd be safe with her sisters. Ilsbeth was the most powerful witch on the East Coast. Not even a mouse could get in her courtyard without her permission. Luca knew in that moment that he needed to bring her home.

"I will go get her, explain the danger. She cannot refuse me. Where did she go, Ilsbeth?" he asked authoritatively. While Ilsbeth was powerful, Luca was older, and emanated his own energy. He could not believe the sheer idiocy of the coven rules. It made no sense that because a person didn't want to be there, they could simply walk out the door with no regard for safety. And the coven would wave goodbye and let her do what she wanted, because the Goddess said so. *Fuck coven rules.* He would go get her and bring her back. End of story.

Ilsbeth slowly rose off the sofa. She'd acquiesce to Luca this once. He appeared to care about the human, her sister witch. *Interesting*, she thought to herself. Everyone who knew Luca would be quite surprised to know he cared about a mortal woman.

"Fine, Luca. We shall do as you wish. But know this; I will not keep her here against her will. Should she refuse to stay at the coven, she's in your charge," she explained. Ilsbeth would not go against the Goddess's rules.

"But of course. However this will not be an issue. She will want to return once I speak with her."

"What makes you say that, Luca? She was quite adamant on her departure that she would not be returning to New Orleans. She is quite traumatized, you know," she said softly.

"Does she remember what happened?" Luca inquired, remembering how Samantha could not stop crying at Kade's that night, dark bruises on her face. He'd wanted to kill the son of a bitch who'd hurt her, but Kade had taken care of it. Unfortunately he couldn't fix the emotional damage left in Asgear's aftermath. The best he could do that night was listen and comfort her by placing his hand on her shoulder.

"No, I do not believe so. Anything she shared with me is her story to tell."

"Understandable. No matter. She must return to the safety of the coven," Luca said without emotion. He walked over to the front door and grabbed the handle.

Ilsbeth followed and put her hand on his. Luca turned to face her. "Luca, be gentle with the girl. She's young and scared. Not a very good combination." She removed her hand, went over to her desk and began to write down the address Samantha had given her.

"Ilsbeth, I may not be fond of human women but I can certainly handle getting one on a plane back to New Orleans. I don't know who tried to attack her but I'll be damned if I'm goin' to just sit by and watch her get kidnapped again. Or worse, die. No," he said shaking his head. "It's settled. I'll go and get her. In the meantime, Kade and Sydney can look for clues as to what in the hell is going on down here, who abducted me."

"Okay, Luca. Please call me if you need my assistance. I can work spells from a distance. Also, call me if she shows any signs of magic." She handed him a business card with an address written on the back of it. "She's in Pennsylvania. In the mountains. May the Goddess be with you on your journey."

Taking the card from her hand he walked into the warm, humid air, breathed deeply and turned back again to Ilsbeth. "Thank you, Ilsbeth. Be well."

Luca had an address. *Samantha.* He would go to her now. He'd take the jet and be there within hours. For a split second he wondered if there was something more about this mere mortal that he was drawn to. Dismissing the thought, he slid his cell phone on and called Tristan. He was the person physically located closest to where she was.

"Tristan here," he answered gruffly.

"Tristan, it's me, Luca."

"Mon ami, so good to hear your voice. Kade told me you got yourself trussed up like a silver chained turkey," he joked. Leave it to a wolf to lighten the mood about his attack.

"Yeah, it was quite the ordeal, to say the least. But I'm back. Sydney and Kade saved my life," he said nonchalantly. He did not wish to discuss the feeding with Tristan, knowing how intimate they were. "Unfortunately, this isn't a social call. I'm in need of your assistance, Alpha." Luca deliberately used his title as a sign of respect.

"Just ask, Luca. What is it?"

"It's Samantha. She ran away from the coven. Apparently things didn't go so well with her training so she split," he stated, unhappy that she'd left.

"Ah...the little witch you rescued. How is it she got away from Ilsbeth?"

"Long story short but essentially, she left of her own accord so Ilsbeth had to let her go. She escaped to your neck of the woods. Pocono Mountains. Do you think you could go find and guard her...as wolf until I get there?" Luca asked. "I don't want her to suspect that I'm coming for her lest she'll probably run again. She may not take kindly to another supernatural like you coming after her either. After all she's been through, it may be best to just blend into nature and watch her from afar. Guard her and don't let her leave."

"No problem. I was looking to take a little run anyway. This just gives me something to look forward to. As I recall, she's a pretty young thing. Hot body and a fiery mane you could run your fingers through," Tristan teased, sensing Luca had a personal interest in finding her. He loved Luca but couldn't resist teasing him, given that he was always so serious.

Luca growled. "Alpha, do not touch her. She's been through enough." What the hell was he doing telling an Alpha what to do in his own territory? Luca forced himself to relax, unclench his fist and gain his composure. "I apologize, Tristan. I didn't mean to tell you what to do. It's just that she's vulnerable right now. Ilsbeth said she couldn't find her magic. She's afraid. She needs our help."

"No worries, Luca. I'm on it. I know you've also been through a lot lately. Text me the address, and I'll meet you there. I'll try to keep it wolf, but if she spots me, I won't tell her you're coming."

"Thank you, Tristan. See you later tonight. " Luca ended the call. He'd go up tonight and be back by tomorrow. Then he'd help Kade and Sydney find whoever had kidnapped him, and rip their throats out.

CHAPTER FOUR

Visions of blood dripping from her mouth clouded her thoughts. She was chained, beaten and naked in a concrete cell that reeked of urine and feces. Yanking her wrists forward, blinding pain racked her body; the unyielding cuffs bit into her skin. Screaming at the top of her lungs; no one came. Cold and alone, she sat in the dark and waited for death, praying her torment would come to an end soon.

The only memory she'd had was a recurring nightmare. Samantha woke in a cold sweat, terrorized, like she had every night since she'd been rescued. Realizing that she was outside at the cabin, she jumped up out of the chair. *Goddammit. I fell asleep outside.*

"Great. I'll probably have a thousand bites all over me," she said aloud to herself. Samantha started rubbing her arms and legs, checking her skin for bumps. "Hmm....candle must've worked."

As she turned to blow out the citronella candle, she heard a branch break. She froze and looked out into the darkness. *Eyes.* She breathed slowly, willing herself to relax. She was only a few feet from the house; she could make it inside. But instead of moving inside the house, she stepped forward out of curiosity. Maybe there was an animal in the woods. *A deer?* Eyes flashed again, and she stifled the urge to scream. Reaching behind her, her fingers blindly fumbled for the door handle. She felt something…a switch.

"I will not be afraid," she whispered to herself. No, she'd had enough of being scared. And she was sick and tired of feeling as though she was a field mouse waiting for the hawk to strike. She was a grown woman and could handle whatever was in the woods. She was in the mountains after all. *There is nothing to fear.*

She blew out a breath and flipped the switch. Light flooded the edges of the forest, and she spotted what she thought was a dog. *A dog? What the hell?* Samantha loved dogs, but there was something strange about the very large mongrel standing between the trees. The dog's eyes glowed a deep amber, and its fur was midnight-black. *It almost looks like a…wolf?*

No, that couldn't be. There hadn't been a report of a wolf in Pennsylvania for over twenty years. Bears, yes. Coyote, yes. Wolf, no. So logically, it must be a dog, she told herself. Maybe it was a breed that looked like a wolf - an Alaskan Malamute or a Czechoslovakian Wolfdog? She steeled her nerves; a dog she could handle.

Samantha slowly moved forward, walking down the stairs. If the dog was lost, he might have a collar and tag.

She held out her hand, palm up and spoke to him in a high voice as if she was speaking to a baby. "Hey doggy? Whatcha doin' out here in my woods all by yourself? Are you lost, baby?" The dog calmly sat staring at her as if he understood what she was saying.

She approached carefully, sensing the animal was uninjured and not aggressive. "Come here, boy. It's okay. Are you hungry?" She blew little kisses towards him as if he was a ten pound Shih Tzu. "Come on, now. Don't be afraid."

She stilled as the large dog stalked towards her. Why the hell couldn't she have just gone inside the freakin' cabin? *Okay, I can do this.* Samantha lowered herself toward the ground so she appeared smaller to the animal. Once again, she offered her hand to it.

The dog loped over to Samantha and lay in front of her. She reached forward, letting him sniff her hand, and then proceeded to rub his head and ears. "That's a good boy. Oh yes, who's a good dog? You're a good dog." She praised him as she caressed his soft fur.

"Now how did you get in the woods, doggy? I've got some food in the house. Are you hungry?" Samantha asked. The dog tilted his head and yipped.

"Okay, then. Let's go inside. Come on. Maybe there's rope inside to make you a leash. I'll help find your owner…" As she turned to try to lead him into the house, she glanced back. *Where is the dog?*

"Hey doggy, where'd ya go?" Samantha called. Out of the darkness, a gorgeous, very naked male walked out of the trees. "What the hell?" Samantha screamed and ran as fast as she could towards the cabin.

Large hands grabbed her arms, holding her frozen. *Oh God, not again. This cannot be happening to me.*

"Settle down, petite sorcière. It's okay. You're safe with me." Tristan had expected that the little witch would not react warmly to his arrival. Her fear permeated his senses. He needed to calm her without revealing that Luca had sent him. He was hoping that he could have gone unspotted. *Damn that branch.* Once she saw him, he couldn't resist walking up to her. Getting a good rub down was a benefit of pretending he was a dog, but there was no way he was letting her leash him. Shifting to human was his next best plan.

"I'm Tristan. Ilsbeth sent me," he assured her.

Samantha exhaled a deep breath, relaxing into his hold. "Ilsbeth? Why?" She looked up to study his face and then her eyes roamed down to his groin and back up again. Her face flushed. "Oh my God. You. You're naked. You're a…a wolf," she whispered, hardly believing the words she spoke.

"Yes on both counts. Now unless you plan on stripping down with me, it's hardly fair that I stay naked for your pleasure. Let's go inside, and we can talk." He winked and opened the sliding glass door, gesturing for her to go in.

Stunned by his flirtatious nature, Samantha walked inside. She struggled to understand why Ilsbeth would send a wolf to her in Pennsylvania. "Tristan, please, I don't understand. Why would Ilsbeth send you here? I'm perfectly safe. Is she okay?"

Tristan made himself at home, grabbing a throw blanket off the couch and wrapping it around his waist. Samantha could not help but stare; his tanned, six-pack abs looked like she could bounce a quarter off of them. He was well over six feet tall, and ruggedly handsome. He looked like a California surfer with his platinum blonde hair brushing his shoulders.

And while she found him attractive, she felt a dull ache in her chest. The knowledge of what she may or may not have done at Sangre Dulce ate at her. She doubted she'd be attracted to anyone in a sexual way for a very long time.

Tristan sat down on the large Italian-leather sofa. He felt sorry for the girl. She had no idea what kind of danger she was in or that she was going back to New Orleans tomorrow. And worst of all, she didn't know Luca was on his way. He thought that he should at least attempt to soften her up for Luca. Perhaps he should plant a few seeds that would make the soon-to-be happenings a little more palatable.

"Petite sorcière, I am Alpha of this area, so I know everything that happens here. And everyone who comes into my territory does what I say. Do you follow me? I want to explain a few things to you…explain why Ilsbeth sent me. Now sit," he ordered as he patted the loveseat adjacent to him.

As if she had a damn choice in the matter. She walked over and sat rigidly in the chair. She glared at him, her pensive lips sealed in a tight line.

"Now that's better, mon cher. Please understand a few important things. First of all, know that you are safe with me. I won't let anyone have at you. And the reason I am assuring you of your safety brings me to my second point. There is no other way to put this; you are still very much in danger. We have reason to believe that they were after you." Tristan could see Samantha's face blanch with fright. He reached over and put his hand on her knee.

"Look at me, Samantha," he commanded.

She silently complied.

"Remember what I said first. I will protect you."

"But..." she interrupted.

"Samantha, I was there that day when we rescued you from Asgear. I know what they did to you. Now, I don't know you very well but if you are tough enough to survive what was done to you, you can survive this. You're not alone."

She wanted to believe him but the images of Asgear beating her bloody flashed through her mind. She could not survive again. She glanced over at the front door and fought the urge to run away. He said he'd protect her. She took a deep breath, willing herself to relax long enough to hear him out. She needed to know why they thought she was still in danger.

"I need to know. Who's after me? I mean, Asgear is dead. What could anyone possibly want from me? They say I'm a witch but apparently I can't do that either. If you've spoken to Ilsbeth then you know that I've felt nothing, done nothing...magically. If I really do have magic in me, I'm a sorry excuse for a witch. Honestly, I just want out of this nightmare. That's why I came here. I need to get away from all that craziness." She put her face in her hands, sighed and fought back a sob; she refused to cry one more tear over what Asgear had done to her.

Tristan took her hands in his, sending waves of calming power over her. "I don't know who took Luca or why they wanted you. But Kade and Sydney are working on it right now. In the meantime, I'll keep you safe. In the morning....well, we'll cross that bridge tomorrow. Now, how about I get you something to drink. A brandy?"

Samantha silently regarded Tristan, feeling numbness wash over her body.

"Okay, you don't need to say anything. Just sit. I'll be back." Tristan rose and strode across the room, quickly finding a bottle of whiskey in one of the cabinets. *Close enough.* At least they had something to drink. From across the room, he could hear her heart racing, probably from both fear and anger. Fuck, if he had told her she was going back to New Orleans tomorrow, she'd probably pass out. No, he'd leave that little doozy for Luca.

After Tristan handed Samantha a glass, she took a long, strong pull of the golden liquid. Immediately, she had a coughing fit, raising her hands to signal she was all right. Composing herself, she regarded the Alpha sitting in front of her. "Little rough, huh, Tristan? You know what, wolf?

I have no intention of being a victim again. No fucking way. If one of Asgear's flunkies is coming after me, they aren't taking me alive again," she resolved.

"Now that's the spirit, ma petite sorcière," Tristan replied.

"Petite sorcière?" Samantha questioned.

"Ah yes. Little witch. That is who you are now. Whether you feel your power or not, it's there. I can literally smell the magic emanating off your skin."

"Yeah well, maybe all that is true, but I couldn't create one little spark when I was at the coven. Couldn't even light a candle. Some witch I am. I'll tell you this for nothing, I am way better at computers than all this mumbo jumbo that supposedly lurks within me. You know, I was good at something, really good at it. Now, I'm afraid I can't even go back to that," she huffed.

"When this is all over, Samantha, you can start anew. There are lots of supernaturals in the area. I can help you find a computer job in the Philadelphia area with folks who understand…who know who you are and what you are." He smiled, taking another swig of the whiskey.

Samantha's head was spinning. *He thought she should go work for supernaturals? Get real. So not happening, Alpha wolf.* She rolled her eyes, and threw back her head, resting it on the sofa.

"Thanks for the offer. But that isn't happening any time soon. I took a leave of absence from my job, so I could get my head together. Heal. And that is exactly what I plan to do. Then I'm going back to my boring, so not magical life. And I can't wait." She placed her empty glass on the end table. She continued talking, determined not to let fear overcome her. "Listen, since there's nothing I can really do at this point if someone breaks in, I'm taking your word that you'll protect me. So here's the plan. I'm going to go over to the kitchen, find a big knife and take it to bed with me. I'm overwhelmed, angry and generally unhappy right now." She gestured to the sofa. "The sofa is all yours, Alpha. Talk to you in the morning."

With those words, she strode into the kitchen, selected the biggest sharpest chef knife she could find and walked down the hall towards her bedroom. Sure, she was afraid. But she was not about to get kidnapped again without a knockdown, drag-out fight. She undressed, throwing on a comfortable cami, and climbed into the freshly lined bed. Reaching over, she placed the knife carefully under her pillow, in easy reach if she needed it, and closed her eyes, praying the nightmares wouldn't come.

A loud knock resounded throughout the cabin's wooden interior. Tristan strode over to the door, throw still around his hips, and opened it. From outside, Luca glared at Tristan, noticing he was wearing next to nothing.

"What?" Tristan asked. He shrugged his shoulders, walked back over to the couch and stretched out, putting his feet up on the coffee table.

Luca followed after him, shutting the door. "What? Really, wolf? I asked you to watch her, not give her a male review."

Tristan laughed. "Hey man, I can't help it if the ladies like to see my goods. Besides, I'm a wolf. Can't exactly carry clothes with me."

Luca sat down and let out a huge sigh. "Okay, just tell me now. Where is she? And why aren't you furry?"

"She was asleep outside on the porch. So I watched and waited. When she woke up, she heard something and flipped on the floodlights. Don't worry, though. She's handled the wolf fairly well. And I can't lie, Luca, the woman gives a good rub," he joked. He jerked his head towards the hallway. "Samantha's sleeping."

"Well, I do appreciate you coming up here to guard her. Tomorrow, we'll return to New Orleans. The jet is ready to go." Luca would be relieved once they were back home.

Tristan smiled and shook his head. "Yeah, about that. You know, you might want to wait a few days before taking her back. Maybe give her a day or two. Get to know her more, earn her trust."

"What the hell, Tristan? Are you kidding me?"

"No, mon ami. I'm dead serious. Just listen. The girl's been through a lot. I talked to her tonight, made her understand how she's still in danger. But you've got to ease her into going back. She doesn't even know you're alive."

"Not happening. We're going back tomorrow. She'll have to deal with it. Look, I'm not a therapist or a babysitter. Do I feel a slight sense of responsibility for the witch? Yes, but only because Kade initially put her into my charge." Luca knew that there might be another reason for why he felt he needed to keep the girl safe, but he wasn't going to share.

Tristan's face tightened and his eyes narrowed. His friend did not seem to hear what he was saying. "Luca. Try to remember what happened to her and what that might've been like for her. I know it's been a long time for you, but try to remember what it's like to be human. The girl was drugged, bespelled, beaten, possibly raped, and to top off her shit sandwich, she can barely remember anything but lying naked in a prison cell. Oh, and let us not forget her being told she's a witch, one who can't seem to conjure up a clue, and whose entire life as she knows it is about to come to an end. Can't you see? It's too damn much," Tristan pleaded.

Luca rubbed his eyes, thinking through Tristan's argument. He didn't want to stay here. This was supposed to be a simple trip. Fly up to Philadelphia, get witch, return to New Orleans. Easy peasy. Not. But Luca could not deny the empathy he felt for the little witch who tugged at his heartstrings. Aside from dragging her kicking and screaming back to the jet, it would be easier if he could get her to agree to go home with him. If that failed, kicking and screaming was always an option.

"Okay. I'll talk to her and stay here for one day...tops. She'll be waking soon, and I should have all day to talk reason into the human." He hated when Tristan was right, but knew he needed to go easy on her. "On our way back, I'll stop at your club to feed. If I stay around her more than a day, I'm pretty sure I would be tempted to taste her. And that's the very last thing I need or she needs. I very much doubt she'd willingly donate her blood." He shook his head as he imagined asking her to let him bite her. She'd probably freak the hell out and try to escape yet again. No, he'd wait to feed at Tristan's club to keep things nice and smooth. Complications were something he was trying very hard to avoid.

"Yeah, I don't think it would go over too well if you asked her to be your donor. Awkward." Tristan laughed. He stood and removed the blanket, unaffected by his nudity, and walked over to the back door.

Luca averted his eyes in an effort not to look at him. It was a good thing the naked wolf was leaving. The thought that Tristan had displayed his generously endowed body to Samantha flew in his head and caused his stomach to clench in anger. Did he just feel jealous? No, that couldn't be possible. He quickly stifled his emotion, not wanting Tristan to sense his feelings.

"Remember Luca, go easy on the female. She'll come round. See you in a day or so." As Tristan shut the sliding glass door, he appeared to seamlessly change into his black wolf, and loped out of sight.

CHAPTER FIVE

Luca paced the room. How was he going to stay here for even a day with the witch? Would she remember him? Would she fear him? Would she fight him? As self-composed as Luca normally was, being here in the cabin, knowing she was in the other room, spurred his curiosity. What did she wear to sleep? Was she cold? Scared? *I should go check on her.* He could hear her soft breathing from a distance. He knew she was just fine. But he wanted to see her again, not later, but now. What would it hurt to just take a peek at her?

Walking down the hallway, he knew what he was about to do wasn't right. He felt like some kind of a pervert, looking in on a woman that he barely knew. Yet he felt compelled to keep going. Once at her door, he laid his palm against it and took a deep breath. Looking at his watch, he confirmed that at five am, she'd still be asleep and not likely to wake. *I really am going to do this.* Slowly he turned the handle, and pushed open the door.

Luca struggled to control his instinct to reach over and touch the lovely woman sprawled out on the bed. Immediately he was filled with desire; his breath caught as he stood frozen, watching her sleep. Samantha lay on her back, her skin exposed from pushing the covers off her body. Dressed only in a white cotton camisole and pink boyshorts, her pert breasts peeked out of the flimsy material. Her long, wavy strawberry hair fanned across her pillow; she almost appeared to smile in her sleep. She was even more beautiful than he'd remembered.

Back at Kade's mansion, after he'd rescued her, she'd appeared quite frail; her thin body marred by bruises and scratches. Her hair was straight and dyed neon red. He'd wondered at the time if that was the real color of her hair. She'd looked like a victim fighting to regain some semblance of normalcy, dignity. No, lying here before him this night was a healthy, resplendent woman who was enticing, alluring and very much human.

His last thought jerked him back to reality. *Human.* No, he would never fall for any woman, let alone a human. Feed from them, try not to screw them and never, ever fall in love with them. It was simply not an option, no matter how much the rise of cock told him that he should do otherwise. He refused to acknowledge that he had any feelings whatsoever for the mortal lying on the bed in front of him. Yet his body reacted as if he should take her right there. *What the hell is wrong with me?*

Luca rolled his eyes and softly sighed. What was he going to do? He wasn't here to fuck her; he was here to bring her back to the coven. Yet he felt the need to be near her, to protect her. He needed to be close to her, tonight.

Spying a brown leather lounge chair in the corner of the room, he walked over, sat down and put his feet up on the ottoman. He decided that he wasn't going to leave her unattended. He could just as easily guard her from the living room. Staying with her here was merely an excuse for him to fill his senses with her; he drank in the sight of her with his eyes, smelled her perfumed skin. He prayed whatever he was feeling would go away.

He hadn't had sex in a long time; well, not for a few weeks anyway. What had happened with Kade and Sydney earlier couldn't exactly be called sex. He'd felt out of control with them. He still couldn't believe Kade had let him feed from Sydney, let alone kiss her, touch her. She was a beautiful woman and a seriously toughened warrior, one whom he respected immensely, but she was not his. Nor did he want her. Sydney had been a means to health, no more, no less. And he was grateful to both of them for bringing him back from the brink.

Samantha shifted on the bed, turning away from him. He inwardly groaned as he admired her perfectly shaped ass; she was killing him. Adjusting himself, he tried to relieve some of the strain of his erection. *Repeat to self, 'Samantha is human'.* Luca was happy that he planned on stopping at Tristan's club on the way back to the airport. He'd pick a donor who'd satisfy his appetite for blood and sex. If he got it out of his system, he'd be able to control himself around Samantha. He relaxed slightly, knowing he'd devised a plan to get the devilish little witch out of his system.

Naked. Pounding music. Slapped across the face. Blinding pain. A pool of blood on a cold stone floor. Samantha gasped for air, jolting herself upright in bed. Another nightmare. She threw herself backward, focusing on the cedar ceiling beams. She was safe. Away from New Orleans and away from vampires. She closed her eyes, practicing the deep breathing she'd learned from Ilsbeth. Tense shoulders, breathe deeply, release breath, shoulders relax. By the time she got to her toes, her heartbeat had slowed, and she considered going back to sleep. Her thoughts began to race once again as she remembered the nightmare. She'd been naked in a nightclub and later had been imprisoned in a cell. *What did I do in New Orleans? I want my life back.*

Thinking she'd go for a run and take a nap later, she decided to get up. Then she remembered that Tristan would be sitting in her living room. Why couldn't they all just leave her alone? Why did they think someone was after her? The attack could have been meant for Ilsbeth, not her. She decided that no matter what Tristan had to say, she wasn't going to agree to return to New Orleans with him. She'd taken a leave of absence from her job so she could get herself together and return to work and her life. And that was what she was going to do.

As she sat up, her heart caught in her chest. A large male sat in the darkened corner of her bedroom. For a minute she relaxed, believing Tristan had come into her room, but then she noticed his hair wasn't blonde. No, not Tristan. Someone was here for her already. Her heart beat wildly as the adrenaline pumped. She would not go without a fight.

Silently, she reached under her pillow and curled her hands around the hilt of the knife she'd taken to bed with her for protection. The man wasn't moving, his feet propped up on the ottoman. In the darkness of dawn, she couldn't see his face. Samantha didn't want to be a victim. No, this time she'd be the aggressor. She couldn't survive being taken hostage again. She'd kill before being taken again. She dragged her legs across the bed in one smooth motion and leapt at the stranger with the knife.

Luca had heard Samantha gasp, watching her sit straight up out of a dead sleep. He'd wanted to go to her, to calm her. But as she lay back again, he heard her heart slow. So he decided to watch and protect. He could not risk touching her while she was barely dressed and in bed. After his arousal earlier in the night, he didn't trust himself to merely comfort her. Her sweet scent called to him like no other human's blood ever had before, yet he swore to not get involved with the witch.

As soon as he lay his head back on the chair, confident she was going back to sleep, he sensed movement. Samantha had spied him and was coming at him with a sharp knife. He grabbed both her wrists and pulled her towards him, so she straddled him. Gently, he applied pressure to her thumb and was relieved that she dropped the knife without incident. Smelling her fear, he sought to assure her of her safety. "Samantha, it's me, Luca."

"Luca...you're alive!" she exclaimed. Samantha was overcome with relief. That day at the coven, she was convinced she'd never see him again. Seeing him brought forth a rush of emotions. He'd been so caring and gentle with her at Kade's house and then had fought valiantly to save her and Ilsbeth when they were attacked.

Wide eyed and shaking, Samantha extended her fingertips and placed them on Luca's cheeks. She couldn't believe he was with her in the cabin and alive. As Samantha adjusted to the dim light, she was captivated by Luca's piercing dark green eyes. His jet-black, shoulder-length hair hung loosely around his handsome, chiseled face. Feeling his strong jawline tense in her small hands, the stubble prickled her fingers.

Luca froze as Samantha reached to touch him. Her hands burned his skin, and he felt as if he was on fire as desire built deep within him. As soon as her skin touched his, he instantly released her wrists, freeing her. Why was he having this visceral reaction to her? He'd hoped she'd jump away from him, and was regretting his action of pulling her onto him. His hands nearly crushed the arms of the chair as he held on for dear life. Blood rushed towards his groin. He breathed deeply, trying to control the rise of his erection. *Christ, I have got to get back to New Orleans.*

"What are you doing here, Luca?" Samantha asked. Instead of releasing him, she moved closer and pressed her forehead to his.

With her lips inches from his, he sucked in a breath and struggled to answer. "Samantha, I've come for you. You aren't safe. I've come to take you home."

Samantha searched his eyes for truth in his statement. Sensing he was entirely serious, she leaned closer still, feathered his lips with a small kiss, then stood up and walked away. She turned to look at him as she entered the bathroom. "Luca, as much as I appreciate everything you've done for me, there is no way in hell I'm goin' back to New Orleans." With that, she shut the bathroom door.

Stunned from her kiss, Luca threw his head back in frustration. He placed two fingers on his lips; how was he going to get her back to New Orleans without fucking her senseless? He cursed his erection and adjusted himself yet again as he pushed out of the chair and walked out of the room. He didn't want to be there when Samantha was finished in the bathroom. His so-called 'protecting' her from her bedroom had officially ended. He could not trust himself. He'd wait for her in the safety of the living room and talk to her there.

Samantha laid the back of her head against the bathroom door and sighed. After being beaten and imprisoned, she thought she'd never think about sex again. Yet seeing Luca right now, she'd kissed him and was most definitely thinking of sex. Maybe she was attracted to him because he'd rescued her from the mage and then again from the attack. Maybe she had some kind of hero complex? No, it was something else. He'd been kind to her on the night at the mansion and later at the coven, had valiantly fought their attackers. It was as if there was some small part of Luca that understood what she'd been through. She could tell he cared by his words and his touch. And even now, instead of waking her and dragging her out of the cabin, which she knew he was capable of doing, he silently waited, protecting her. It was obvious to her that he'd been watching her sleep, waiting for her to agree to go willingly.

Looking deep into his eyes, she'd sensed sadness, hesitation, but also lust. From the second she'd touched his face, she'd felt the chemistry and soon after, she'd felt him grow physically hard beneath her. But then he said he really just wanted her to return to New Orleans, and she just could not do that. She understood from Tristan that she was in danger, but she wanted time to figure out another way to escape it. Any way to do that would satisfy her, as long as she didn't have to return to New Orleans.

Samantha huffed and stared at herself in the mirror as she brushed her teeth. She wondered if her nightmare would ever end. For a split second, she contemplated sneaking out of the cabin but knew her effort would be a futile attempt at freedom. She'd learned that vampires could sense the tiniest sound or scent. Even if she somehow managed to get out of the house without Luca hearing her, he'd soon realize her scent was gone and would just follow her.

Samantha pulled on a pair of black spandex yoga pants, and topped it off with a royal-blue tank top. As she looked at herself in the mirror once again, she decided to stay and deal with Luca. She refused to run. Contrary to whatever he thought, he wasn't the boss of her. She'd calmly explain that she was staying in Pennsylvania and convince him to leave her alone.

Luca was staring at the lake when Samantha walked into the living room. He sensed her enter but chose not to look at her; what he needed to say would be better said if he wasn't distracted.

"Samantha, we need to have a serious talk. Perhaps when I told you we needed to return to New Orleans, you thought it was a request. However, I assure you it's not. Quite the opposite, in fact." Luca turned to face her; his face hardened. "It's simply a matter of fact. We'll leave tomorrow morning to return to New Orleans. You can come willingly or not, but you'll be returning with me."

Samantha's eyes flashed angrily at him as she grabbed an apple out of a bag on the counter. "What the hell is that supposed to mean, Luca? How exactly do you intend to get me on a plane if I don't go *willingly*? Are you going to kidnap me just like Asgear did? Bespell me?" As she continued to rant, she paced back and forth in the kitchen.

"Oh, I know what you vampires do. What do they call it? Enthrall me? No way, Luca, no one is going to mess with my mind. I thought you were different from the others." She stood and hung her head in despair. She was barely getting her thoughts back in order and now he was threatening her too. He was just like the rest of them.

Samantha's words cut to his core. Maybe he didn't care for humans, but he was not as cold-hearted as she'd just described. Why couldn't she be reasonable and see the danger? Regardless, he felt he owed her the truth.

"I am vampire, Samantha. Nothing more, nothing less. I won't lie to you. If given the choice between leaving you here unprotected or bringing you back to safety, I will enthrall you to get you back on that plane. I'm sorry if you're angry with me, but this is how it must be. When the danger has passed, you can return to this area and Tristan will help you get settled, living as a supernatural." Luca felt bad about having to be so strict with her, but he needed to keep her from danger.

He approached her slowly and placed a finger under her chin, tilting her face upward. His eyes met hers. "Trust me, Samantha. It will work out for the best. Please, just come back to New Orleans, willingly, until we figure out who attacked you. I promise to make this as pleasant as possible. I don't want to enthrall you. I just need you to be safe."

A tear fell from Samantha's eye as she looked up at Luca. "Okay, Luca. I'll go. But I don't want to go back to the coven. Maybe no one told you, but I can't do anything remotely witchy. The witches don't even like me there, and frankly, I don't want to be there. Ilsbeth is fine but I'm just not comfortable staying with the coven. Can I return to Kade and Sydney's? Maybe I could stay with them until we get this figured out?"

Luca did not think it was a good idea for her to return to Kade's house with Dominique milling about the place. When Samantha had been bespelled, she'd silvered Dominique to a table in Sangre Dulce. Dominique could have cared less that Samantha had no control, and she wanted very much to tear into her throat and drain her dry for what she'd done to her. She was incredulous that Kade had saved her and taken her to the coven. If Dominique saw Samantha, it was likely blood would be shed.

"No, there's no way you can *safely* stay at the mansion with Kade and Sydney. As much as Sydney would love to have another human visit, Dominique is at their place way too often, and she's looking for payback. She probably won't kill you, since Kade has made it clear you're off limits, but I'm afraid I couldn't trust her not to at least attack you," Luca continued, knowing he was going to regret his next words. "You're welcome at my home, however. I live next door to Kade within his compound. There's plenty of room, and I have a spare bedroom."

Samantha nodded in relief. "Thank you, Luca." She toyed with the apple in her hands and broke eye contact. "You have to realize that things are so out of control for me. I just need to have a few things I can control, like where I live." She rolled her eyes. "I can't believe this is happening to me. You know, I haven't even told my family. My mom and dad live outside of Baltimore, and I haven't even gone to see them since I got back. I just called my sister, Jess, to tell her I was the unfortunate victim of a 'mugging' per the story Sydney set up with the police and my employer. I told her to tell mom and dad I was staying in New Orleans on a consulting job and would call them when I got a chance. I'm lying to her…I'm lying to everyone. What am I supposed to tell them?"

She walked away from Luca, looking around the floor for her shoes. "Luca, you don't need to say anything. I know you didn't cause this to happen. I'm just frustrated. I need to think."

Luca couldn't resist her any longer. She reminded him of a wounded puppy, albeit a very sexy one. He confidently strode over towards Samantha and put his arms around her, raking his hands through her hair as he brought her face against his chest. Settling his lips into her mane of hair, he kissed the top of her head. He wrapped his other hand around the small of her waist as he spoke gently to her. "Samantha darlin', it's goin' to be all right. We'll find who's responsible for this attack and you'll get your life back. I promise you."

Surprised by Luca's tender embrace, Samantha hugged him back, enjoying the feel of the sinewy muscles of his back. Somehow within his arms, she knew she could trust him. He made her want to feel again: desire, lust, love. But he was vampire. Strong and lethal. At six foot five, he could easily overpower her and drag her to New Orleans, bend her to his will. But instead, he was comforting her in the best way he knew how...with words, with an embrace.

The growing desire within her chest frightened her. How could she be so attracted to Luca? She inwardly laughed, knowing that it was not so hard to be physically attracted to him. He was ruggedly gorgeous but not a pretty boy. No, nothing boy-like about him; he was pure virile male. Samantha could feel his tight abdomen against her own and longed to see the hard planes of his chest without clothing hindering her view. Whilst he was muscular, he was also lean, with a spectacularly athletic build.

Reluctantly, she stepped out of his arms, and sat on the ottoman, struggling to understand what was happening to her when she was around him. She blushed as she scrambled to put on her running shoes.

"Thank you, Luca. Um...for comforting me," she stammered, trying to tie her shoes as quickly as possible.

"And where do you think you're going? It seemed just a minute ago that we'd come to an understanding," he said, raising a questioning eyebrow at her.

"Going for a walk around the lake," she replied as she walked back to the sliding glass door leading to the back deck. "Our deal is that we leave tomorrow. So for today, I'm going to do my best to relax. You're welcome to come with me. If not, you could stay here or meet me down at the pier when I'm done. I promise to yell should I see any bears," she teased.

"I'll watch you from the deck. I don't sense any supernaturals in the area right now, so you'll be okay. But stick close to the lake and I'll meet you down at the pier in ten minutes. I just have to make a few calls. I want to let Kade and Sydney know when we'll be arriving. I have to call Tristan too."

"Okay, meet you down there." Samantha bit into her apple, walked outside, closed the door and headed down the path towards the lake.

Watching Samantha like a hawk, Luca took a deep breath, grabbed his cell and called Kade. He explained to him that he'd be back down tomorrow and purposefully left out the part about Samantha staying with him. He couldn't believe that he'd offered to let her stay with him, but at the same time, he secretly wanted to spend more time with his little witch.

After calling Tristan to let him know they'd be stopping by his place early in the morning, he opened the door and headed towards the water. He didn't relish having to stop at Eden, Tristan's club, but he needed to feed and Tristan had promised to keep a blood donor waiting for him. He wasn't about to feed on Samantha; she'd been through far too much trauma over the past weeks. His fangs elongated at the thought of tasting her sweet, magical blood. *Goddammit. I have to keep it together.* He retracted his razor sharp teeth, not wanting to risk Samantha seeing them.

As he got halfway down the path, he watched her stretch on the dock. He halted, admiring her firm ass as she bent forward to grab her right calf. His cock jerked to attention as he fantasized about ripping off her clothes and taking her from behind on her hands and knees right out in the open on the wooden pier. No one would see, he surmised, looking around at the isolated woods. Shaking himself from his thoughts, he sighed. He could not get involved with this human. He knew how fragile they were, how easily they could die. Luca refused to let that happen again.

Just as he thought he'd regained control of himself, his mouth dropped wide open. With her back facing Luca, Samantha crossed her arms in front of her and removed her flimsy, stretchy tank top. *Jesus, what was she doing?* He continued to watch in awe as she kicked off her sneakers, hooked her thumbs on the waist of her pants and stripped them off until she was standing on the end of the dock stark naked. She reached a hand up into her ponytail and freed her fiery mane; the soft tendrils scattered over her creamy pale shoulders, teasing the small of her back. The perfectly-formed globes of her buttocks called to him; his erection pressed tightly against his zipper.

Luca could not believe she'd stripped nude in front of him and every small creature in the woods. He couldn't help but smile as she launched herself off the dock in a perfect dive. Did she know he was watching her? How could she not have known? He'd told her he'd keep an eye on her at the lake. Little temptress, what was she doing?

With preternatural speed, he arrived at the dock just as her hands breached the shimmering dark-blue water.

Samantha bobbed up to the surface and spun to face him. He could hardly believe the reckless abandon she demonstrated, given that she'd been held up in a strange coven less than a week ago. She was resilient, young and full of energy, representing a zest for life that he'd long forgotten.

Samantha smiled as she waved to him to join her in the deep abyss. She called out to him, "Come in, Luca! The water's great!" She laughed and dove again; her white bottom peeked out for a second before submerging yet again.

"Darlin', I've got no suit. Besides, vampires don't swim." He wanted desperately to go in after her, but knew it would lead to so much more than a morning swim.

"You've got your birthday suit. Please, you're not gonna make a girl swim alone, are ya?" she purred.

"Is it cold?" He was starting to waver in his firm decision to stay on shore.

"Naw, it's plenty warm. It's late August, had plenty of time to heat up. Come on!" she begged.

"You a good swimmer?" Luca asked.

"Yes. Why're you asking?" she replied.

"Because I'm coming in to get you!" Losing all control, Luca quickly pulled off his white t-shirt and began to undress.

As he unzipped his pants, Samantha screamed playfully and started to swim away. Stripped naked, Samantha admired his rippling abs out the side of her eyes. She knew he'd be coming for her.

Breaching the water, Luca cursed. "Damn, it's cold. You lied to me, woman. You'd better swim fast because I'm goin' to catch you!"

Luca dove under the water once again, determined to catch up with the very slippery, naked woman who'd enticed him to jump into a cold mountain lake in the middle of the day. It had been at least a hundred years since he'd indulged in such a childish activity, but he simply could not resist her. While vampires could be exposed to sunlight, he was weakened to the state of a human during the day. Breaking the surface, he searched for her and spied feet splashing several yards from him. He dove once again, knowing he'd soon catch his prey.

Samantha gasped for air after racing away from Luca. She spun in a circle, treading water as she looked for a trace of him. The smooth lake gave no clues as to where he was. She knew he was somewhere. Somewhere close. Looking towards the cabin, she screamed loudly as hands came around her waist.

Luca pulled her close to him and began to tickle her mercilessly. "Ah, little witch, you lied to me. The water is nearly freezing. And since I can't spank you in the water, this is your punishment." He continued to tickle her as she laughed hysterically, thrashing in the water.

"I'm sorry," she pleaded. "Uncle! Uncle!"

Luca stopped tickling her but didn't let her go. Instead he let his hands move from her waist to just under her breasts, encircling her ribcage. Samantha relaxed back onto him, letting her head fall back onto his shoulder as they both floated on their backs in the peaceful reserve.

"I'm happy you joined me. I love it up here in the woods. It's so peaceful." Samantha wrapped her arms around his, fully aware of where his arms supported her. As they moved as one in the water, she could feel the hardness of him brushing her bottom. Yet she wasn't afraid. She was aroused and excited that he'd joined her in such a very human activity.

"I'm happy you convinced me to swim with you," Luca responded. "I haven't done this in such a long time. I'd forgotten how wonderful it is to skinny dip."

"How old are you, Luca?"

"Very old, indeed, my dear Samantha. I was turned in the eighteen hundreds. So I'm well over two hundred years old….give or take a few years."

"Do you miss being human?" Samantha asked.

"No, darlin'. Being human is so ordinary. And now that you're a witch, you've joined our little club of supernaturals. I sense your fear. But I promise you that you'll be all right. In fact, you'll probably love it once you find your magic." Luca squeezed her tightly and kissed her shoulder.

"Ah, and there's the rub my friend. I have no magic. Nothing. Ilsbeth seems to think there's something about me, but I can't do a thing. Believe me, I've tried. Nothing happens," Samantha huffed.

"It will come, Samantha. I can smell the magic on you, and it's as sweet as honey. It's there. Maybe it hasn't shown itself yet, but it will."

"You sound so confident, Luca. I wish I could be like you. But I feel so defeated. Seriously, Luca. I've been kidnapped, forced into working at a sex club, beaten and then told I was a witch. I've had to take a leave of absence from my real life. I can't tell anyone human what's really happened to me. And now, on top of everything, you think I'm in danger, and I have to return to that God forsaken city where it all started. I just want to lie back in this lake and forget everything," she confided.

"Do you remember what you told me that night we were at Kade's?" Luca asked.

"Yes. No. I don't know. I said a lot of things. I was crying. I was upset. What do you mean? What did I say?" Samantha laughed a little, knowing how confused she sounded.

"You said you were a strong person. And while I don't know you very well, I believe that's true," he continued. "Since you've been here at the cabin, you've stared down a wolf, talked with an Alpha and held a knife to a vampire. You're either crazy or strong, and I can tell you that I know it's the latter. You'll survive what's to come. You can do this, Samantha."

"Luca, where have you been my whole life?" she joked. She smiled, realizing there was something about him that made her feel better. "Maybe you're right. Maybe I can do this, but I can't do it alone. You make me feel like I'll get through this as long as I'm with you." She'd never known such encouragement in her entire existence, and here was a man who had faith in her even when she didn't have it in herself.

Luca's heart beat against his chest at her words. He knew he shouldn't fall for a human, but she was chipping away at whatever resolve he had left to stay away. Unable to resist her any longer, he kissed the side of her neck and slowly trailed his lips behind her ear. She moaned in arousal as he slid his hands up to caress her breasts. He wanted to take her there in the lake.

"Luca," she whispered as he kissed and touched her. "Yes."

With her words, he turned her around to face him, pressing his lips to hers. Their tongues swept together as they passionately kissed. Samantha wrapped her legs around Luca's waist, aroused by the feel of his rock-hard cock bobbing up against the crease of her ass. She fingered his long hair and kissed up his cheeks as he licked her neck.

"Luca, please," she panted. God, she wanted him. She wanted to forget everything in that moment but him.

"Samantha." Luca wanted to stop, to tell her that they shouldn't continue. She was so vulnerable after what had happened. As much as he wanted her, he didn't want to take advantage either. And then there was his vow not to get involved with humans. But she tasted sweet as peaches on a warm summer day. So soft and slippery in his hands.

"Mmmm...you're so beautiful," he murmured, unable to stop kissing her. He needed to have all of her.

As he was about to suggest they go inside the cabin, Luca tensed. He immediately released Samantha to stop and sniff the air. *Smoke.* He growled, baring his fangs.

"Luca, what's wrong?" Samantha asked, frightened.

"Swim Samantha," he ordered. "The cabin. It's on fire."

Luca and Samantha immediately swam toward the dock. Luca reached it first and effortlessly leapt up onto the wooden surface. Extending a hand, he pulled Samantha out and they both dressed within minutes. Luca held Samantha's hand as they ran towards the black smoke billowing from the cabin. Orange streaks of fire danced towards the trees as they stood helplessly by and watched the inferno.

"Luca, who would do this?" Samantha gasped.

"I told you that you were in danger. Looks like whoever attacked us in New Orleans has just found you in Pennsylvania." He released Samantha's hand and began to search around the edge of the house for evidence. "Stay back from the flames. I just need to check. I might be able to scent whoever did this."

Samantha stood silently for a moment, looking at the blackened embers; the flames licked toward the sky. Part of the exterior walls remained even though the front of the building was completely gone. Luca walked over to the entrance while Samantha relegated herself to the perimeter of the woods.

Looking down toward the walkway, Luca's anger rose as he read words scrawled on the slate. *"Where is the Hematilly Periapt?"* Luca frowned. What the hell was that supposed to mean? He knelt down with his cell phone and snapped a picture. Then he ran his fingers over the clotted, blood-red substance; he held it to his nose and sniffed. Bat's blood. What the fuck was someone doing with bat's blood out here in the middle of the mountains? It was a common ingredient used in witchcraft, usually made with indigo dye, cinnamon, myrrh, and a few other benign ingredients. But the sanguine ink was genuine blood from the veins of a freshly slit bat's throat; it was used for revenge. Someone had intended to burn them to a crisp in that cabin; fitting retribution for a witch.

What is the Hematilly Periapt? An amulet, he pondered. Ilsbeth had said nothing to him about her owning it. Could Samantha have such an object? Did she know what it was? And if existed, what did it do? Who would want something so badly they'd be willing to kill for it in broad daylight? Deciding not to tell Samantha about the writing, he smeared the fluid across the sole of his shoe, blurring the words. He wiped his finger on his jeans, looked up into the flames and sighed. They needed to get out of there.

Samantha's eyes pricked with tears as she watched her rental cabin burn. She looked up to the surrounding trees, which had begun to catch fire. Anger burned deep within her soul. She'd had enough of the evil and destruction. Luca was right about one thing; she was strong, and she would find a way through this. Not only that; in that moment, she resolved to be part of the solution and not idly stand by while life happened to her. She remembered what Ilsbeth had told her about how she had magic within her but she was the only one who could call it to be. It was her decision, her power.

Closing her eyes, Samantha reached out her hands, palms up toward the heavens and focused on her need to put the fire out. She called to the elements as if they were servants; instinctually, she knew that they were within her control. She felt the tingle in her fingertips as her eyes flew open. The clouds had already drawn close, and lightning flashed in the distance. "Rain, come," she commanded.

Nothing happened, and she looked up again as if readying to scold an insolent child. Anger surging, she encouraged the tendrils of magic to dance over her skin until she was within a mystic trance. Unconsciously, she chanted over and over as the words came to her from within, "Aqua Dei tui eu nunc. Aqua Dei tui eu nunc. Aqua Dei tui eu nunc!" She shook with power as the water began to fall from the sky.

Luca stood back as a bright aura surrounded Samantha. Although he'd known her magic existed, she had doubted its existence. As streams of light pushed from her palms, he knew she'd found it. He blessed the rain as it poured down in droves, putting the fire out within minutes. When it was clear all the embers were drowned, he called out to Samantha, "It's done Samantha. You can let go, darlin'. You did it."

Samantha barely registered Luca's words as the power within her died. She slumped over, holding herself up by propping her hands on her knees. It felt as if she'd run a marathon. Colors danced in the whites of her eyes as she fell into blackness.

"You did it!" Luca exclaimed. "You put out the fire." As he turned to smile at her, he panicked; she'd collapsed into the muddy mixture of dirt and ash. He rushed over, fell to his knees and gently cradled her in his arms. "It's okay, you did it. Come on now, wake up, Samantha." He kissed her head and pulled away, realizing they needed to get out of there. He traced his fingers from her temple down around her chin.

Her eyes fluttered, "What?"

"You scared me. You're okay now, let's get going." He stood up with her cradled in his arms. She pressed her face into his chest, afraid to look at the cabin.

He walked with her over to his SUV, opened the door and carefully sat her in the front seat.

"Stay here, Samantha," he told her. "I need to get my keys. Is there anything you need out of this rubble?" Luca knew full well there wasn't much left worth salvaging. But after all she'd been through, he would've tried to save anything important to her.

She silently shook her head no and stared out the car's front windshield, not wanting to face what had happened. Denial could be quite a peaceful state if she only embraced it; alas, she could not tear her eyes from the debris. A dazed veil fell over her face as she silently contemplated the fire, her magic. It was as if her inner light dimmed as the cold splash of reality dowsed her. She was still in danger, and if she'd had a doubt before, her magic, while unpredictable, was intact. It was a wicked blow to the fragile sense of balance she'd worked hard to build over the past week.

Samantha, still in shock from creating the rain, shook her head silently. She hadn't brought anything of importance with her to the cabin. She hadn't had a chance to replace all her credit cards since New Orleans. The only thing she'd replaced was her smartphone, which had all her financial information on it via the apps. And luckily, she'd worn it on her walk so she could listen to music.

Luca trod into what was left of the home, watching carefully where he stepped. The crunch of the charred wood beneath his feet resounded in Samantha's ears as she watched the smoke-filled sky dissipate from gray to blue. The smell of burnt wood engrained itself in the surrounding woods and grass; there was no direction either of them could turn where they could not detect the evidence of what had happened.

Luca came out of the house with nothing more than a single set of keys. "Got the keys!" he grumbled. He quickly strode over to her, got in the car and started it. "Let's go. You're in shock and we've got to get out of here before whoever did this comes back. It's odd. I can't smell a vampire or a wolf, no magic either." *Smells undeniably human.* He didn't want to tell Samantha that wolves, shifters, vampires and those of the magic persuasion could all use human minions to do their dirty work. "Samantha, this may not be the best time to discuss this, but your magic back there…the rain. Do you wanna talk about it?"

"No. Yes. I mean, not right now. I don't even know what I did, those words I spoke. I just was so upset about the cabin. Something just happened in me. Let's just drop it, Luca. I'll call Ilsbeth when we get to New Orleans. I'm just so upset right now that someone would burn down the cabin." Samantha just wanted to crawl into a hole. Some good her so-called magic was. She didn't really even know what she'd done to bring the rain. She needed to talk to Ilsbeth about what had happened, but right now she wanted to hide, sleep and forget. She hadn't asked for this life, and felt a great sense of loss; she'd never be normal again.

Looking over at Samantha, Luca realized how small and fragile she appeared curled into the seat, leaning her forehead against the passenger side window. He wondered what thoughts swirled behind her pale blue eyes; she looked a million miles away, silently considering what had happened perhaps. Luca swore silently for indulging himself with her in the lake. He'd been foolish to allow himself the pleasure of holding her soft pliant body: kissing her swollen pink lips: tasting her sweet honey-like essence. *What was I thinking? I've been thinking with my dick.* God, he needed to get it together. She was defenseless, innocent to his ways. No matter how much he wanted to make love to her, he couldn't allow himself to do it. He could not allow himself to kiss her again. Even though she was technically a witch, he wasn't sure if she'd ever accept her circumstances. And what of her life expectancy? Would she do what she needed to do to become immortal?

He knew that Kade had resolved that issue with Sydney, giving her his blood to keep her youthful and healthy. But Sydney was a toughened cop who'd fought side by side with him and Kade. She'd faced death time and time again. And while he'd initially hated that Kade had let a human go after Asgear, Sydney had proved her worth. Kade was determined to marry Sydney, and Luca respected their special connection, knowing Sydney could hold her own in the supernatural world.

But Samantha? No, she was like most humans. She was delectably, wonderfully normal: a computer analyst, for Christ's sake. Her only experience with supernaturals was being bespelled, possibly raped, beaten and now being turned into a witch. And now she could add 'passionately kissed by a vampire' to her done list. He reckoned that she could find a much better mate than him. He rolled his eyes even thinking of the word: *mate*. In over two hundred years, he had never even considered marrying, mating, bonding or any other supernatural or human word that meant commitment. Never again.

Raised in Australia, Luca had known that loving someone brought nothing but heartache. In the late seventeen hundreds, his father, Jonathon Macquarie, a marine, had taken his family to the colony of New South Wales so that he could work on the development of the penal colonies being set up by the British. It was a rough life for the soldiers and their families as well as the prisoners; life in a strange new world was not kind, and often inhumane. During the summer of his twenty-fifth birthday, he'd found comfort in the arms of a lovely woman, Eliza Hutchinson. She was the abandoned daughter of a prisoner who'd been brought to the island ten years earlier, caught pickpocketing on the streets of London.

When he'd turned eighteen, Luca's father had secured a guard position for him. A few years into the position, he was stationed to guard the factory where Eliza's mother had worked. One day, he'd caught Eliza sneaking in food for her mother, but hadn't had the heart to turn her into the authorities. Instead, he'd courted her every chance he got at her farm stand in the market, where she sold fresh honey and wool.

Using his influence within the marines, he'd worked hard to secure a 'ticket of leave' for her mother, ensuring her freedom as long as she stayed out of trouble. Within months, Luca and Eliza fell very much in love, and she agreed to marry him. Then one night on their way home from dinner, a drunken group of soldiers had cornered them in an alley. They'd taunted Luca and Eliza, as they expressed interest in sexually assaulting her. While Luca was a trained guard, he was outnumbered five to one. In a brutal fight, he'd lost consciousness as a bottle smashed upon the back of his head.

Luca had woken in his parents' home to find that Eliza had been raped and killed. His legs had been broken and his skull fractured, but somehow he'd survived the attack. During the months he'd spent under his mother's care, convalescing, Luca was despondent, determined to leave Australia. He'd grown up in the brutal colony watching soldiers punish convicts. Sometimes they were beaten, humiliated or hanged for the smallest infraction. He'd planned to leave someday with Eliza and take them back to London where they'd escape the constant stress associated with forging the path to civilization in the settlement. After her murder, he'd had nothing: no love, no desire to live, and no faith in humanity.

As soon as he could walk again, he'd spent his savings on a passage back to Mother England. Upon arrival Luca immediately 'took the King's shilling', and enlisted as a soldier for the War of 1812. Because of his experience as a guard and his father's service in the marines, he entered as an officer.

Hopeless and wrathful, Luca had wanted to kill and looked forward to each battle, seeing the face of Eliza's murderers in every opponent. There would never be enough blood shed to satisfy his need for vengeance against a faceless nameless enemy who'd never seen the shore of Australia. But it hadn't mattered to Luca. He'd heard that Eliza's true murderers had been hanged. However it would never be enough to quench his rage and the burning loss he'd experienced. Battle after battle, he'd fought with the utmost intensity, earning the respect of his fellow officers. One fateful night, however, it was his blood that had been shed.

On January 8, 1815, Luca had pushed out with his unit into the darkness of night as the fog clouded his vision. As chaos erupted in the field along the Mississippi, Luca had fallen to the ground in a barrage of musket fire, as had many other officers of the British army.

The next day, as he was saying his last prayers, a stranger had happened upon him. Sensing his impending death, Kade had offered him immortality in exchange for his loyalty. Luca, no stranger to adventure, had accepted his proposal and thus began his life as vampire.

Luca shook his thoughts free of his troubled past. Eliza was merely a distant memory, albeit an everlasting reminder of how fragile mortality was. Since turning vampire, he'd pledged his loyalty and friendship to Kade. Over the years, they'd done almost everything together including fighting, feeding and fucking. Yes, they'd shared quite a few women over the years, but those days were over now that Kade was getting married. And while Luca was glad of Kade's new-found happiness, he had no plans to follow in his friend's footsteps.

No, he'd been perfectly content over the past two hundred years with his non-committed sexual escapades. The closest he'd ever come to commitment was with women he'd considered to be 'friends with benefits', long before the saying was popular. He was devastatingly handsome, so finding women who'd throw a night of passion his way was never an issue. If they acted as though they were in love, he could just enthrall them to think otherwise.

As vampire, he was as physically strong as anyone could be, yet emotionally he'd never be strong. The death of Eliza had brought him to his knees, and he'd never forgive or forget what humans could do. Nor would he forget how it felt to have his heart ripped from his chest, to lose someone he loved with all his heart. He'd rather stake himself than go through the pain of loving and losing a mate again.

Whatever he was feeling for Samantha needed to be squelched. The seed that had been planted inside his heart had to be crushed and the best way he knew to do that was to find another woman who could sate his needs for blood and sex. Perhaps then, he'd lose interest in the red-headed witch seated next to him.

CHAPTER SIX

Samantha startled as she woke; driving rain and booming thunder seemed to shake the large SUV as it sped down Broad Street. She looked over to Luca, who was distracted by the city traffic. How long had she been sleeping? If they were in center city, it must've been for hours, she thought. Sitting up and combing her hand through her dried frizzy curls, she tried to get a bearing on where she was. "Hey, Luca, where are we? South Philadelphia?" She'd answered her own question.

"Uh huh, we're goin' to Tristan's club, Eden. It's only three in the afternoon, so we should be able to get showered and have something to eat before leaving. The plane is cleared to take off at nine tonight, so we have a few hours to wait. I was hoping to leave earlier but they had to make some minor repairs to the jet," he replied, glancing towards her. "You okay?"

"Yeah, I'm okay. You?"

She licked her lips, and Luca tried not to notice. He grew hard with arousal, dreaming that her soft pink lips were wrapped around a particular part of him. He shifted in his seat. Damn, even after nearly dying in a fire, the woman looked sexy.

"I'm vampire. As soon as I get a little blood, I'll be more than fine," Luca grumbled.

Samantha wondered what was making him so irritable, and assumed he was hungry. She had honestly never given a thought that he might need food or that she was considered a part of his food chain. Samantha pushed the thought to the back of her mind, knowing that regardless of her qualification as a meal, he'd never hurt her. And she needed his help to find whoever was after her so she could get her life back in order.

"I'm hungry too. And I smell like a fine combination of smoke and lake water." She crinkled her nose in disgust.

As they pulled into a driveway, she noticed they had driven into a subterranean garage. After going down two levels, Luca pulled the car into a large parking spot next to a set of elevators.

"This is it. Let's go," he ordered as he turned off the car and got out. "Listen, this is a club for paranormals and humans. It's pretty much a meat market in there." He didn't want to sugarcoat the situation. He also didn't want her getting hit on or going off with strangers. "So when you go with me into the open part of the club, stay close to me. Or stay with Tristan. You never know who might be around. Not to mention someone just tried to turn us into French fries."

"Yum. Fries," she joked. She couldn't stop thinking of food. She'd only eaten an apple all day. "I really am hungry." She smiled up at him, hoping she could sway his foul mood.

Seeing her smile at him melted his anger, and he lifted the corners of his mouth in a wry smile. "Okay, hungry girl. Let's see if we can go get cleaned up and find you something to eat."

He flipped up a security pad located near the doors and punched in a code. The elevator opened, and he placed a hand on the small of her back, guiding her into a small, mahogany-lined lift. Samantha felt a flip in her stomach and couldn't decide if it was from going up so quickly or from Luca's touch on her back. Following the commotion over the scorched cabin, she'd forgotten the desire she'd felt while kissing Luca in the lake. She blushed, thinking of how he'd tasted her mouth and caressed her breasts. She grew aroused at the thought of taking it further, touching his naked body once again, feeling him inside of her. She tried shaking the thought, knowing this wasn't a good time to resume what they'd been doing. They hadn't even spoken about what had happened between them, and she wasn't sure if it was such a good idea to talk about it here, at Tristan's.

Luca's eyes flashed red and then back to green, sensing her thoughts. Scenting her arousal was hard to ignore in the tiny, private elevator. He balled his fists and then stretched his hands, as he caught a glimpse of her hard nipples poking through her exercise top. He considered kissing her against the wall but was prevented by the ding of the doors opening.

"Finally," he muttered and strode across the room, hoping that putting some distance between them would help temper his rock hard erection that was begging to be set free.

"Where are we?" Samantha asked as she walked into a royal-blue room furnished with a large cherry desk and a black leather sofa. Very rich and masculine, she thought to herself as she admired a spectacular bronze wolf sculpture on the fireplace mantle. It was delicately balanced on a black marble base. Samantha recalled Tristan in his wolf form, black fur with amber eyes.

Luca walked over to a large wooden door and opened it. Pointing across the room, he addressed Samantha. "We're in Tristan's private office. Listen, there's a shower over there across the room. Go ahead and shower, and I'll send someone up with a fresh change of clothes once I talk to Tristan. After you're done getting dressed, come downstairs. Just follow the long hallway out towards the staircase, and you'll be downstairs."

"What about you? Where are you going to shower?" Samantha was hoping for a repeat performance of today. She'd love to see the strength of him that she'd only felt in the slippery cool water.

"There's a men's locker room downstairs. I'll shower there. See you at the bar." He waved and shut the door. Luca took a deep breath and blew it out. For a long minute, he'd been ready to take her in the elevator and now she was asking about the shower. She was fucking killing him. *Shit. Looks like I'll be having a cold shower.*

Samantha watched Luca leave with a puzzled look on her face. She knew what she'd felt in the lake had been real chemistry. But now Luca seemed like he couldn't get away from her fast enough. She knew she shouldn't trust a vampire, but she felt safe with Luca. Lying back in his arms in the lake felt like the first time she'd relaxed for weeks. He was so strong yet gentle. They'd talked like old friends but felt like new lovers. She'd never experienced such a passionate kiss in her life. Sure she'd had a few lovers, but no one that had evoked such a fiery, passionate reaction in her. And certainly no man had kissed her with such fury, naked beneath azure waters.

Samantha poked her head into the bathroom and found it surprisingly clean for a bachelor's. She looked on the shelf and saw herbal shampoo but hoped for a razor and if she got lucky, a toothbrush. She pulled open the vanity drawer: condoms, a single toothbrush, straight edged razor and deodorant. This bathroom definitely belonged to a man, she mused. Opening the second drawer, she found a stash of disposable pink razors and new toothbrushes. A ladies' man's bathroom, she corrected herself silently and laughed.

After taking the most delightful shower in a strange bathroom, Samantha dried herself with a clean towel. She heard a door open, and butterflies danced in her stomach. Luca had returned. She checked her face and rushed out with the towel wrapped around her.

"Hello there." A stunning, tall female held up clothing with a smile. "It's okay, Samantha. I'm Kat, Tristan's sister. Tris said you could use some clothes, so here I am," she chirped.

Samantha walked over to her, extending her hand. "Hi Kat, I'm Samantha. I really appreciate you bringing me something to wear." She was disappointed Luca hadn't returned for her but hid her feelings from the stranger.

Kat shook her hand and placed the clothes on the desk. "I brought you a choice: yoga pants or sundress. Tris said you were a petite little thing, and he's right. I co-own a shop a few blocks over, Hair and Heels. We're a beauty salon and spa but also sell clothes and accessories. I'm pretty sure both will fit. So what do ya think?" She put her hands on her hips, waiting for a response. Kat played with the red sundress, holding it up to herself by the spaghetti straps.

Kat was naturally beautiful; an exotic woman with long auburn hair and deep brown eyes. Even though Tristan had platinum blonde hair, he and Kat had the same intense eyes and straight nose. Samantha wouldn't have known they were siblings if she hadn't been told, but now saw a slight resemblance.

"Since I've been in yoga pants all day, I guess the sundress will work. But I don't have any shoes except sneakers," Samantha answered.

"No problem. I've got some flip-flops in my bag," she added, smiling.

"Thanks so much. I really appreciate you taking time out of your day to help us." Samantha used the word 'us' as if she and Luca were a couple, even though a more accurate description would have been traveling companions, or friends due to circumstances.

"Like I said, not a problem at all. A friend of Tristan's is a friend of mine. We take care of each other. Especially us girls," she winked.

Oddly, Samantha felt at ease with the lovely woman and wondered if she was a wolf like Tristan. She smiled at Kat. "Well, thanks again." She waited on her to leave.

"Come on now, Samantha. Don't be shy. Lord knows, us wolves aren't. I'm staying; at least until I make sure the dress fits you. I've gotta get back to the shop soon, but I've got time for a bit of a chat," she said, plopping herself in the overstuffed leather sofa.

Samantha never thought of herself as shy, but she didn't know the woman in front of her from Adam. But she really didn't have much choice, given that Kat wasn't moving. Deciding to go with the flow, she stripped off her towel and pulled the cotton sundress over her head. Looking down and feeling around to make sure it wasn't too tight she smiled over at Kat. "It's lovely," Samantha declared, running her hands down her sides. "Thanks again."

"No problem." Kat came over and stood in front of Samantha, admiring the smooth fabric and the fit of the dress. "Looks great on you. That plastic bag over there has the flip-flops in it and a pair of undies. Good thing the dress has a shelf built into it 'cause I don't sell bras. Well, I better get going."

Samantha waved as Kat opened the door. "Thanks again, Kat. I actually live in Philly too. Maybe when I get back, I'll look you up," she offered.

Kat just smiled and waved back as she shut the door.

Samantha walked back into the bathroom and began to comb out her wet hair. Thinking about her conversation with Kat, Samantha felt quite relieved to have a normal conversation with a human-looking woman...even if she really was a wolf. She smiled to herself wondering if all wolves were as friendly as Tristan and Kat. Taking one last glance at herself in the mirror, Samantha felt satisfied with her attractive new dress. Clean and clothed, she was refreshed and ready to go downstairs; she wanted to find Luca and get something to eat.

Shaved and showered, Luca walked into the main club room and sat at the bar. From behind it, Tristan faced the wall and reaching up, grabbed a bottle of Martell Cognac off the top shelf and two glasses, and set them on the brass bar.

"So, long day, huh?" Tristan asked. He poured two fingers into each snifter. Even though it was four in the afternoon, happy hour started early in Eden on a Friday night. Patrons were already starting to pour through the front entrance, but no one had come to the far end of the bar yet.

"Yeah, you could say that. Someone torched the cabin and left our witch a little message. Something about a periapt." Luca took a long draw of his drink. "It was written in bat's blood. Real bat's blood. But I didn't scent any supernaturals so it must have been a puppet. Haven't told Samantha yet."

"A periapt, huh? Could be for anything, but what does this one do and why would someone want it so badly and why would Samantha have it?" Tristan mused.

"And those, my friend, are all very good questions I've asked myself. Perhaps Ilsbeth can help us. I don't know. To be honest, I really just need to feed right now and maybe fuck. This whole situation's wearing on me, and I need to blow off some steam, before I get onto that plane and head down to New Orleans." He tapped nervously on the edge of his glass.

"Yeah, about that…" Tristan hesitated and looked up at his sister. She bounded down the stairs toward them, silently signaling to Tristan to be quiet, obviously wanting to surprise Luca.

Luca spied a female refection in Tristan's eyes. Immediately recognizing her scent, he spun on his bar seat and held out his arms. "Kat!"

Kat jumped into his arms as he spun her about as if she weighed nothing. "Luca, baby!" she cooed. "I'm so glad to see you. I can't believe you're here. I've only got maybe twenty minutes 'til my next appointment, but I've been looking to go down to visit ya."

Things were about to get interesting. Luca and Kat had met years ago when Kade's ex-lover had kidnapped and tortured her in the mid-eighteen hundreds. Luca had been there that day to rescue her and bring her back to Tristan. As the years passed, Luca and Kat had had their fair share of romantic moments, but it was always free and easy; neither of them was looking for commitment.

As they hugged tightly, Kat kissed him on the cheek, and pulled away, leaving her arm around his waist.

"You knew she was here?" Luca questioned Tristan.

"Yes I did. And you know, if you're going to New Orleans tonight, I've been thinking maybe you could take Kat with you," Tristan suggested.

Luca looked at Kat and then back to Tristan. "What's up?"

Kat looked at her shoes, not wanting to recount what was happening.

Tristan's eyes narrowed. "Kat, here, has an unwanted suitor. And it's none other than Jax Chandler, the Alpha from New York. Now, he's been told that he can't have her, but he's not one to take no for an answer. I don't want anything happening to her."

"What? Are you afraid he'll kidnap her?" Luca asked.

"Well, that I'm not sure of, but I think if she takes a little trip down to see our brother Marcel, it'll help to bolster my verdict on this. I don't want him thinking he can get stupid and try and take her." Tristan hopped over the bar and put his arm around his sister. "Kat wants Marcel to call the pack out on this, and I agree. So what say you? Can you take her with you?"

"Certainly. But she can't stay with me. She'll have to stay with Kade or Marcel." There was no way he was going to let two females stay at his house. He had a feeling that Samantha wouldn't take too kindly to having him let a former lover stay with them. Nor did he want the two women ganging up on him. No, she'd have to stay with Kade or go to her brother's.

"Thanks Luca!" Kat kissed him again; this time on the lips.

"Okay, it's settled then. Now let's see what I can do about a donor. I'll go check the list," Tristan announced.

Eden's maître d' kept a donor list at the front desk of willing human and shifter donors who wished to experience the orgasmic bite of a vampire, sex, or both. They wore beepers around their necks that buzzed should they be called to 'volunteer'. There were private rooms upstairs for these activities that accommodated pairs and groups. The rooms were video monitored for the safety of guests to make sure all activities were consensual and safe. It was against the law to kill during a feeding, and Eden's state-of-the-art security system kept things legal.

Kat stopped Tristan from leaving and looked over to Luca. "Luca, I'll feed you," she offered.

"You sure? I thought you had an appointment. And you need to get your stuff together. We've got to leave soon," Luca said.

"I'll call the shop and give Sherri my client. They're expecting me to leave soon anyway. Now they'll just have to rearrange the schedule a little more quickly. Call it a perk of being an owner. And I don't need anything else but my purse and cell phone, which I have. As soon as I get to Marcel's, I plan to go wolf for a while. Any clothes I need, he'll provide from the pack," Kat answered without hesitation.

"Tristan, you mind? This isn't our first time, but she's still your sister." Luca was old-fashioned in many ways and felt it necessary to get her older brother's permission.

Tristan trusted Luca with his life and his sister's. Luca and Kat had been tight ever since Luca rescued her, and while he hadn't exactly talked about sex with his sister, he was pretty sure that they'd been together several times over the years.

"No problem. Go have fun, kids. Don't do anything I wouldn't do," he quipped.

Luca grabbed Kat by the hand and started up the stairs toward the private rooms.

As they walked down the hallway, looking for an open feeding room, Kat grabbed Luca's arm tighter and giggled, hoping she'd have at least an hour to make love with him before they had to take off. It had been years since they'd been together, and she was looking forward to reminiscing.

Luca, thirsting for blood, could feel his fangs pushing through his gums. Kat's blood, heady, woodsy and potent, would surely sate his thirst. As he went to turn the handle to one of the feeding rooms, he froze. *Samantha.* She stared straight at him down the long, dimly lit hallway. There he stood arm in arm with another woman after he'd kissed her only hours earlier. The instant he locked eyes with Samantha, he registered the pain he was causing her.

Samantha stopped dead in her tracks, observing Kat hold Luca's arms as if they were long-lost lovers. Rationally, she knew that he needed to eat and that he'd use a donor. She hadn't offered her own blood to Luca. After everything she'd been through, she just couldn't bring herself to do that. She honestly thought that she understood what it meant for him to feed off of someone else, but there in the hall, seeing another woman wrapped around his waist, she felt jealous. Her anger flared.

She felt like a fool for kissing him, for believing that they could have possibly had a connection. At the cabin, he'd kissed her passionately. He'd acted like he was ready to make love to her. It must have all been a ruse to get her to go with him back to New Orleans, she thought. Obviously he hadn't felt the same toward her if he was letting Kat put her hands all over him. She felt sick to her stomach at the thought of him kissing that woman, holding her in his arms. But what could she do? He did need to eat. And a display of jealousy would be akin to showing weakness. She would not let herself be a victim again. Biting her lip, she steeled herself and began to walk toward them.

Luca watched her contemplate what was happening. He felt a strange, unfamiliar feeling in the pit of his gut. *Guilt.* No, he refused to acknowledge it. Just as Samantha came within twenty feet of him, he acknowledged her presence with a nod, opened the door, pulled Kat inside and slammed it shut.

Luca growled in hunger as he caged Kat against the door. In anger, he pressed his lips to hers, pushing his tongue deep within her mouth. Sensing his predatory nature in full force, Kat submitted, keeping her arms down and against the door, and kissed him back. Luca knew immediately something was off as soon as he kissed her. That damn witch had cursed him; he was sure of it. He had kissed Kat many times in the past, but now the only picture in his mind was Samantha. Luca bared his fangs, threw his head back and roared.

Kat reached up slowly, pulled off her t-shirt and bared her neck to him. She wasn't sure what was wrong with Luca but it wasn't the first time she'd seen him upset. She could tell that she probably wouldn't be having sex with him like she'd been anticipating, but understood that Luca had something on his mind.

"You're sure, Kat?" Luca asked. No matter how many times he fed, he always asked his donor. He wanted to make sure he wasn't taking someone against their will, no matter what their original intentions.

"Yes, Luca. Take me," Kat whispered.

A split second later, his fangs sank deep into her neck. As he drank, he tried to block Samantha, but couldn't stop thinking of her.

Kat pressed her flattened palms against Luca's chest. Then her fingers clasped his shirt tightly as she felt an orgasm rip through her. She reached down to feel Luca's hardness and had him in her grip, when he pushed her hand away and released her.

His eyes remained red as he fell down onto the sofa. "Fuck!" he yelled.

"Luca, what's wrong?" Kat panted. She was still riding hard from the explosive release. She knelt before him.

Luca laid back with his head resting on a pillow and his feet up on the armrest. "I can't, Kat. And I don't want to talk about it, okay. Just don't ask." He closed his eyes, wiping her blood from the corner of his mouth.

"Luca, it's fine. You know I want to, um, finish, but if you're not into it today, that's okay. Your bite is quite satisfying," she teased and put her hand over his chest. "Whatever it is, we can talk about it later, when and if you're ready."

With a pat, she jumped up and put on her shirt. "Luca, since I have the time, I'm gonna run over to the shop and just check in before I leave. I'll be back in forty-five minutes. I promise it won't take long." Kat leaned over and kissed her friend's forehead.

Luca barely saw her walk out the door, but heard it slam shut. He opened his eyes, which had returned to green, and stared up at the stark white ceiling. He'd gone centuries feeling nothing, and it had served him well. Now he was good and fucked. Guilt. He was sure he felt guilt about being with Kat. And why? Because he'd had a kiss and tickle with Samantha in the lake? No, he'd known there was something there between them ever since the first time he'd stroked Samantha's hair in Kade's basement. And now that he'd kissed her, he couldn't forget the taste of her sweet, soft mouth and the feel of her breasts in his hands.

"Shit! Shit! Shit!" he said aloud to himself. Feelings. Very human-like feelings could threaten his entire existence. Yet he knew in his heart that he was done for. It didn't matter what his mind said or the logic it possessed; his heart spoke and knew what it wanted. He had to have the witch.

From across the room, Tristan could tell that Samantha had been crying. Her face was reddened from her attempts to dry her eyes. He wasn't sure what was wrong, but pain washed over her aura. He knew that she'd been through a lot of trauma over the past few weeks, but she'd seemed relatively calm during their encounter at the cabin. Perhaps she was having a meltdown after watching the cabin burn? Or maybe she was just hungry? He knew he got cranky when he didn't eat.

Deciding not to leave her to any of the sharks looking for a hot date, the Alpha strode over and pulled her into an embrace. "Come on, ma petite sorcière, whatever it is, it'll all work out. What'd I tell you up at the cabin? Go to New Orleans for a little while and then come back. I'll help you get settled back here at home." He rubbed his hand over her hair. She was quite petite indeed, maybe five-three, he thought to himself. The top of her head barely reached his neck.

"Thanks, Tristan. I know it may not seem like it to you, but I'm a relatively strong person in spite of the fact that my life has turned into a living hell, and I have no control over what's happening." She spoke into his chest, pulling herself closer to him.

Samantha knew Luca had come here to feed, but couldn't believe it when she saw him with Kat. They clearly were well acquainted with each other, and she knew damn well that vampires often had sex when they ate. She suspected more than feeding was going on tonight in 'those rooms'. She couldn't believe that after what they'd shared this morning, kissing and touching each other in such an intimate way, he'd take another woman to bed as if it was nothing. But then again, she didn't really know Luca or any of the supernaturals that well. She was attracted to Luca, lusted after him, but all those feelings did not amount to a hill of beans when it came to men. Conflicted, she silently sighed. Even though they hadn't known each other very long, Luca seemed honorable. He certainly didn't seem like the kind of man that would touch a woman's breasts and kiss her and then fuck a different woman less than six hours later.

Sensing her tumultuous thoughts, Tristan rubbed his hands over the top of her head and then slowly moved them down her back, sending out waves of calming reassurance into her skin. Given the temperamental nature of wolves, Tristan was well-trained in using his powers to both excite and pacify supernaturals and humans alike. He could feel her muscles relax as they began to slow dance on the floor. She held onto him tightly as if she needed security, a lifeline to hold onto.

"Tristan, I'm okay, really. Thanks. You...you're a really good Alpha." She giggled and looked up at him. "I can't believe I just said that. Okay, I admit that I really don't know what an Alpha does and you're the only Alpha I know, but you're a good person. I would really like it if we could be friends when I come back." She honestly had never met someone as grounded and down to earth as Tristan before; he was a caring leader.

"That sounds like a fine plan. Tell you what...I'll teach you all about wolves when you get back...everything you want to know, baby," he flirted and spun her around quickly as the music changed into a sultry R&B song.

Samantha laughed out loud and threw her head back and then rested her forehead against his chest. "I just bet you would, Tristan." He was incredibly handsome and charming and seemed to know all the right words to make everything seem all right.

A stranger's hand on her shoulder and a loud growl jolted her back to reality.

Tristan's face hardened as he pulled her tighter against him.

"Stand down, Luca, my friend. Remember where you are," Tristan said calmly with an even-toned voice.

She looked up to see Luca, his eyes a fiery red. What was wrong with him?

"Did you eat yet, Samantha? We don't have much time before we have to leave for the airport," Luca asked, irritated that she'd found comfort so easily in another man's arms.

She reluctantly pulled away from Tristan, yet still kept one hand on his forearm. "No, I haven't eaten." She spoke in a businesslike manner as if she'd just met him.

Tristan looped his arm through hers and began walking them towards the bar. "Ah, see here, Samantha. Dinner is ready now. I wasn't sure what you liked, but I figured most girls like a steak dinner, salad. And who can say no to chocolate cake?" He pointed to a place setting at the bar.

"Thanks, Tristan. It looks delicious. I'm starving." She kissed Tristan on the cheek and sat down, but not before shooting Luca an icy look that could have frozen water on a hot summer day.

"Luca, over here," Tristan commanded, pointing to the end of the bar.

As they both sat down, Tristan glared at Luca. "What in the fuck is wrong with you? Don't you get that she's been traumatized? I know you don't care for humans, but you've got to give this witch a break. I thought you'd be in a better mood after being with Kat."

"I like a particular human a little too much these days. That's the problem," he mumbled. He caught a glimpse of Samantha, who was voraciously eating her steak and totally ignoring him. Then he looked over at Tristan, who was smiling like the cat who ate the mouse.

"I see," he laughed. "Luca, if I hadn't seen it with my own eyes, I wouldn't believe it."

Luca shook his head silently.

The look on Luca's face made Tristan laugh even harder. "Oh my God. Wait...wait until Kade finds out!" He extended his hand and put it on Luca's shoulder. "You're jealous. And you know what that means, my friend? Oh yeah, that's right my man, you're developing feelings. That icy excuse for a heart beating in your chest is starting to melt."

"No, no, no," Luca protested.

"Yes, yes, yes. Let the Alpha guess what happened. Hmmm. Let's see. You went upstairs with my lovely sister expecting to get your rocks off and your fang on, and you couldn't do it. Luca Macquarie cannot fuck and feed, because he's falling for a little red-headed witch. I never thought I'd see the day."

Luca shoved his hand away, disgusted by the truth of the situation. "Fuck you, Tris." He gave him a small smile. "Okay, so maybe you're right. Maybe I'm in deep and not sure what to do. It's not like I have experience with this...with relationships. Hell, most of my relationships consist of 'hey, do you want to have sex? You wanna bite? Okay, done and done'. Now I'm turned on my head. I don't even know what to say, to do. And she's pissed at me. I've been around long enough to know when a woman's jealous. I am so fucked."

"Perhaps you are. For a while, anyway." Tristan grinned broadly. "Don't worry, you'll figure it out, Luca. You're an honorable, decent man. Always have been, always will be. But I can't say I envy you your plane ride back to New Orleans with Kat and Samantha. That's gonna give a new definition to turbulence."

Luca shook his head again, looked at Samantha, and then to Tristan. "Yes, I'll have my hands full on the way back. So, how about you give us a ride to the airport once she's done eating? I'm ready to face this head on. What other choice do I have?" He shrugged.

"Not much. It'll work out, mon ami. I'll call the driver and ask him to get the limo ready," Tristan said.

"Hey Tris."

"Yeah," Tristan answered, standing up, wanting to go check on Kat.

"Thanks buddy. Sorry about going all vamp on the dance floor. I'm out of sorts. And I appreciate the chat. Besides Kade, you've always been there for me. I'll never forget it," Luca said.

"Back at ya. Now, let me go round up my favorite sister. I wanna make sure all of your women are accounted for so you can have a good time for the next few hours." Tristan laughed and punched Luca's arm.

Yeah, it's going to be a laugh riot, Luca thought to himself. As he looked back at Samantha, she glared at him then quickly looked away. He could see the hurt and passion in her eyes and was determined more than ever to go to her. But as he started over to explain things to her, Tristan walked in with Kat.

All four of them looked at each other, and Samantha rolled her eyes, shoving a piece of chocolate cake into her mouth. It was going to be a damn fine flight home to New Orleans, indeed, Luca brooded.

CHAPTER SEVEN

Flying in luxury was not all it was cracked up to be, Samantha thought, as she stared out the small porthole window. The plane was beautifully decorated, with plush tan leather seats, mahogany tray tops and undertones. In her life, she'd never known such decadence; she was used to being crammed like a sardine into a coach. But she knew that it wasn't the plane that was the problem.

Learning that Kat was coming on their trip and that she'd be trapped in a tin can for three hours with the two of them made her want to spit tacks. The four-seat luxury jet was not nearly big enough for her to breathe, let alone survive an entire trip with Luca and Kat. Perhaps if she just settled in against the window and tried to sleep the entire flight, she would not have to look at or talk to either one of them. On the way into the plane, Samantha chose to sit away from them in a cabin chair nearest to the front of the plane, essentially separating herself. Luca and Kat sat side by side in their individual bucket seats with only the aisle between them.

In the elevator on the way down to the limo, Luca had informed her that Kat was coming with them; Samantha had silently nodded and pulled a mask of indifference over her face. Whatever had happened at the lake was clearly an insignificant bleep in Luca's social calendar. She wondered if Kat was Luca's girlfriend and perhaps she was the other woman. Did Kat know Luca had kissed her mere hours before making love to her? God, she felt so stupid for ever opening herself up to him.

After nearly an hour of total silence, Kat wondered what the hell was up with Luca. He hadn't said a word since leaving the club and wasn't acting his normal self. And while she didn't know Samantha, she felt an icy coolness wash over her as if she'd killed her cat. The last time she'd seen her in Tristan's office, it had seemed like they were on their way to a friendship. Not able to take one more minute of the tension, she broke the dead air.

"Luca, are you feeling all right?" She reached over and put her hand on his arm.

Luca flinched at her touch, but Kat held firm. "I never thought I'd see the day when a vampire was jumpy. Too much coffee, dear?" she teased.

Hearing the term of endearment, Samantha's eyes flashed up and held Luca's gaze. Her tight-lined mouth and intense stare told Luca all he needed to know about what Samantha thought of Kat.

Pulling his arm away from Kat, Luca unbuckled his seatbelt and stood up. "I'm fine. Just have a lot on my mind. I'm going back to the office to make a few calls. I want to make sure Marcel is ready for you and that Kade and Sydney are aware of our ETA," he responded. He made his way toward the back of the plane and shut the office door.

Kat looked over at Samantha, who gazed out the window into the darkness of night. "Okay, I know witches don't have night vision, so what could possibly be so interesting out there? You've been boring a hole into the window ever since we left."

"Huh? Yeah, well, it's better than staring at you all. I feel caged up in this tiny excuse for a plane," Samantha replied tersely. She hadn't meant to sound so rude, but she was losing patience with the situation.

"You can put your claws back in, kitty-cat. What's everyone's problem around here, anyway?" Kat was taken off guard by Samantha's snarky attitude.

"Sorry, Kat. I just need to get this over with and done. I guess I'm just nervous," she lied. "So, what's with you and Luca? I was supposed to stay in his guest room when we get there, but I can go to the coven if that'd make you all more comfortable." She silently cursed herself for asking, but she couldn't take not knowing what was going on between the two of them. Were they lovers? Engaged?

"No need, I'm going to my brother's house. Marcel. He's the Alpha in New Orleans. I...I've been having a bit of guy trouble lately," she continued, looking out the window and then back to Samantha. "There's this Alpha in New York. He wants me as his mate. Tristan and I have both told him it's so not happening, but wolves don't always play fair. I'm worried he might try to take me. So, I figured I'd go see my other brother, and have him talk with my persistent suitor. Two brothers are better than one. Plus, I'll get to go wolf for a while down there, run with the pack in the bayou. I miss it."

Samantha studied Kat's face, confused by why she needed to escape to New Orleans and why Luca wouldn't just help her if they were together. It didn't make sense.

"But what about Luca? Why can't you just tell the New York Alpha you're with him?" she asked.

"Samantha, I'm not sure what you think you saw at Eden, but Luca and I are not mated, nor will we ever be. We're just very good friends who enjoy a good roll in the hay every now and then. Don't get me wrong, the man is yummy, but I should not have to lie about my relationship in order to rebuff an overly assertive Alpha who doesn't know the meaning of respect." Kat was starting to put two and two together. Samantha's cold demeanor; Luca's distant emotions combined with his lack of desire upstairs at Eden; his evident angst. Luca and Samantha were involved. It was all starting to make sense.

Samantha's eyes pricked with tears hearing Kat practically admit they'd had sex. She wanted to tear off her seatbelt and parachute out of the plane, so she could be anywhere but near the two of them. She managed to get control and took a deep swallow.

"It's none of my business, Kat. I'm glad you could get a ride with Luca so you'd be safe on your way to your brother's." Samantha tried to sound gracious, but in reality, she wanted to vomit. Part of her liked Kat, which made it all the worse knowing her and Luca had slept together.

"Hey, Samantha. I just..." Kat searched for the right words. "I just want you to know that Luca and I did not have sex today. I mean, I did come, but that was all. Oh God, that didn't come out right. Geez. Okay, it's like this. The man has got to eat. And I offered. And sure, I was hoping to get my freak on with him a little. I am single, after all. I mean, I had no idea you were together or anything. If I'd known, I would have never..."

"We are not together," Samantha spat out.

"Whatever you say, but I want you to know the truth. Luca, he didn't. We didn't. He just fed. Sure, I came but that's just a side effect of his bite. I'm sorry," Kat apologized. She came over to where Samantha was sitting and sat crosslegged in front of her on the floor. She placed her hands on Samantha's knees.

"Samantha, Tristan told me all about you, ya know. I thought we could be friends, because I know what it's like...what happened to you. Well, a very long time ago, it happened to me too. God, it seems hard to talk about even now." She rubbed her eyes and raked her fingers through her hair. "Simone. She took me too. And others. Tristan went to Kade for help. He and Luca found me. Luca dragged me out of that hell hole and brought me back to Marcel. We share a special bond because of that, he and I. And now, you and I. All I'm saying is that it gets better over time."

Samantha felt like a jerk for being so jealous and mean-spirited towards her. Maybe not Luca, because he damn well knew how she'd felt at the cabin.

"Kat," Samantha put her hands out to Kat's. "Thanks. No one else could possibly know what it's been like for me, and it helps to know there's someone else on God's green earth who understands what happened to me. It's been difficult." She blew out a breath and continued. "As for Luca, I wasn't lying. We really aren't together. We just shared a moment, and I thought it meant more than it did. But I appreciate you telling me what's going on with you two. As much as it pains me to admit it, I felt...I felt upset." It was the best Samantha could do at the moment.

"Hey, don't worry 'bout it. Whatever's goin' on with Luca, I suspect it wasn't 'just a moment' as you put it. I mean, he seems wound tighter than a two dollar watch. And for that man to turn down sex with moi," she laughed, "he'd have to either be a damn fool or starting to fall for someone else. And I'm guessin' the latter, girl."

Samantha smiled, feeling like a weight had been lifted off her. She might not know where she really stood with Luca, but it felt good to bond with another woman.

"Thanks, Kat. The only thing I'm sure of right now is that I've got to stay safe and help find whoever wants me dead. Piece of cake, right?" she joked, just as Luca came through the door.

He raised a questioning eyebrow at Kat as she buckled herself back into her seat. "Everything okay here?" he asked.

"Fine," both women answered at once. They both laughed and looked out the window.

The air in the plane felt lighter, but he wasn't sure what'd just transpired between the two very special supernatural ladies. He'd been on the earth for over two hundred years and still couldn't say he understood women. He did understand enough, though, to know he'd be having a very long conversation with Samantha when they got home.

Kat hugged Samantha tightly, before getting into the waiting limo. They had exchanged email and phone numbers so they could stay in touch. Luca waited until Samantha was done before embracing Kat. He was worried about the situation with the New York Alpha, but knew she'd be safe with Marcel.

"Listen, Kat. Call me if you need anything. I talked to Marcel, and he's going to help straighten out this mess." He kissed the top of her forehead. "Now, get going little wolf. Make sure those gators don't get your tail in the bayou," he teased as she ducked into the limo and shut the door.

Samantha and Luca got into the back of the other limo, and she purposefully put space between them by sitting on the side which faced the trunk. She was still irritated with him and questioned his intentions, but at the same time, she couldn't help noticing how great he looked tonight in his loose fit blue jeans and black t-shirt. His biceps were exquisitely carved, and she noticed he had a black tribal tattoo on the right one. She remembered the strength of his arms holding her up in the water, and wondered what it would be like if he bit her. Would she offer herself?

Her thoughts were broken when Luca shifted and sat beside her. She felt his jeans brush her bare leg, and struggled to act nonchalant.

"What are you doing?" she asked.

"What does it look like I'm doing? I'm sitting next to you," he smiled at her.

She shot him a look of annoyance. Moving closer to the window, she tried not to let her bare leg touch him again.

"So little witch, I think you and I need to have a bit of a talk," he said.

"Don't call me that," she insisted.

"You are testy, aren't you?" He took a deep breath. She wasn't going to make this easy. "I'm sorry for what happened at Eden."

"For what?" she feigned ignorance.

"Let's not play games," he countered.

"Games? Games? I don't know what you are even talking about, Luca." Samantha's normally soft voice was growing louder and louder.

"Yes, games. I know you're mad at me, and I know why. I just want to talk about it, so we can…"

"So we can what, Luca? What? I mean, this morning at the cabin we kissed; that was all. You don't owe me any explanations. Besides, Kat told me everything," she interrupted.

"Did she now?" he chuckled. *Women.* "I told you when I went to Eden I needed to feed. I prefer to have live donors. You see, when vampires feed..." He stopped himself from explaining any further as she looked straight at him and held up her hand to him.

"Just stop. I don't want to know," she stated.

"Okay, well here's the bottom line. Kat and I are friends who've known each other a very long time. I'm not going to lie to you, Samantha. In the past, we've been lovers, but we have never been a couple. And today, I just...I just needed to feed. And as much as I would love to taste your sweet blood, and believe me, I would, Kat was there."

"And you were going to make love to her?" Samantha asked.

"Yes," Luca answered quietly and truthfully. "But Samantha, I didn't." He reached over to run his fingers along the side of her face, and she brushed his hand away.

"But you wanted her?" Samantha challenged.

"No, Samantha, that's the thing. I wanted you," he whispered. He moved back to sit across from her as the car pulled into the driveway. Samantha's eyes widened in disbelief, and he wasn't sure what else he should say in the few minutes they'd have in the car. He decided to wait until they got settled before continuing the conversation.

Samantha didn't know how to respond. She was confused. Why would he take Kat instead of her if he did indeed want her like he said? She tried to think of how she would have reacted if Luca had asked her to let him feed from her. Would she have said yes or have gone running in the other direction? As much as she liked him, she couldn't honestly say that she would have said yes. She felt so raw from her abduction that she just wasn't sure she could trust someone to bite her, to risk putting herself in danger, to risk pain.

As they pulled into the Issacson compound, she gaped at the huge southern Victorian mansion. She didn't remember leaving there, but could still remember the luxurious prison cell accommodations located in the lower level of the home. She couldn't help but wonder what the rest of the place looked like.

The car circled around the front of the mansion and took a small, almost hidden road that was lined with breathtaking, majestic live oak trees. The private road went on for about one hundred feet until they reached a secondary Greek revival styled mansion, which was equally impressive, with its white columned entrance greeting its guests.

As the limo stopped, Luca got out of the car and offered his hand to Samantha. She stepped out of the car, and silently followed him to his home. At the front door, he flipped open a security panel, typed in a code and placed his face and palm into the box. Within seconds, the lock clicked open.

Samantha was impressed. "Biometric facial recognition, iris security and palm identification?"

Luca smiled. She was sexy and smart. "Yeah, well, you can't be too careful. Unlike Kade, I don't have any security personnel working in my home. What you can't see is the instantaneous DNA detection in the palm identifier. Look." He pointed to a black panel with a neon green outline of a hand on it. "It's hard to see, but there's a microscopic needle that extends into the thumb of the user. Facial recognition is great, and while this software is essentially hack-proof, there's still a small percentage of failure."

"Yeah, I read hackers have been trying to demonstrate failure. Even though it's a small percentage, I could see how if you were to invest in such a system you'd want redundancy," she commented.

As they walked into the foyer, Samantha was amazed to see Luca's finely decorated home, adorned with antiques and paintings. "Wow, Luca, your home is beautiful. It looks like a museum in here," she gasped.

"Thanks. I don't use the upper levels, though. It's pretty much for show. If I entertain, I use this first floor area for guests. But I don't live up here. Come on, follow me." Luca walked down a short hallway, punched another security code into the wall, and a door with an antiqued face opened. "This is it. Ladies first." He held out his hand to usher her down.

Motion detector lights illuminated the circular oak staircase which deposited them into a great room, which appeared more as Samantha had expected Luca's style to be; an ultra-modern bachelor's dream: sleek with minimal décor. A single chrome wall ran the length of the area; it was decorated with black and white still-life photos. The other three whitewashed brick walls complemented the cherry hardwood floors. A large overstuffed black leather sectional sofa directly faced a ninety-inch flat screen TV. Across from the living area, a half-moon, black granite bar swept around a small kitchen area. Royal-blue, spiral-shaped lights hung down from the ceiling from fine silver chains; the delicate illumination danced and reflected across the chrome walls.

His home screamed masculinity, refinement, and wealth. Yet as he tossed his phone on the bar, and pulled open the refrigerator, he seemed casual, relaxed and very much at home.

"So, this is where I spend most of my time. You can stay upstairs in the guest room, but I'd prefer it if you stay down here with me. I don't sleep much, so you can stay in the master bedroom, and I'll take the couch." He pulled out two bottles of water and set them on the counter.

Samantha ran her hand across the bar and sat down on one of the black and chrome stools. "Are you sure, Luca? It's bad enough that I agreed to stay with you. I feel badly putting you out of your bed." Luca. Bed. As she said the two words in a sentence she realized she'd much rather be saying a different sentence with those two words. *Luca, take me to bed.* She blushed, grabbed the water, opened it and drank it slowly, while looking up at Luca.

He could sense what she was thinking, and he needed to take this opportunity to set things straight with her. She was in his home now; his domain. He had control, and she was his. He walked around the bar, put his hands on her shoulders and began to rub her neck. Inhaling her feminine scent, he instantly hardened.

"What I said in the car, I meant. It's important we're clear." He continued massaging her as she released a tiny moan of pleasure.

"Today at the lake, I did not forget what had happened between us. How could I forget? But you must understand. For over two hundred years, there has been no one for me. Lovers, yes. But human lovers have been few and far between. I don't do relationships. And now, there is you." He shook his head, but she couldn't see because she held her head downward as he caressed her muscles. "Today at Eden when I saw you in the hallway, I felt guilty. I know that isn't what a woman wants to hear, but I could not ask you to let me feed from you. And I know Kat, and well…she was there. And if I'm being honest, I was trying to forget you."

Samantha slowly raised her head but just stared forward, afraid to look at him. "Why forget me?"

Luca stilled his hands and his breath hitched. He slowly swiveled her stool around so she was facing him. She instinctively reached out and placed her hands on his hips, but kept her head down.

"Because, my dear Samantha," he cupped her face, tilting her head upward to meet his gaze. "I want you more than I've ever wanted any woman in my life, and it scares the living hell out of me."

Luca took Samantha's hands, gently lifting her onto her feet. Reaching around the nape of her neck, he ran his fingers into her hair and pulled her towards him. Luca kissed her slowly, hungrily, wanting to savor her intoxicating essence. She was everything he remembered from the lake and more. So soft and pliant; he couldn't wait to sink himself deep within her.

A thousand butterflies danced in Samantha's tummy in anticipation of making love to Luca. She opened her lips as his mouth engulfed hers. He wanted to be with *her*. No, there would be no other women, just her. She'd decided in that moment to give herself to him, body, soul and blood.

Their tongues intertwined with one another as the kiss deepened, and Samantha rose on her toes, pressing herself tightly against his muscular torso. She could feel the hardness of his arousal against her belly and the growing ache between her legs.

Swiftly, Luca picked Samantha up, one arm behind her back and one under her knees. For a brief second, they stopped their kiss to gaze into each other's eyes. Samantha saw the fire burn within his eyes as they quickly flashed from green to red. This was who she wanted: her vampire. She reached up, cupped his cheek and let her pointer finger slide down into his mouth. He roared in erotic lust as his fangs elongated, and she stroked one of them.

"Samantha, are you sure?" he asked in a breathy, rugged tone. He was close to losing control, finally giving into his desire for his witch.

"Take me, Luca. Now," she softly demanded.

Luca carried her down the long hallway and kicked open the door to his bedroom. Candles along the shelving flickered into life at Luca's command. Samantha caught her breath at the sight of Luca's dominating presence. He was primal; pure unadulterated male. She grew wet awaiting his touch, the feel of him deep inside her sex.

He placed her feet on the floor and stood close to her, barely touching her, then brushed his face against the side of hers, smelling her hair. Luca's cock twitched at her feminine scent. He was turned on seeing her in an overwhelming state of arousal, her cheeks flushed, her breath quickened. She was ravishing. Never breaking eye contact with Samantha, he glided his palms down her shoulders, the sides of her arms, her hips, to the edge of her dress. He grabbed the hem of her sundress and deftly pulled it upward until she stood before him all but naked; she wore only a pair of black lace panties.

Samantha went to cover her breasts, but he grabbed her wrists and placed them back to her sides. "No. Leave your hands to your sides," Luca ordered. "Let me look at you. So very, very beautiful, you are. I was a fool to ever believe I could stop thinking of you."

Even though Samantha had gone skinny-dipping earlier, she felt oddly exposed standing perfectly nude in front of Luca while he was still dressed. Yet his request drove her mad with need, and she complied. Samantha moaned softly as Luca dropped to his knees and grabbed her ass, pulling her smooth taut stomach to his face.

Luca thought he'd died and gone to heaven. The smell of her silky soft skin against his face drove him wild. He wanted to taste every last inch of her. He could tell she was ready for him. Kissing her belly, his tongue celebrated the feel of her body against it as he made love to it. He'd tried so hard not to want what he shouldn't have. But now that he'd resigned himself to his feelings, he would take what she so freely offered.

"Stay very still, darlin'," he whispered. He ran his hands up her calves to her thighs and hooked his finger around the top of the lace. He teased her by running his pointer finger back and forth along the rim of her panties, barely brushing the top of her curls.

"Ah, Luca," she sighed. She went to wiggle away but Luca held her hips firm in his hands.

"Hmmm...you're so delightful, Samantha. I can smell your desire, you know. I can hardly wait to be deep inside you, but first...I must taste you." Luca removed his hands from the sides of her panties and placed them behind her knees. Slowly he kissed the top of her belly, along the line of lace. Sliding his hands up the back of her thighs, his fingers slipped underneath the flimsy fabric until each hand was full with a curve of her ass. His thumbs hooked around her hips, jerking her towards him as his tongue teased an inch under the elastic in the front.

"Please, Luca," she pleaded. "You're driving me crazy. I need you, please touch me."

Grabbing the sides of her panties, he slowly eased them down and off her legs until she stood completely naked to him.

"I want you so much. I need to know you want this as much as I do. I won't be able to stop once I taste you." With his forehead pressed to her stomach, Luca waited for her approval. He wanted to make love with her, to taste her blood, to possess her.

"Yes, Luca, take all of me." Samantha's heart pounded against her chest as her adrenaline spiked. She felt a rush of excitement. She knew there was no going back, and she didn't want to. Her human life was over as she knew it, and Luca was her future. She'd known it from the minute he'd held her at the cabin. She waited in silence for Luca to respond.

He responded by softly kissing along the crease of her legs, as he gently sat her on the bed. Then he spread her legs open until he was comfortably caged between her knees. He quickly lost control as he teased her outer lips open with his tongue.

Samantha moaned loudly at his sweet invasion. Her hands fisted into his long raven hair as he kissed her sex mercilessly.

Luca flicked over her clit with the tip of his tongue, and heard Samantha release a small scream. She tasted delicious, so sweet and wet for him. Running his fingers into her soft red curls, he parted her so he could kiss her deeply. His tongue darted into her core as he brushed the pad of his thumb over her sensitive nub.

Samantha felt her blood rushing as Luca tormented her with oral finesse. She threw her head back in delight. "Yes, Luca. That feels so good. Please don't stop," she begged.

Luca inserted a finger, then two, pumping into her as he licked her sensitive petal. He was careful not to nick her with his fangs, not yet. As she began to quiver in his arms, he could feel she was close.

Samantha began to shake as her arousal built. She bucked her hips up to him as he took her over the cliff of pleasure. She thought she saw stars dance as her orgasm tore through her. "Oh God, Luca. Yes!" she screamed.

Luca sucked on her clit as Samantha shook above him. Releasing her for merely a second, he licked over the smooth skin of her inner thigh, and bit into her. As the blood trickled into his throat, he groaned in delight at the taste of her. He wanted more of her magic-laced liquid, but restrained himself, licking the wounds shut.

In a silent haze, Luca stood up, while Samantha lifted her heavy-lidded eyes to meet his. Without speaking a word, she unbuckled his pants, never looking away. He pulled off his shirt, and Samantha grew aroused once again, admiring his rock-hard abs. His chest was smooth and muscular, his shoulders broad. He watched her with great intensity as she unzipped his pants. His cock sprung forward into her small soft hands.

Luca hissed as Samantha jerked him toward her slightly so she could lick the tip of him. His head rolled back when she cupped his testicles and began to run her tongue up and down his shaft.

Samantha hadn't given oral sex to very many men. But the instant she saw Luca's virile masculinity, she craved the taste of him. She deliberately glided her tongue along the sinewy length of him, and could detect a slight pulse as she swirled her lips over his tip. She held him firm with one hand as she parted her lips, seductively taking him into her mouth.

They held each other's gaze as she gently sucked him, back and forth, pumping him in and out; her warm soft lips firmly viced on his straining sex. This witch surely was performing a spell on him because he felt helpless in her hands. He growled as he struggled not to come.

"Darlin', you've gotta stop. Please. I want to be inside you." He put his hands on her shoulders, trying to cease the intense sensation. "Now." He gritted his teeth, resisting the urge to come.

As she released him, he pulled her to her feet, and they spilled into the bed together. She eased backwards on her hands and feet, feeling like a lion's prey, yet smiling, as if she was thoroughly enjoying the chase.

Luca stalked over to her on his hands and knees, until she was caged against the bed. He felt a primitive need to claim her, so she'd never know another man. With a hungry urgency, he leaned over and captured her lips.

Samantha deliriously explored his mouth, lost in his animalistic kiss. She wanted him so badly, feeling as if he were her first. And she knew in that moment, that there would be no other for her. Captivated by his raw power, she submitted to the overwhelming pleasure she felt within his snare.

Breathing heavily, he tore his lips from hers, yet again silently seeking her acceptance. She nodded, unable to speak, and he lowered his head to suckle the rosy tip of her breast. Samantha screamed in ecstasy as he bit gently and teased the shimmering bud.

Unable to submit to the glorious torture any longer, she found her voice. "Please Luca, I need you in me."

Reluctantly releasing her breast, Luca gazed into Samantha's eyes, and he slowly sheathed himself inside her. Samantha's eyes widened as she gasped. He halted his entrance to give her time to adjust to his substantial size. She started to rock up into him, letting him know she was ready for him. Luca groaned as he joined his body to hers fully.

"Aw, yes. You feel so warm and wet. You're amazing." He sucked her lip, until she opened for him. They kissed in rhythm as he began to pump in and out of her.

Samantha had never felt so womanly in all her life. No man had ever made her come before, and Luca's finely-tuned movements started to build yet another climax in her womb. He knew exactly how to brush his pelvis against her clit, teasing her senses, mounting her arousal and waning it back again.

Luca kissed up and down the alabaster skin of her neck, feathering kisses behind her ear down to her breast. He dipped his head down and suckled a sensitive peak.

Holding himself up with one hand, he caressed the other aching bud. Samantha moaned with pleasure as he pinched the taut nub between his fingers. She responded in turn by wrapping her legs around his waist, driving him deeper into her tight moist heat.

Completely enveloped by her, Luca felt on the precipice of his own release. He began to hasten his movement, thrusting himself in and out of her softness.

Samantha couldn't hold herself back any longer as he slammed into her hard. She screamed against his throat as the climax rippled throughout her body. The pulsating sensation was so intense she shook against him.

Luca felt her tighten around him, massaging his hardness. Surrendering to the exquisite pleasure, he exploded within her. He felt as if he'd been hit by a lightning bolt, realizing his orgasm was like nothing he'd ever experienced in all his two hundred years. He wished it was her magic making him feel this extraordinary pleasure but knew it was his heart; she was taking it, and there was nothing he could do to stop himself from falling.

CHAPTER EIGHT

Luca opened his eyes and glanced down at the beautiful woman in his arms. After making love the previous night, they had both fallen into a deep sleep. It was a rare indulgence for Luca to sleep with a female. He listened to her heartbeat and felt the rise of her belly with her every breath. Samantha had somehow touched his heart, and he couldn't even say in that moment that he regretted giving it to her. After two hundred years of a self-imposed moratorium on love, he couldn't resist Samantha. She was vulnerable, yet intelligent and strong. She was a survivor, and Luca admired her spirit and resolve.

Thinking of Eliza, he knew she would want him to move on and be happy. It had been such a long time. And while he truly did love Eliza, it was a young man's love that had attracted him to her. He wondered how he would have felt after years of marriage to her if they hadn't been attacked. Yet it had been a different time then. Women were very proper, and he'd been quite the respectable lad. The truth was that he'd never known Eliza in a biblical sense. They'd only kissed, which had been appropriate for that time period.

As he lay spooning Samantha, he pulled her closer to him. Luca might not have wanted a human lover, but now that he'd made love with her, he was certain he'd never let her go. Deep inside her last night, he'd fought the urge to claim Samantha. If he'd bitten her during climax, they would begin to bond. But he wasn't sure how Samantha felt about him. Did she want to live with him? He was vampire, and she'd barely adjusted to the fact that she was a witch. She was adamant about returning to her life in Pennsylvania.

He found himself dreaming of her, what it would be like to have her live with him; turning the mansion into a home instead of a showcase of expensive antiques and paintings. Could they have children? The idea of Samantha having his children excited him, as he regretted never having had any before he was turned. While most vampires were sterile to humans, he'd heard rumors from the witches that they could be impregnated. One night while attending a coven party with Ilsbeth, he'd been told that because of a witch's magical blood, they, in only very special circumstances, could accept the infertile vampire sperm into their body and infuse it with their life-force, creating the perfect conditions for fertilization. He made a mental note to check with Ilsbeth to see if this was simply an urban legend, or a real possibility.

While Luca stroked Samantha's delicate hand, her eyes started to flutter. She didn't want to wake up from the wonderful fantasy she'd experienced last night. Encased in Luca's well-built arms, she felt safe, happy and loved. *Loved?* The minute the thought popped into her mind, she tried to push it away. No, vampires like Luca don't do love. He'd already told her that he didn't get involved with mortals, let alone fall in love with them. Yet she couldn't shake the thought. Luca was such a caring and sensual lover, like no other man she'd ever been with. She'd only been with a handful of lovers over the years, but none had ever made her come. Most men just quickly came, and then asked her if it was good for her. But Luca was different; he knew exactly what he was doing and played her body like a virtuoso played a Stradivarius. She tingled, thinking about the mad earth-shattering orgasm she'd experienced under his hand. He was a master.

Growing aroused, Samantha pushed her bottom backwards, feeling the hardness of him. She began to rock back and forth, brushing against his erection.

Luca squeezed Samantha as she began to grind against him. "Good morning, my little witch," he said, kissing the top of her head. "This is the finest way I've woken up in a long time. But are you sure you're ready for me?"

"Ummm….yes Luca. I can't seem to get enough of you," she purred as she increased the pressure.

Luca reached both hands around her and cupped her breasts, gently caressing her pink flesh. "I can't seem to keep my hands off of you, either. I need to have you, be in you." He kissed the back of her neck, sending chills down her arms. Luca's straining shaft eased into her warm heat in one hard thrust from behind.

"Ah, yes, Luca!" Samantha screamed.

"My God, you feel so good. I won't last long this morning. You're so tight. Hmmm." Luca massaged her breast in one hand while he reached into her warm, wet folds. He began to rock in and out of her, slow and steady while he feathered his fingertips over her clitoris.

Luca's fangs elongated; there'd be nothing more satisfying than drinking her sweet blood while climaxing inside her. But if he did that, the bonding would begin. He fought the urge, retracting his fangs, and kissed along the back of her neck instead.

"Please Luca," Samantha begged. "I need to...I have to..." her breathless words trailed off.

He knew what she needed, and he needed it too. Losing control, Luca increased his pace and felt them going off the cliff of pleasure into a simultaneous release. Samantha yelled out Luca's name as they both rode out the incredible final moment of ecstasy.

Luca just held Samantha, not wanting to let her go. "Samantha, you're so intoxicating, darlin'. I...I just want you to know that I'm glad you came down here with me." He wanted to tell her how he felt, but registered the oddest sensation of fear, a rare feeling indeed for a two hundred year old vampire. What if she wanted to leave and go back to Pennsylvania? He'd never see her again; he knew a long distance relationship would never work.

"I didn't want to come down here, but I can't say that I'm upset right now. What we shared Luca....it was incredible. Thank you," she whispered.

He could feel Samantha's breathing slow; she was falling asleep again. Easing himself from the bed, he went to take a shower. He needed to get the upper hand of his emotions before he lost control to the seductive female in his bed.

Samantha woke alone, experiencing an odd sense of loss that he'd left her. She looked around the spacious room, noticing the sleek, modern furnishings. His black, king-sized platform bed stood alone save for a long matching bureau and armoire. It was a sharp contrast to the antique furnishings upstairs, and she found herself wondering if he'd decorated both. While he seemed to consider this subterranean domicile his primary home, he clearly must have had a hand in the magnificent interior décor on the first floor. Perhaps this suited Luca's dynamic personality. On the one hand he was stoic, refined and dominating, yet he'd showed her that he could be caring, erotic and loving.

At the cabin, he didn't mince words when he gave her no choice in returning, even threatening to enthrall her, and then last night, he seemed to open up about what had happened at Eden, when he could have simply ignored how she felt. He'd made love to her with primal fury, yet he'd made sure she was in agreement about moving forward at every turn. He'd showed a gentleness and tenderness she hadn't experienced from any man in her life, ever.

Softly padding across the wooden floor, Samantha felt her stomach grumble. Vampires might not need actual food, but she needed to eat something soon. She also realized how sore she was from all the lovemaking with Luca. She sighed and smiled, thinking of how she'd lost all sense of responsibility with him. He was a gloriously irresistible male.

Pushing open the bathroom door, she was impressed by the oversized charcoal, soapstone shower lined with beveled glass blocks. A shelved wall held black, neatly folded, clean towels. Two gray pedestal sinks stood in front of a single, wall-sized square mirror. Masculine and luxurious, she thought. She reached over to the shower head and turned on the water. After waiting a few minutes, she stepped into the hot steamy spray, enjoying the beat of the droplets on her back.

She startled, hearing a door open, but settled when she saw the outline of her sexy vampire through the glass. Luca poked his face into the shower, taking a long drink of her bare creamy white skin. Smiling back, she wished he'd join her.

As if reading her mind, he grinned. "Hello darlin', as much as I'd like to join you, if I do I'm afraid we won't get any work done today. It's nearly three in the afternoon, and we've got an appointment with Ilsbeth at six. We'll start with her, and then go from there. While you were asleep, Sydney stopped over and brought you a goody bag. Clothes, toothbrushes, good stuff like that. Anyway, she and Kade haven't found any leads, but they're on call if we need them. We have some things to discuss with Ilsbeth, including having a little chat about that rain making trick you did at the cabin." He winked at her, sending a thrill up her spine.

"Okay, sounds good. I'm anxious to get this over with," she said, using both her hands to apply the conditioner through her long mane. As she leaned back into the spray, her firm breasts pushed out toward Luca, beckoning him into the shower.

Luca raked his fingers through his hair. "You're killing me. You know, I'm finding it hard to resist you, let alone wet and naked."

She shot him a wry grin. "Then why don't you join me?" She turned her face into the drizzle, wiggling her behind at him.

Luca adjusted himself as he blew out a breath. They'd never get anything done, making love all day. "Later, temptress. I've got brunch out here for you, courtesy of Sydney. Now come on and hurry up. We've got work to do."

Samantha squeaked as she felt a firm spank on her butt cheek. She laughed and complied, turning off the water. She was hungry, and Luca was right. They needed to do research and get information out of Ilsbeth. She was tired of being a victim. Whoever was doing this had sorely underestimated her ability to fight back.

Eating a wonderful array of fresh fruit, beignets and bacon, Samantha listened to Luca tell her about the writing at the cabin.

"Hematilly Periapt? What's that?" she asked.

"A periapt is an amulet. They're usually made by someone of magic, like a witch, warlock or mage. So for example, if it was blessed with white magic, it would be used for something good, like protection. But I'm guessing that it has been created by someone using black magic, and has a nefarious purpose like hexing or perhaps a curse. To be honest, I've got no idea what it does or why someone would want it. But it must be pretty important to someone, given they followed you to Pennsylvania and burned down a building to try to get it."

"But why would anyone think I have it? I mean, I don't remember much of what happened to me, but I can tell you that I don't have it. This is the first I've heard of it. I swear. I don't even know what it looks like or what it does."

"I'm not sure. But this has got to do with Asgear. He probably has something to do with this, or should I say, had something to do with it."

"Can't we just search his house? What about that warehouse Sydney told me about?"

"No. Kade and Sydney searched all his properties after the crypt was destroyed. He owned the warehouse in the business district, which has since been demolished, thanks to Kade. They also ran a search to see if he owned any other properties and came up empty. Now he may have owned or rented other properties under an alias, but so far there's no evidence of their existence. The periapt could literally be anywhere in or out of this city," Luca speculated.

"Well, I can't just sit around doing nothing until we go see Ilsbeth. If this thing is real, maybe there's something about it online. I know that the witches were in the process of converting some of their books over to digital versions, in case of flood or fire. Of course, I wasn't allowed access to anything when I was at the coven, but I heard them talking about it."

"We can ask Ilsbeth to let us see the books when we go there tonight," Luca suggested.

"No offense, Luca, but the witches aren't going to let a vampire look at their books. The one thing I learned in my week there is that they are very secretive. And since I didn't agree to join their sisterhood, I wasn't allowed in the library either. We can ask Ilsbeth, but I know she'll say no. Don't get me wrong, she can be very kind. But she also can be a tough as nails bitch. She does not bend rules, period. Besides, I think we should try a backdoor approach at the same time we're playing nice."

"What do you mean, backdoor?" He smiled at her, knowing she had something up her sleeve.

"Well, if they are putting all the books into a database, then we just take a peek," she proposed. "You know, hack in and look at the files and then sneak out. I can do this, Luca."

"Very impressive, tell me more."

"I'm considered a 'white hat' hacker. That means I purposefully spend time trying to hack into systems to expose their weaknesses, so that I can help clients and our company. There are some folks out there who are considered 'black hat' hackers. They do the same thing, but they're not doing it to help anyone. They might be stealing or just trying to cause trouble. There are other titles in the hacking world too, like 'grey hats' who break in and then offer to fix systems for a fee. Regardless, I've had to learn all kinds of hacking techniques when I'm testing. The only caveat is that hacking isn't always as quick as they make it seem in the movies. If I can't find a gaping hole in their system, I may need to try a few other tactics that might take longer," she explained.

Prior to her abduction, Samantha had worked as a high level computer engineer for a large government contractor and was known to be one of the best 'white hat' hackers in her division; she regularly attempted to hack their own computer systems as part of quality assurance. If the *Hematilly Periapt* existed and its information had been recorded digitally, she could find it.

A business call interrupted them, and Luca took it in his office, leaving Samantha to work. Borrowing Luca's laptop, she ran a search on 'Hematilly Periapt', suspecting that initial searches would turn up nothing. She had a hunch that this item was only known in supernatural circles and wouldn't show up on poser sites. People who knew about the amulet were not wannabe witches or vampires. And whoever was threatening her and looking for this item knew that it held seriously potent power; they'd been willing to kill for it.

Samantha knew the coven had a huge physical library that she hadn't been given access to yet. Ilsbeth had told her that she'd be given the key once she'd completed her training and had sworn allegiance to the coven. Rowan, a young but powerful witch who worked as the librarian, had befriended Samantha. Although she was kind during Samantha's training, she had gone out of her way to tell Samantha to stay away from the mystical athenaeum. At the time, Samantha hadn't thought twice to ask about the room, why she couldn't go in there or what kinds of archives were stored within. She just knew that she wasn't allowed to go in the library, and that there would be serious consequences for breaking coven rules. But now she wanted very badly to see what was hidden behind those doors.

The one thing that Rowan had let slip during tea one day was that the witches had started moving information to online storage, as it could be safely backed up. Critical data could be kept safe from all kinds of natural disasters and recovered easily. If for some reason their wards failed to protect the coven house, a fire could take out their library within minutes.

Contemplating where to search next, Samantha typed in the name of the coven, *Cercle de lumière Vieux Carre*, and waited. A single site popped up in her Google search and she clicked. A blank screen flashed onto her computer with two blank spots for identification and password. Knowing she wouldn't have the identification, she'd need to obtain another witch's security information, or find a weakness in their system. Samantha switched windows, and logged into her home server, so she'd be able to pull over the software she needed to hack in.

Within minutes, she ran a vulnerability scanner on the coven's site. She was hoping easy in, but it didn't show any cracks. *Damn.* "I'll find your secrets," she muttered to herself. "It may take a while, but I'll get in."

Picking up her cell phone, she moved forward with a typical 'black hat' hacker approach and called the hosting system administrator's number that she'd been able to search out. Unfortunately for Samantha, they'd been well trained and had not given up the security information despite her name-dropping and helpful attitude. She had to give them credit for not falling for her tactics.

Being one never to give up, she decided to resort to her most reliable but time-consuming method for breaking into computer systems. She accessed both Rowan and Ilsbeth's email addresses and sent them an email letting them know about the cabin burning and that she was looking forward to seeing them tonight. The email looked innocuous enough, but in reality she'd attached a worm to it. When opened, the worm would infiltrate their systems and attach a key-logging application with a Trojan horse to keep it hidden. The second Ilsbeth or Rowan accessed the online site, their keystrokes would be recorded and sent via messaging to Samantha's iPhone. They'd never be any the wiser, and eventually Samantha would get the passwords.

She felt a little badly for taking advantage of their kindness, but she knew they'd never simply agree to give her access. It had been made clear that unless she was a fully-fledged member, she would not get access, online or otherwise. Knowing that having information on the *Hematilly Periapt* was a matter of life or death justified the hacking, in Samantha's mind. She would ask Ilsbeth in person tonight again for access, and if granted, she'd remove the software. But until that happened, she'd wait for the passwords to pop up on her hack.

Samantha shut the laptop and decided to go upstairs to look around Luca's mini-museum. It was almost five in the afternoon, and they needed to leave soon. She peeked into Luca's office and told him she was going upstairs to look around. He was on the phone, clearly listening, but yet he gave her the okay sign when she told him where she'd be.

Her breath caught as she entered the great room on the main floor. The tan walls were offset by the cream wainscoting; the entire first floor was richly decorated with both paintings and sculptures. Samantha resisted the temptation to run her fingers across the floral upholstery of a lovely French empire settee. Its mahogany arms were rolled and adorned with acanthus leaf carvings. She'd never seen anything so beautiful or intricately designed.

Samantha's eye caught a spectacular oil painting which had been set in a sophisticated gold leaf frame. She studied the landscape, admiring the way the artist appeared to capture the sun's rays.

"You like?" Luca came up behind her. Samantha jumped, but calmed under the touch of his fingers on her shoulders. "Paysage vers Canes-sur-Mer by Renoir. Lovely, isn't it?"

"Stunning. I can't believe you have all this stuff. No wonder you have such a serious security system. It's like the Smithsonian in here."

Luca chuckled. "All memories. Keepsakes. But I see nothing here as beautiful as you." He released her shoulders to move over to the baby grand piano. He'd been accumulating all the art pieces for well over a century. Kade had suggested he needed a hobby, so he'd started collecting, piece by piece. "Some pieces are souvenirs. Others I just wanted for my collection. Kade said I needed to find something constructive to do with my time, immortal as I am, so I started antiquing. I live in New Orleans after all," he joked.

"That you do," Samantha said in amazement as she walked over to look at a marbled bust of a woman that sat on the hearth of the old fireplace. "She's beautiful." She touched the cheek of the marble and then quickly withdrew her hand, fearing she'd break something. "She must be a very important lady to command the attention of the room."

Luca frowned. "She was...she was my fiancée, Eliza."

Samantha's stomach dropped. He'd been engaged. She had never thought that Luca might have been married. She silently admonished herself for being jealous of a dead woman. "Your fiancée? I'm sorry. I assume she's passed."

"Yes, it was a very long time ago. She was killed before I had the chance to marry her...before I was vampire. I had an Italian artist create this in her memory. Such a long time ago but the memories remain." Looking out the windows to the gardens, he didn't want to say any more about Eliza to Samantha. It didn't seem the right time to tell her all the sordid details of how she met her demise. He felt he'd told Samantha enough of the truth for now. If and when they grew closer, he'd share the story with her.

Samantha resisted pressing him for details, realizing Luca didn't want to talk about it. She knew what it was like to experience loss, and understood that there were times in life when you just needed to let things go. When he was ready to talk about it, he would tell her. She was about to tell him not to worry about telling her the details, when a tall gorgeous woman burst into the great room, looking pissed as hell. It took all of two seconds before Samantha realized the angry female was a vampire.

Glaring at Samantha, the woman bared her fangs and hissed. "You little bitch! I knew you survived Asgear, but I heard you'd left. What the fuck is she doing here, Luca?" she demanded to know. "No, don't even tell me because I don't care. I told you I'd get her back for what she did to me and now it's game on."

The livid female vampire raced across the room with preternatural speed, knocking the wind out of Samantha as she grabbed her around the throat and held her against the wall. Samantha's eyes bulged as she watched Luca snatch the other vampire with one hand and throw her across the room. He growled as Samantha held up a hand to him indicating she was okay.

"Dominique!" he yelled. He strode across the room, where the woman shot daggers at him, looking like she was ready for round two. "Enough! It's over. You will apologize now. And if you ever touch her again, I'll stake you myself."

The woman vampire acquiesced and quickly stood up, holding both her hands up in surrender. "Me? Apologize? Luca, how can you take her side? You know what she did! How could you?" she pleaded.

"She is mine," Luca declared. "And you will not touch her. You will treat her with respect. She doesn't even remember what happened to her. Samantha," he glanced over to her and back. "This is Dominique. Unfortunately, when you were bespelled, you silvered her. And while she did suffer that night, she is no worse for wear as you can see. She most definitely does hold grudges but she will be respectful in your presence. Isn't that correct, Dominique?"

"Goddamn you Luca. I can smell you all over her. Yes, I will try not to kill your plaything," Dominique spat through her teeth with a sickening sweet smile that promised retribution. She hated having to follow Luca's order but would do it for him. He was her superior.

"Now that we're done with introductions, I believe you'd best get back to Kade's to continue working. Dominique is the Director of Public Relations for Issacson Industries. We have a downtown office, but she spends a lot of time here if Kade is working from home. She also helps me with security when needed." Luca came to stand next to Samantha and put his arm around her shoulder; he wanted it to be clear to Dominique that Samantha was his. "We're going over to see Ilsbeth. I'll contact you later if I need your assistance. Goodbye, Dominique."

Dominique shot Samantha an icy scowl and nodded at Luca. "Goodbye, Luca. I hope you know what you're getting into with this one," she huffed. As Dominique walked out the door, she slammed it in defiance.

"Are you okay?" he asked, checking Samantha's neck for injuries.

"I'm fine, just a bit shaken up is all."

"Dominique can be a bit of a handful, but she's very loyal. I promise that she won't hurt you now that I've talked with her."

"I sure as hell hope so. That was one pissed off vampire bitch." Samantha rubbed her neck. "I don't even remember her, but I certainly will now."

"I'm really sorry about her. She'll get over it, though. I meant what I said to her, and she knows it," he assured Samantha.

"Thanks, Luca. I appreciate you saving me. She's kinda scary," she admitted.

Luca couldn't resist pulling Samantha against his hard chest. He caressed her back and neck. Her shiny red hair now smelled of peaches, and he smiled, remembering how responsive she'd been the night before. She'd nearly killed him when she took him into her mouth. Growing aroused, he knew it wasn't the time to start something he couldn't finish. They needed to go soon and get some answers. He reluctantly released Samantha, putting some needed distance between them.

"Darlin', as much as I'd like to play museum curator and show you all my fun toys, we'd better get going over to the coven. I'm barely holding onto control. If we don't leave within the next five minutes, I might be tempted to have my way with you yet again," he teased.

"And I might like that very much," she countered. She blushed, thinking about how they'd made love the night before. She'd never met a man who could make her climax during intercourse, let alone make her feel as if she'd gone directly to heaven. It was as if he intimately knew every square inch of her body so well that he could send her into a blinding rapture with just his lips.

Luca could tell Samantha was silently reminiscing about how incredible last night had been for them both. The mind blowing sex wasn't something he'd soon forget.

He couldn't remember ever having been with someone who was so vibrant and loving. Envisioning her beneath him, writhing in pleasure, he groaned, willing his erection to subside. He needed to think about something else besides making love to Samantha.

"So did you have any luck getting into the database?" he asked, grabbing his keys off of a hallway desk.

"Yeah, about that. I tried breaking into the coven database, while you were on the phone. It was pretty tight, so I have to take a more indirect approach. I sent both Rowan and Ilsbeth emails that have a hidden key stroking tracking worm attached. I'll be alerted once they go online and then we can nab the password. It might take a little while but the method is tried and true." Samantha was confident they'd have the passwords within the day. Ilsbeth might not go online that often, but she was sure that Rowan would do so, since she actively worked in the library.

"Smart and beautiful." Luca hugged her and brushed a light kiss on her lips. "We'd better go now, before I decide to take you back downstairs and ravish you senseless." Luca wished he was joking but knew she was quickly becoming an irresistible vice.

CHAPTER NINE

Samantha and Luca sat in the parlor waiting on Ilsbeth. Feeling her hands tingle, Samantha wondered if maybe she was feeling her magic. The only other time she'd felt a similar feeling was at the cabin. In an effort to dull the sensation, she closed her eyes, breathed in a deep breath, held it for five seconds and then blew it out. She reasoned that she might know shit about magic but she was pretty good at meditation. Relaxation seeped through her veins as she repeated the exercise.

It was not that she hated the idea of the existence of a witch's coven; she just hated what it personally represented. It was where she'd been sent to be cleansed of the dirt that had tainted her very soul. Whatever Asgear had done to her was beyond human reason, possibly demonic. She shuddered, wondering what could have happened if the evil had been allowed to grow within her. Would she have stolen? Murdered? Learned and utilized black magic for her own gain?

The thought of deliberately hurting someone made her sick; it all seemed unbelievable. Even after she'd left the coven to return to Pennsylvania, she'd felt normal, perfectly human. But she couldn't deny the surge of electricity and power that she had called when pushed into a fit of rage. Seeing the cabin ablaze had given birth to an uncontrollable reaction.

"Luca. Samantha. So glad to see you safely made it back to New Orleans." The lilt of Ilsbeth's voice jilted Samantha back into reality. Ilsbeth sat in a chair across from Luca and Samantha, who sat side by side on the sofa. Noticing their closeness, Ilsbeth quietly smiled. "Samantha, you are welcome to move back into the coven and continue your training," she offered.

"No thank you," Samantha refused kindly. "I...I'm staying with Luca." She looked to him for comfort and then returned her gaze to Ilsbeth. "We came because we need your help with a few things. The first is my magic. I did something in Pennsylvania that I think you should know about. The cabin I was staying at. Well, someone set it on fire. I was so angry and scared, and before I knew what was happening, something called to me within, like my skin was crawling. I felt out of control, like electricity was bolting through my body. I felt this need...to call rain. And it worked. It rained and put out the fire. I guess I just wanted you to know..." Samantha's voice trailed off as she stared at Ilsbeth. *God, I sound crazy. Although I'd take crazy over 'witch' right now.*

Laughing out loud, Ilsbeth stood and began to pace the length of the room. "This is wonderful, Samantha! Don't you see? Of course you don't. How would you know?" She quickly returned to her seat and held Samantha's hands. "It sounds as if you are an elemental witch, my dear. The elements: fire, water, earth and wind. They will come to you when needed and when called. You may not have good control right now, but with practice, you will be quite powerful someday. Please consider returning to the coven. It will be great fun to teach you."

"Thank you for the offer, Ilsbeth. But right now, I need to stay with Luca. He's keeping me safe. Nothing has happened since with my magic. I'll let you know if something else does. I guess that I'm just...I'm just not ready for this. Maybe someday." She sounded unsure, but after all, she didn't seem to get a choice about when or how the magic came. She didn't want Luca to send her back to Ilsbeth. "I promise to think it over, but right now we've got a more pressing problem. Whoever is after me wants something called a *Hematilly Periapt*. Do you have any idea what it is, or why someone would want it?" she asked.

Ilsbeth's face hardened; her lips pressed together in a fine line. An icy sheet fell across her face. "Now listen here, I am not sure who told you about that, but the *Hematilly Periapt* is not to be trifled with. It's a very powerful amulet, and it belongs in the care of a coven. No one currently knows its location and thankfully, it is probably lost or destroyed. Whoever is asking for it is nothing but trouble. Now, I suggest you forget about it."

Samantha hesitated then pressed forward. "Ilsbeth, I'm sorry if this line of questioning bothers you. But someone could have killed us and they wanted that amulet. And for some ungodly reason, they think I have it. So please forgive us, but I have to ask about it. Could you tell us, you know, if you had to take a wild guess, who might have it or where you think we should start looking for it?"

"Samantha, maybe I am not making myself clear. There are certain things that are not up for discussion. You are welcome to train with us, to be accepted within the sisterhood. By doing so, there are many secrets that will become known to you. Until that time, I am sorry, there is nothing I can do to help you," Ilsbeth replied coldly. She stood as if expecting them to leave. "Is there anything else I can help you with? I'm very busy."

"Would it be all right if I went up to my old room? I think I may have left some notes there, and I really would like to collect them. I wanted to keep a journal of my transformation," Samantha asked. It couldn't hurt to look around to see if perhaps she'd left any clues during her time at the coven. Samantha barely remembered the first few days she'd spent there, but there was a small chance she'd left a note about the amulet. It was a long shot, but grasping at straws was about the only thing she could do, now that Ilsbeth had clammed up about the *Hematilly Periapt*.

"Please, feel free to search your room. However, I believe the sisters have cleaned the area of any belongings you may have left behind. I'm serious, Samantha. No more talk of the periapt. Sometimes just talking about something can affect our universe," she warned.

Samantha nodded and hurried up the stairs.

Luca stood to walk Ilsbeth to the foyer. "Ilsbeth, I do have one more question, which may seem quite odd. Definitely off topic."

"Yes, what is it, Luca?

"It's rumored that it's possible for witches to bear the child of a vampire. Is this true?" He knew Ilsbeth would put the puzzle pieces together and surmise what he was thinking. At the same time, he needed to know if it was possible for him to father a child.

Ilsbeth's face softened, and she smiled slightly. She put her hand on Luca's forearm. "Yes, it's true, Luca. It is uncommon but has occurred a number of times over the centuries...very rare, though. I certainly would not plan a future based upon it. Witches bear children to humans and witches...sometimes shifters. It is the natural course of our kind. Luca, I'm not sure what you're thinking, but please be cautious in how you proceed in your relationship with Samantha. I can see how she trusts you. I must counsel you to be honest with her before you decide to claim her. She's getting stronger, but she's still fragile," she advised.

"She may have once been fragile, but she is not as delicate as you would think. In fact, she's quite a bright and capable woman," Luca acknowledged.

"Luca, today you are full of surprises. I never thought I'd see the day when you would come to care for a human woman, albeit a witch. Very interesting indeed," Ilsbeth smiled slyly. "Take care, Luca. Please keep her safe." Shaking her head in disbelief, she turned and walked behind the shimmering curtain that blocked the view of visitors from seeing further into the coven's home.

Luca considered Ilsbeth's insights. Yes, Samantha was emotionally delicate. But that was only because of the unwanted circumstances that had been thrust upon her; she'd suffered a loss of control. Luca reasoned that any human would have crumbled, given the same situation. Samantha could have chosen to give up, but instead, she'd fought with him to get her life back, to find out who was after her. Luca knew that Samantha was substantially stronger than he'd initially judged. She'd proven herself resilient and resourceful at each step of the journey; she was more determined than ever to find the *Hematilly Periapt* and get her life in order.

Upstairs, Samantha feverishly searched her guest room for evidence of an amulet or some kind of clue. When she'd spent time at the coven, she'd written herself little notes every day, hoping that one would spark her lost memory. She was certain that she had left a few in the room when she left for Pennsylvania. Yet, scouring the room, she could barely find a speck of dust in the cleaned out desk, let alone any of her memos. No wonder Ilsbeth had allowed her to search her room; everything she'd written had been thrown in the trash.

Samantha walked down the circular, cedar-lined hallway. As she approached the library, Rowan, the librarian, sat working at her desk, guarding the entrance. She sat in front of the ornately-carved wooden doors, working on her laptop, appearing not to notice Samantha. Rowan's long, frizzy black hair cascaded over her petite figure. She was oddly attractive, dressing as if she was a college student, in a mini-skirt with a sharply pressed white oxford shirt. While she looked as if she was only in her twenties, Samantha knew that she was nearly fifty years old.

Casually approaching the witch, Samantha cleared her throat. "Hi Rowan, long time no see."

"Ah you're back, Sam. Are you moving back into your old room?" she inquired.

"Uh...no, well not yet. Right now, I'm staying with a friend," Samantha responded. "I was just looking for my notes in my old room, but I guess they were thrown out. I really need to get going but I thought I'd stop by and say hi on the way out. I'm not sure when I'll be back. Do you have my cell number? Maybe we could go out for coffee sometime," she suggested.

"Yeah, sure." Rowan cautiously eyed Samantha, wondering why she was roaming around the coven hallways unescorted. She made a mental note to discuss this incident with Ilsbeth. Samantha was nice, but she wasn't a sister. They couldn't afford that kind of security lapse. Rowan got up from her desk and stood protectively in front of the library doors, guarding its entrance.

Typing numbers into their cell phones, Rowan and Samantha politely exchanged numbers. Samantha wanted to ask Rowan to let her into the library, but knew it would never happen. She might be friendly, but she was nothing short of ruthless when it came to protecting coven secrets. Explaining that she had a friend waiting, Samantha quickly ran down the coven steps and into Luca's waiting arms. On an intellectual level, Samantha knew the coven was supposed to feel like home, but on an emotional level, it felt like a prison and she couldn't wait to leave.

Luca turned the ignition and tried to figure out how he'd pitch his next idea to Samantha. They had come up with practically nothing at the coven. It was clear that Ilsbeth didn't want them to have the amulet or speak of it, but besides that, they didn't have much more information than before they came. If the object scared Ilsbeth, that was not a good sign.

Luca wondered what the amulet did that caused Ilsbeth to insist they stop looking for it. He knew one fact for certain; it was important enough that someone would murder in order to get it. It was possible that Asgear had had the amulet and then that Samantha had stolen it at some point. Perhaps she'd hidden it? Samantha's memory had failed her so far, and Luca wasn't sure he wanted her to remember the rest of the gory details of her abduction. Overnight, Samantha had appeared to grow stronger, and he didn't want to risk a relapse.

The problem, Luca surmised, was that there weren't many places he was aware of that they could even search. The only two locations she'd been at for certain were the mausoleum in St. Louis cemetery and Sangre Dulce, where Samantha had been bespelled into posing as a waitress and submissive. The mausoleum was out of the question, because it had been destroyed. Dominique and Ilsbeth had taken care of that.

As for Sangre Dulce, Luca was concerned about taking her back to the club. If they went back, there was a risk she could be traumatized all over again. When she'd been in Kade's basement during her initial interrogation, she'd nearly fainted after being shown pictures of herself nude, serving drinks. She only had a vague memory of having a drink with a man, James, who was really Asgear. No other memories existed for her.

Shifting in his seat, he drove towards home and sighed. "So listen, Samantha," he began. "Since Ilsbeth was a bust, we don't have many options. I have a plan, but I'm not sure you're going to like it." He didn't bother looking over at Samantha to gauge her reaction, and kept his eyes fixed on the road.

"Well, let's just say, I'm open to suggestions. There was nothing in my old room. In fact, they'd cleaned the place out. And until Ilsbeth or Rowan try to log into the coven site, we can't hack into their server. So, whatever's on your mind has got to be better than the whole lot of nothin' we've got now." She shrugged and glanced over at him.

"Okay, if you're open to it, here goes. I'm thinking it's a real possibility that Asgear stole or found this amulet. Maybe he knew what it did, maybe he didn't. I'm also thinking that maybe you took it and hid it before or during being bespelled. Just because he bespelled you, it doesn't mean you liked him. He could have told you what it did, and you inherently knew he wouldn't put it to good use. Now, how someone else knows you were with him or that you might have had it, is a true mystery." Luca steeled himself before telling Samantha that they were returning to her living hell. "I think that we need to go back to Sangre Dulce to take a look around, maybe talk to the other waitresses, look for clues. We know you were there."

Samantha silently contemplated his proposal. She loathed the idea of returning to that club. It had forever fucked up her life: one decision to go out with friends, one decision to have a drink with a stranger. Going back could bring back her memory or not. She wasn't even sure she wanted to remember. She could literally pick up with her life and move on, not having to worry about the frightening lost memories. Yet if she went back to the club, she might possibly find evidence to lead them to the amulet. Whoever was looking for that damn thing would not leave her in peace until they got it. There was a real possibility that she had done exactly what Luca had postulated. She would never know until she tried.

"Yes. Let's do it," she agreed.

"You sure?" he asked.

"Yes. Until we find this amulet, I'll never get my life back. I need this, Luca. I need normalcy. Maybe supernaturals are used to living in a state of constant stress and chaos, but I'm not. I want my boring, Starbucks drinking, nine to five working life back. It wasn't much but there's one thing I've realized; when you lose everything…your job, your home, your identity, the only person who can put the pieces back together again is you. I've got to do this." She caught Luca's eyes and put her hand on his thigh.

He reached down and covered her small hand with his. Slowly rubbing the inside of her palm with his calloused thumb, he realized how protective he'd become of her. She was so beautiful and brave, willing to return to Sangre Dulce. She wasn't a weak human lying down in defeat. No, she was a fighter. A quick glance at her smiling up at him melted his heart. *What was she doing to him?*

He hadn't even known her very long but felt a deep connection to Samantha that he didn't think he'd ever be able to break. His thoughts drifted to Ilsbeth's words; it was rare, but they could conceive. *A baby.* Silently admonishing himself for even thinking about it, he blew out a breath. What the hell was happening to him? Luca didn't do humans or love and here he was thinking about babies? While growing aroused at her touch, he was more concerned about the tightness he felt in his chest. *I'm falling for this little witch.*

"What are you thinking about? You okay?" Samantha broke his train of thought.

"Just planning our next move," he lied. "When we go to Sangre Dulce, I'll be by your side the entire time. You're not the person you were when you were Rhea. Rhea was mere illusion, someone you were forced to be. We'll go in, do our business and get out," he promised.

"You know, when I saw those pictures, at Kade's, I was just shocked that I could have been made to parade around naked like that in some kind of a magic stupor. I felt like a fool. And then there's that whole submissive thing. I mean, it's not like I'm not open to fantasizing in the bedroom, but what I did wasn't exactly private." She rolled her eyes and shook her head in embarrassment.

"You have nothing to be ashamed of, Samantha. Seriously. Number one, you were not in control of yourself. Asgear forced you against your will. And number two; even if you were a submissive, it's nothing to be embarrassed about. A lot of people experiment with fantasies. It can be fun." He winked at her, trying to lighten the mood.

"I, uh, I don't know, Luca," she hesitated for a moment before continuing. "It's just that I really haven't ever been so intimate with anyone...until you. What we did last night, it was amazing. It's not that I haven't, you know, had sex. God, this is embarrassing. Okay, I'm just going to say it. There's been no other man who made me, you know, come like that." She giggled a little. "Oh my God, I can't believe I'm telling you this." She raked her fingers through her hair, twisting the ends nervously.

"Well darlin', I'm glad to hear it. And if I have my way, I'll be the last man who makes you come 'like that' as you put it," he smiled at her, turning into his driveway.

"Look at what you do to me, woman." He moved her hand from his thigh onto the hard evidence of his arousal. "We're never going to get anything done," he sighed. "Seriously, as much as I'd like to take you inside and make love again, we need to get over to Sangre Dulce," He groaned due to his uncomfortable state of arousal. "When we get home, I'll call Sydney and see if she can bring over something suitable for you to wear to the club. I also think we should bring Étienne and Xavier for backup. I'm not expecting trouble, but after what happened the last time we were there…Let's just say that I'm not risking anything happening to you."

As Luca pulled his car up to his home and turned off the engine, Samantha jumped out. As he approached her, Samantha wrapped her hands around Luca's waist, pressing her face into his chest and hugging him tightly.

"Thank you, Luca. Thank you for talking me into coming back here to get my life together. Thank you for helping me. I don't know what I would've done without you."

"Well, I did threaten to enthrall you to get you home, so I guess that counts as talking you into it," he joked, and kissed her head.

She playfully pushed his chest with the palm of her hand. "I'm here, aren't I?"

"Yes. Yes, you are. And I couldn't be happier that you're with me." He gathered her into his arms for a brief embrace and then released her. If he started kissing her, they'd never get to the club. He was two seconds from tearing off her clothes as it was.

"Come on now. Let's get dressed." He lightly smacked her bottom as she quickly walked up to the porch. Adjusting himself, he fantasized about how delicious it would be to spank her pink while taking her from behind. He couldn't seem to stop thinking of Samantha and all the delightfully naughty things he wanted to do to her.

Knowing they had work to do, Luca decided it was safer to stay upstairs rather than follow Samantha down to his bedroom. He could barely keep his hands off of her for two seconds. She was driving him mad. It wasn't as if he could stay in a cold shower forever. He needed to get himself together, which was not going to be easy, considering they were about to go to a sex club. He sighed, resigning himself to the fact that he was going to remain uncomfortably hard for the next several hours. It was going to be a long night.

Samantha tugged at her short dress as they walked toward Sangre Dulce. Sydney had come over to Luca's to help her get dressed. After vehemently refusing to wear a little, very little, see-through number, she'd settled on a royal blue spandex mini-dress with a draped skirt that was gathered at her waist by rhinestones. One-shouldered, it exposed her creamy, pale skin; her golden red hair was straightened and tied back in a ponytail. Samantha enjoyed the black patent leather platform heels she'd borrowed. They made her feel more confident and tall, despite only adding a few inches to her five foot three stature.

She knew that the club catered to both humans and supernaturals; that was partly what had enticed her to go there in the first place. They'd all thought it would be fun to maybe see someone being bitten or spanked. Samantha didn't recall either. Still, with the knowledge that there could be vampires there, she nervously stroked her neck as if to protect it. Sydney had given her a silver chain in case of an emergency, which she kept stowed in her small clutch bag. She'd tried to get her to take a stake, but Samantha trusted Luca to keep her safe. She reasoned that not knowing exactly how to stake a vampire could be more dangerous for her, if she tried using the weapon without practice.

Luca put his arm around Samantha's waist and possessively pulled her against him. He planned to make it clear from the minute he stepped out of the car that she was his. He could practically feel her smooth skin through the barely-there, stretchy material that was her dress. He'd nearly had a heart attack when she came out of the bedroom tonight. With her hair swept up, he admired the fine lines of her neck; how he'd love to pierce her and taste her honeyed blood again. The spandex dress showed off every last curve of her luscious body without revealing a hint of cleavage. Samantha was simply stunning.

As they walked through the door, the pounding techno beat blared. Samantha slowly practiced her deep breathing, trying not to let Luca notice. She had said she wanted to do this, and she was determined to see it through. Samantha put on a mask of coolness as she observed naked girls serving drinks to customers. Straining to observe over a sea of bodies, it appeared a Domme and her sub were gearing up to engage in a public scene. A tall, lithe woman, dressed head to toe in spandex, led a good looking, muscular man around the room on a leash and proceeded to cuff his wrists to a Saint Andrew's cross.

Watching the preparation, Samantha lost her concentration on her deep breathing. Inexplicably drawn to what was happening to the sub, her heart began to race. Was this what she'd done? She couldn't help but notice that the man didn't struggle. He willingly followed his mistress and held his arms out to her, his jutting excitement conspicuously revealed to the audience. Samantha wasn't quite sure whether she was aroused by the sight of the virile stranger or disgusted, knowing it could have been her, a memory better forgotten. Conflicted, she could not tear her eyes from the unfolding exhibition. A cry of delight roared through the room as the Domme alternated between stroking him mercilessly and cracking the flat end of a riding crop against his reddening bottom.

Luca put his hand on Samantha's elbow, jarring her from anxiety. He could tell from the fascinated look on her face that she'd never seen anything like she'd just witnessed. On the one hand, he cursed Asgear for fucking with her memory. Yet it was probably best she didn't remember whatever had happened in the club.

Studying her face, he could see she was mesmerized by the intense sexual display. He observed her warring emotions. Was she excited by it? Perhaps. But her eyes told him she was also uneasy, anxious. She was worrying about things she couldn't remember nor control. He needed to get her refocused on their purpose, so they could get out of there.

Luca guided her around a semi-circular bar and signaled the bartender. They were addressed promptly; two bottles of water were placed on the bar. Samantha had made it clear that she wasn't drinking anything that didn't come in a sealed container. After what had happened last time, she wasn't taking any chances. Luca nodded at her and pointed to a small area that had been cordoned off by ultra-modern chrome leaf screens. It was partially open to allow the wait staff to enter and leave, but had no door.

"Over there. I'll stand right outside the entrance while you search the area. Are you ready to do this?" he asked.

"Born ready," she feigned confidence.

"Okay, let's do it quickly."

Several nude waitresses were leaving the break area as they approached the opening. Samantha winked at Luca and entered. The room was the size of a small walk-in closet, and she guessed that no more than four people could fit in there at a time. *One way to keep the waitresses working.* Plastic orange chairs lined one wall with a mini-fridge and plastic cups on the other side. Folded purple towels and blankets were piled high in a corner. Quickly she rummaged through the linens and refrigerator, but couldn't find anything.

Disappointed, she exited the room, and Luca caught the crook of her arm.

"Nothing, I found nothing," she commented tersely.

"Come dance with me," he whispered into her ear.

Nina Simone's *I Put a Spell on You* began to play as Luca pulled her out onto the dance floor. She felt herself melt into his body as he put a hand to the small of her back and held his other hand to her throat, slowly brushing his fingers down the hollow of her neck. Without words, he pressed his lips to hers, tasting her, deepening the kiss as she reached her hands around his neck.

Within seconds, she'd lost control, digging her hands into his hair. Desire pooled below, as she began grinding against his hardness. She wanted to make love to him there, not caring who was watching.

Grudgingly, Luca began to withdraw. Closing his eyes, he pressed his forehead down to hers. "Ah Samantha, I want you so much. But we can't do this here. We've gotta go back to the room where Dominique was silvered.

Check it out." He was breathing hard, struggling to compose himself. A year ago, he'd have had no problem having sex in a club like Sangre Dulce. He wasn't in the lifestyle but liked to play lightly every now and then. When a vampire had lived as long as he had, he or she was always looking for something on the edge to spice up life. But now was not the time to get carried away; he'd only brought her out to the floor to talk with her briefly before they went to the private rooms.

"Back there." He nodded towards an entrance covered in red-beaded fringe. "We'll walk back together. Hold my hand and stay close. Sometimes people gather at the rooms to watch; we'll just walk around them."

"Any chance I can use the ladies' room before we go? Somebody has me all hot and bothered," she teased.

"Yes, come on, let's go. I want to get home as soon as possible so I can finish what we've started on the dance floor." It was more of a promise than a joke.

Léopold watched the mortal girl dance with Luca, cursing their pleasure. They were supposed to be finding him the *Hematilly Periapt*; instead, they were mauling each other like oversexed teenagers. He was sure Asgear had given it her, and she would lead him to it, even if he had to grab her by her long red hair and drag her through the streets of New Orleans himself.

Anger raced through his veins; he was incensed with their cavalier attitude. Obviously, she needed a reminder of her task. He'd thought the fire would have been enough to frighten her into this much-needed search. He required the amulet...now.

Luca spied Étienne and Xavier sitting at the bar, and casually nodded. He planned on introducing Samantha to them another time, letting them remain in the background. He watched as she took off down a long open hallway to the rest room. It was dimly lit with black lights and tea-light candles that sat in ceramic luminaires. As he turned back, Étienne and Xavier had crossed the room to meet him. He wanted to quickly brief them on the plan. They'd stay twenty feet behind them and watch for an ambush.

Samantha patted her face down with a paper towel and prided herself for holding it together. Not remembering a damn thing helped, she mused. But she didn't regret spending time with Luca. She found herself wanting to stay in New Orleans with him. She wasn't sure if he really meant it when he said that he didn't want to let her go.

The more time she spent with him, the more she said goodbye to her old life.

Exiting the ladies room, dark smoke filled the hallway. Before she had the opportunity to register the cause, she found herself shoved against the wall. A large hand covered her mouth, while the attacker's body flattened against hers, effectively caging and immobilizing her. Unable to speak or move, her eyes widened at the stranger.

"Do not make a sound. I am going to release your mouth. If you scream, I will take you out of here. If you're quiet, I'll let you go. If you understand, nod your head," Léopold instructed.

Samantha did what he said, quietly pursing her lips together. She wanted to scream, but wasn't convinced he would not hurt her. There was something otherworldly about him. His hardened raven eyes seemed to pierce right through her, pinning her in place, like a dried butterfly stuck to a display board. She could see the slightest hint of candlelight glinting off the sharp edges of his fangs. *Vampire.*

"Maybe I haven't been clear, Samantha," he began.

"How do you know my name?" she interrupted.

"Do you know the meaning of quiet, witch? Do you? All you need to know is that I need the *Hematilly Periapt*, and you are going to find it for me. Now no more fooling around with the vampire. Find. It. Now!"

"But…but I don't know where it is. I don't even know what it is. Please just leave me alone," she pleaded.

"Listen to me, little girl. Asgear gave it to you. I don't give a shit what you have to do, but you will find it." He released her and shook his head. She was the only one who could find it. "Now go to your vampire," he ordered.

"But how will I find you if I get it?" she asked. She felt braver. He hadn't hurt her. There was something about him; she couldn't put her finger on it. He was powerful. Lethal. Yet he hadn't attempted to kill her or even bite her.

"Don't worry your pretty little head, Samantha. I will find you, so you'd better keep looking," he threatened.

Samantha looked up the hallway, and could see Luca's back to her. Readying herself to scream, she glanced back at the stranger, and he was gone. Vanished. She ran up the hallway, and embraced Luca tightly. "Luca, Luca. He was here. "

Luca growled. "Who was here? Who touched you?" An uncontrollable rage filled him at the thought of another man's hands on Samantha. Luca signaled over to Étienne and Xavier, who sensed something was wrong. They immediately came over to find out what had just happened.

"Are you hurt? Look at me. Tell me everything." Luca wanted to know every detail. This bastard had almost burned them to death, and now he was here in the club. How the hell did he get past him?

Without giving Samantha a chance to answer, he barked out orders to Étienne and Xavier. "Go down the hallway, and search for the man. Scent her first."

"Where did he touch you Samantha?" Luca asked through gritted teeth.

"He put his hand over my mouth, and pinned me to the wall, but he didn't hurt me. He wants the periapt. I told him I didn't have it, but he thinks Asgear gave it to me. He's a large vampire; I could see his teeth. At least as tall as you, Luca, so maybe six-five. Black eyes. I don't remember much else; it was dark," she quietly finished.

Xavier and Étienne leaned in, sniffing her dress. Samantha rolled her eyes upward, trying not to notice two strange vampires that she hadn't even been formally introduced to, within inches of her breasts. She huffed as they backed off and went down the hallway.

"We should go home," Luca suggested. "This is too dangerous."

"Excuse my French, Luca, but no fucking way." She had come this far and was not leaving without at least checking that room. "I'm telling you, he is not going to leave me alone until he gets that damn periapt. I've had enough of this shit tonight. Vampires looking for amulets I don't have and then disappearing into thin air. Seriously? Enough." She shook her head in disbelief. "Let's go to the room and then we'll leave. Please Luca," she begged.

Xavier and Étienne were back within minutes. "There are no vampires down there that match his scent. He's gone," Étienne said.

"Listen up. We're going down to the last room on the right, the one that Dominique was silvered in. Étienne, you go ahead of us. X, you bring up the rear. No stopping for shows or looking around. We're going to move fast and then get outta here. Understood?" he asked.

They all nodded and one by one passed through the red-beaded curtain, making their way to the room. Samantha held onto Luca for dear life, hearing screams of pleasure and pain as they crept down the darkened hallways. Finally, when they reached the room, they found it occupied by two very naked humans. The man had the woman bent over a spanking bench and was entering her from behind.

Samantha's mouth gaped open at the sight, while Luca strode in and interrupted them. He bared his fangs and roared. "Out!"

The people froze mid-coitus, the blond woman's mascara-streaked face staring at them defiantly. Luca knelt down to the man, who appeared not to have heard his order, and glowered. "I said get out. Now move! Move! Move! Move!" he yelled.

The couple scrambled around for their clothes. Upon seeing Étienne and Xavier's exposed fangs, they stopped looking for clothes and ran out the door. Samantha grinned. *Vampires are scary when they're angry.*

Luca slammed the door behind him, scanning the room. "This room's all we've got, so let's tear it up. There's got to be something here. Xavier, check all the floor panels. Étienne, you check the walls and light fixtures. Samantha, you've got the sofa. I'll take the equipment," he instructed.

They spread out and started searching. Samantha was more than grossed out by the plastic-covered sofa. She shuddered to think who and what people had done on it. "Gloves," she called out, finding a box of surgical gloves on a small table in the corner that also housed towels, sanitizing wipes and a bowl of flavored condoms. Snapping on the latex life-savers, she began to rip the cushions off and delved into the cracks, looking for a clue.

Xavier inspected the heavily worn, oak floor planks. While the floor appeared well used, it presented as if it was in good condition. Aside from a few squeaks, he couldn't find any loose boards.

Étienne scrutinized each brick in the wall, running his fingers along the grout. Not one stone was wavered. Save a few high hat lights, there was no other illumination in the room. Each one was tightly mounted and left no room for an opening.

Having already examined the Saint Andrew's cross and spanking bench, Luca moved on to the massage table. On first glance, the padding looked clean and uncracked. Running his fingers underneath, he felt only smooth particle board until he came upon a section that was worn. Losing patience, Luca flipped the table upside down, exposing its warped underside. He noticed that one of the corners did not seem to evenly match the rest of the seams; it was slightly raised. Digging his fingers into the juncture where the particle board met the padding, he tugged until it popped. *What the hell?* Someone had put chewing gum inside the backing as makeshift glue. It had hardened into nothing more than a small tacky spud, yet it had held tight.

Luca peeled back the panel until he spied a flattened cocktail napkin. He carefully removed it and called the others over. "Got something. A napkin. Looks like there's writing on it, but it doesn't make sense. Samantha, take a look." Luca surmised it was not a foreign language, and sincerely hoped it wasn't nonsense. It simply read, "*NIJE QN QSMGIOT.*"

Samantha gently took the tissue paper into her hands and unfolded it. Her eyes widened in surprise, unexpectedly realizing she'd written it. "Oh my God, Luca. I wrote this; it's my handwriting. I know what this is; it's a code. A code to conceal a message. Knowing me, I probably created a cipher. My co-workers and I sometimes play encryption games with them. You know, create codes and see who can break it. I wouldn't have used something easy, though."

"Can you break it?" he asked.

"Probably, but I need to think about how I created it, and I can't think in here." She fingered the napkin and held it to her chest as if it was made of gold. This clue could give her back her life. Excitement coursed through her body; she could feel the tendrils of magic stirring under her skin.

"Let's go everyone, we've gotta get out of here," Luca ordered. "The back door. It leads to an outside alley. Although it looks like someone decided to lock it up good, since the last time we were here. Stand back while I break it." Luca went over to the door, the same one Samantha had used to leave after she'd silvered Dominique. Obviously management wasn't crazy about people using it as an exit, so they'd put a chain and lock on it. Whoever thought a chain would stop a supernatural was a dumbass, Luca thought. He knew a simple steel chain wouldn't keep vampires from breaking it, so why bother? Luca wrapped the steel chain around his fists, grunting as he broke it apart. He kicked the door open, and they all took off down the alleyway.

Samantha started to analyze the code as soon as they got into the car. She couldn't wait to get home to crack it. On the precipice of solving the mystery, she smiled to herself. Inwardly, she celebrated the fact that despite all Asgear's efforts to control her mind, some small part of her couldn't be controlled. The code was evidence that she probably had stolen the periapt, and had taken great care to hide it from him. Yet despite her small victory, its clandestine location had drawn a very powerful and dangerous vampire into her circle. She prayed she'd find it before he found her again.

CHAPTER TEN

After taking a hot shower, Samantha checked her cell phone for the hundredth time. Neither Rowan nor Ilsbeth had attempted to log into the database. She was still feeling exhilarated from finding the code. Wrapping herself warmly in Luca's robe, she held it to her nose and inhaled his masculine scent. Samantha shook her head, knowing that Luca was stealing her heart. She could feel herself falling for him, and wasn't sure how or if she wanted to stop it. All she knew for certain was that she was going to find it very difficult to go back to Pennsylvania without him after they found the amulet.

She sighed in defeat, conceding that her heart might break into a million pieces if she didn't have him in her life. Even though they'd only just made love, she felt as if she'd known him forever. She wasn't one to just have sex with any guy. But on a whim, she had given in to her most carnal desire and let him make love to her. In the aftermath, she couldn't shake the feeling that he was the one for her. She wished it wasn't true. He probably had a thousand women on speed dial who'd come willingly running to service him...to be his donor or whatever else he needed. *How could she leave her heart open to a vampire?* The answer didn't matter, because it was already done. Samantha contemplated whether or not she should move to New Orleans. As the thought popped into her head, she laughed to herself. Just a day ago, she'd been kicking and screaming to stay away from that city. But now there was Luca. And Luca was in New Orleans.

As she walked out into the kitchen, he was putting out sandwiches on the large granite bar. There was something heartwarming about seeing a large, sexy man preparing food for her.

"Hi there, the sandwiches look great," she said.

"Hey, beautiful. Thought you might be hungry. I had Kade's cook bring over something to eat, so you'd have strength to work. And to play with me," he joked, pushing a plate towards her. "But work before play. So first, let's take a look at the code while you eat, shall we?"

She took a healthy bite of turkey, and looked at the code: "*NIJE QN QSMGIOT*" What did it mean?

"So here's the thing. When I do my ciphers, I usually use something called a date shift cipher. That way, I can stack the ciphers when I'm trying to make it really hard to decode. Also, all I have to do is change the dates and it will change the codes. I wrote a program that can run through figuring out a date cipher, so that's not the problem. The real challenge is finding out what date I used."

"I've heard of date ciphers. It's going to make this tough to crack without the date," Luca commented. When he'd joined the war, they'd often put their messages into codes; if captured by the enemy, they were indecipherable without the key date.

"Yes, you're right. So what code would I have used?" she spoke aloud to herself.

"A birthday?" Luca suggested.

"No, too easy. I did this all the time at the office. Sometimes I would use someone else's birthday, but given that I don't know anyone down here, I don't think I would have done that. A family member's birthday would, again, be too easy. Sometimes I'd pick dates of important events. Things that only I would know," she explained.

"Your graduation date, perhaps?" Luca realized in that moment that he didn't know that much about her past; something he fully intended to investigate once they'd found the amulet.

"Maybe. I have used my high school graduation date in the past. Can you get me your laptop? I want to pull over my date cipher program from my home server, and try it." Samantha was starting to worry that she wouldn't be able to find the date. It literally could be any date, past, present or future.

Luca booted up the laptop and set it in front of her. He watched as she typed away; she chewed her lip, concentrating on what she was doing. He loved seeing her in his home, wrapped up in his black velour robe. She pushed the reddish curls of her freshly washed hair behind her ears as she waited for the program to open.

"Okay, read me the code," she instructed and typed it into the space designated for it. "I'm going to try my high school graduation date, which was June 23, 1999. So what happens is that the computer will take all this information and work backwards to see if we come up with something that makes sense based on the code and date variables. In a date shift cipher, the date is generated sequentially without the slashes over and over. The letters of the alphabet are assigned to each number. So then you take your message, and the code assigns a letter based upon how many spaces you need to shift," she explained.

"Can you give me a quick example before it runs?" It had been a long time since he'd deciphered a code on the battlefield and wanted to make sure he correctly understood.

"Sure. So my graduation date would be written like this." She wrote down the number sequence, six, two, three, nine, and nine and continued, "So I would write the numbers over and over again until I had a little more than the alphabet. Like this." She drew out the numbers until they were all the way over. "Then I would add the alphabet underneath, like this. So if I was looking to code the word, "sex" for example, I would go to the *S* which tells me to move over spaces. So the S turns into a *B*, the *E* turns into an *N* and the *X* turns into a *G*. So the code would be BNG. But still, you'd need to know the date I used in order to crack the code. But again, if you'd been given the secret code, BNG, you would need to know the date in order to solve the code."

6	2	3	9	9	6	2	3	9	9	6	2	3	9	9	6	2	3	9	9	6	2	3	9	9	6	2	3	9	9	6	2	3
A	B	C	D	E	F	G	H	I	J	K	L	M	N	O	P	Q	R	S	T	U	V	W	X	Y	Z	A	B	C	D	E	F	G	H	I	J	K	L

BNG

Luca laughed. "You're brilliant! Perhaps in need of some lovin', but brilliant," he teased. He came around the bar and sat next to her to watch what happened online.

She smiled over at him but turned serious again as she watched the progress of the program. Within seconds, it finished bringing up the message. It made no sense, which meant the date was incorrect.

"Shit. That's not it. You know what they say? Garbage in, garbage out. We need the right date," she huffed.

Samantha closed her eyes and put her hands to her forehead trying to rack her brain for the correct date. Luca rubbed her neck while she concentrated. *Think. Think. What date would I have used? I was in a hurry. In danger. Scared.* It occurred to her that maybe she'd used the day she was taken by Asgear. It would have been fresh in her mind, something she'd want to remember. She reached back into her mind to search for the date but couldn't seem to do it without a visual calendar in front of her.

Opening her eyes, she pulled up her calendar on the screen. "August. I was taken in August. August 11, 2012." She flipped back to the cipher program and typed in eight, one, one, two and pushed enter.

Luca and Samantha watched patiently as the program worked backwards through the sequence to find out the code. Within seconds, the screen came up with a message: *MAID OF ORLEANS.*

"Maid of Orleans? What's that?" Samantha asked.

"Maid of Orleans," Luca said thoughtfully. "The Maid of Orleans is a statue of Joan of Arc. It was given to the city by France in the seventies. I'm not sure what we'll find there but we've got our next lead. You did it, Samantha!"

Samantha was overwhelmed with relief that Luca knew what the message meant. She was one step closer to freedom. "Where's the statue? Why would I have been there?"

Luca went over to the refrigerator and pulled out a bottle of champagne. He talked as he uncorked it and poured it into flutes. "The statue's in the French Quarter over near the French Market on Decatur. It's not far from Sangre Dulce. Maybe wherever Asgear took you first, he had to walk you past it to get to the club. I'm not sure, but perhaps somehow you got away long enough to hide it. It might have taken only a few minutes to feign an escape, plant another clue or the amulet and then agree to go to the club."

"Joan of Arc, huh? Kind of ironic, isn't it?" Samantha commented.

"Ah yes, Joan of Arc. She was accused of witchcraft, and yet a very real witch chooses her as the place to drop the next clue." He grinned wryly, handing her a glass.

"Let's not forget she was burned at the stake," Samantha reminded him. "I'd like to avoid that if at all possible."

"Well, let's just take a few minutes to celebrate. It's getting really late, and I for one am growing tired of this chase. You see, I'd much rather be chasing you." Luca set down his glass and came up behind Samantha, putting his hands on her shoulders. As he massaged her neck, she let out a loud groan.

"Ah, Luca, that feels so good. I'm not used to walking around in heels like that all night. Or being in that kind of club. Seeing some of those people do what they were doing; it made me feel…I felt…" Her words trailed off; she wasn't sure whether or not she wanted to talk about it.

"Tell me Samantha. How did it make you feel to be in the club again?" Luca questioned her. He was worried she'd have a flashback or panic at the club, but nothing had happened. She was one cool cucumber. But he knew that beneath the surface, thoughts lingered. Fear? Anger? Arousal?

"I…I felt…I don't know. I was scared to be in the club at first. But nothing happened. I didn't remember anything. And then there was the whole meeting with 'mister freaky vampire'. He was really scary at first. But it was strange. He was very angry, but controlled. By the time he was finished telling me to get the amulet, it was as if I knew he wouldn't hurt me. I know it sounds crazy. I can't explain it. And then seeing the submissives parade around naked as if it was nothing. And the sex. I guess it was okay." Samantha sounded unsure of her own thoughts. She'd witnessed and experienced so many strange and new things.

Luca put his fingers around her pallid neck, tracing his fingertips from her hollow to the back of her shoulder blades. He wouldn't let her off so easily. He wanted to know what she really desired.

"Did the domination scene excite you, darlin'? I saw you watching," Luca whispered into her ear. She shuddered, feeling his warm breath against her.

"Luca, did you go to that club often? Is that something you like? Do you do those things? Do you do what that woman was doing to that man?" she asked.

"Answering a question with a question? No. Quid pro quo. You first," he answered.

"Fine," she sighed. "I found it erotic. I don't think it's something that I'd do every day, but I wouldn't mind playing at home with someone I trusted. But there is no way I'd do that in public like they were doing. I don't mean to sound judgmental, it's just that it's not me. When I saw them, naked, and her touching him so intimately, I was aroused, but also upset. I kept picturing me in that club. I can't believe that I did that, served drinks that way. I guess it's not too bad, not at this point, considering I can't remember. It's like you're telling me I did it. I see a picture in my head, but it doesn't seem at all real to me. Then, later tonight, dancing with you on the floor; that was real. Okay, enough about me. Now your turn. Dish."

She got up, walked around the stool to stand next to him and put her arms around his waist.

Luca looked down at his beautiful woman. He was falling for her. He planned on telling her about the bonding, about everything. But tonight? Gazing into her eyes, he knew it was right. She was his and he knew in his heart he'd never let her go.

"Samantha, I'll be honest. I don't ever want to lie to you. You know I've lived hundreds of years, and yes, I've had sex with many women. But I haven't loved anyone since Eliza. I really want to tell you about her sometime, but tonight all you need to know is that there's no one in my life right now except you. As for the club…well, yes, I've been there a few times over the past couple of years with friends. I've played in the rooms, sometimes dominated women who were looking for fun with a supernatural. But it's not something I do all the time or feel compelled to do. Until you came along, I was just passing the time. I work for Kade, collect antiques, travel and that's about it."

"And do you want to do that to me? Do you want to tie *me* up?" she said, flirtatiously rubbing her breasts against his chest. Samantha hugged Luca, and he embraced her back, holding her tightly in his arms.

"Perhaps. Are you interested in playing with me, little witch?" His sultry voice washed over her.

"Um, yeah, that might be fun. Playing with you, experimenting with you actually excites me a lot. Is that wrong?" she giggled.

"No, it certainly is not. I'd love to play with you in all ways possible. But Samantha," he continued, "before we make love again, I need to talk with you about something. You know, there's a connection between us."

She nodded.

"Well, you need to know that I want more than just a casual affair. I want to be inside you, tasting you, bonding with you. I want you to be mine."

Samantha didn't really understand what he meant by bonding with her, but she knew for certain that she wanted him to make love to her. Her heart pounded against her ribcage, hearing him say that he wanted her. She'd been unsure about how he felt. Every minute she spent with him made her never want to leave. Her prior life and job in Pennsylvania were becoming a distant memory as he was becoming her future. She admitted silently to herself that she wasn't sure of the consequences of what he was asking. She only knew that she wanted him: to make love to him, to be with him, to be his.

Samantha looked up at Luca who was patiently awaiting her answer. With great anticipation, he heard a single word from her soft lips. "Yes."

Intense green eyes locked on Samantha's as he leaned in to kiss her. Her heart raced, anticipating his kiss, his every touch. With trembling lips she opened to him as he fiercely captured her mouth. His tongue danced with hers, tasting her magical spirit.

"Yes," was the only word he heard in response to his proposal; Luca lost control. Passionately and provocatively, he took her with a hungry urgency. It wasn't sweet. His mouth claimed hers, savagely taking what was his. The intoxicating nectar of Samantha only made him kiss her more deeply. He wanted her in a way that he'd never wanted any woman. Determined to possess every part of her body and mind in the moment, he would claim her tonight. She'd be his forever.

Luca tore his lips from hers. "Bedroom. Now," he commanded. Leading her by her small soft hand, he stopped her before they got to his bed.

"I will have you tonight, Samantha. After tonight, you'll never forget that you are mine. And I will be yours."

Samantha silently nodded in response. She was ready to commit to this man, this vampire. Luca was everything she'd ever wanted in a male: strong, loving, trustworthy, and passionate. She knew in her heart that giving herself over to him was all she desired now and for her future.

Luca unraveled the belt on her robe, slid his fingers underneath the soft fabric and slowly pushed it off Samantha, letting his hands glide from the smooth skin of her shoulders to her hands. As the robe pooled at her feet, he gently took her hands in his. She stood bare before his eyes. "You're enticing, Samantha. I cannot seem to get enough of you. So the question is, do you want to play with me tonight? Be honest with me, darlin', because I plan to take you to places we've never been before."

Samantha felt womanly, exposed to Luca. She trusted him completely as he released her hands and placed his on her waist. "Luca, please, hurry. I can't seem to keep my hands off of you."

"Well, I guess we'll have to do something about that," he smiled knowingly. "Turn around, face the wall. Don't move unless I tell you. It's time for some fun."

Without question, she complied and waved her bottom at him, shooting him a sultry look that said, 'come and get me'.

Luca loved how responsive she was under his direction. He didn't ever bring women into his home, and certainly engaging in a little light bdsm was something he rarely did anymore. Yet he'd wanted to do this to her since the minute she'd danced with him in the club. Luca slid his hands slowly up the sides of her waist, under her arms, pushing them upward and placing the palms of her hands against the wall. With the same precision, he glided his hands back down her arms, waist, until finally, he reached her bottom.

"Samantha, you are everything I've ever wanted in a woman; beautiful, smart." She let out a small moan; he rubbed his hard aching bulge against her. He wanted to fuck her right now, but he wouldn't dare. No, he planned to make her beg for mercy as he slowly brought her to orgasm over and over.

Though he was still fully clothed, she could feel his magnificent erection against her bum. She wanted him in her now; she grew wet from the intense ache between her legs. "Please, Luca."

His hands slid from her ass around to lie just beneath her sensitive bosom. She moved slightly to urge him to cup her breasts. He smiled, smelling the overwhelming scent of her desire, but he wanted to draw out the anticipation, tease her with delight. "No, no, no, darlin'. Not tonight. You don't get to decide when or how the pleasure happens. You wanted to play, so play we shall," he whispered into her ear. Goosebumps ran over her skin in response to his hot breath. "Tonight is about wanting what you can't have until I give it to you. It's about me savoring every stroke of your flesh. The ultimate pleasure, tasting you while you come, screaming my name. Now, do you want me to touch your lovely breasts? Tell me, Samantha."

"Yes. Please Luca, please touch them. I need…" Struggling to keep her hands pressed to the wall, she threw her head back in sexual frustration and sighed.

"Since you asked so very nicely." Luca glided his hands over her sweetly curved flesh, while rocking his aching shaft against her behind. "So firm. Just right. And your perfect little nipples; they demand my attention too. You want me to pinch them?"

Samantha was lost in the sensation. He was driving her mad with need. She could feel her throbbing tips growing hard, but she was helpless to relieve the ache. She managed a strained response. "Yes, oh yes."

"Such a good pet." He tweaked her hardened pink tips and released them, then repeated it several times until he heard her moan. "This? Is this what you want?" Luca slowly brushed the pads of his forefingers across the straining peaks.

"Mmmm…more, Luca. Please," she begged.

As much as Luca delighted in the sweet torture, he needed more too. He took each pink tip between his thumb and forefingers, and pinched even harder.

Samantha screamed in a heightened mixture of pleasure and pain. She rocked her hips back into Luca's incredibly sexy and very hard male frame. She longed to touch the muscles that she knew rippled down his arms, flat stomach and strong legs.

"Like a little pain with your pleasure? Interesting." Luca couldn't resist kissing along her neck behind both of her ears. "How about a few spanks for my beautiful woman? Tell me, Samantha, is that something you want?"

"I don't know. I've never…" She was embarrassed to admit that she was excited about the idea of his firm hand on her cheeks so close to her core.

Luca shook his head, sensing her desire. So his little witch wanted a spanking? He smiled. Without giving her warning, he stood to her side, letting his left hand slide down into her hot, moist folds, and then, in an alternating, successive order, he delivered four sharp slaps to the sides of her ass. He rubbed the inflamed, creamy skin with one hand as he inserted a finger inside her with the other.

"Ah, Luca, yes!" Samantha spoke between ragged gasps. "I know I shouldn't want this but I do. Oh my God, please," she was begging.

Luca felt the surge of wetness flow between her legs as she responded to his hands. He wanted to give her everything she needed but was finding it difficult to contain his own arousal. He'd like nothing more than to sheathe himself within her and fuck her senseless. Deciding to proceed with her pleasure, he inserted two fingers and began pumping them in and out, resting his chin on her shoulder as he whispered into her ear. He loved watching her lose control, giving into her darkest fantasies.

"Aw darlin', you're so nice and wet for me. I'm going to fuck you so good and hard." Panting in pleasure, she snapped her head toward him; her eyes locked with his. "That's right Samantha; I said I'm going to fuck you. You like when I talk dirty to you, don't you? And you liked it when I spanked your ass too. Do you want more, Samantha? Come now, tell me."

She sucked in a startled breath when she felt his thumb brush her clit. "Yes," she said through gritted teeth.

He smiled at her, gazing deep into her eyes. "Get ready to let go, Samantha. I'm going to spank you while I finger your sweet pussy. Do you understand?" Her mouth opened, not sure what to say to his crass words. She'd never been one to say anything during sex, let alone something dirty. But his words were more of an instruction than a random thought. She was aware that he knew the words made her grow even more ready.

"Yes, please," was all she managed to say before she felt four more spanks to her ass and Luca's thumb pressing hard into her sensitive nub. She heard herself screaming as she plunged over the crest. In a molten sensation of release, she shuddered; her fists balled against the walls.

Releasing her, Luca spun her around and erotically kissed her, fisting his hands into the back of her hair. She reached for the hem of his t-shirt and pulled it up over his head; they separated for only seconds as the shirt flew across the room, and then recaptured each other's lips in a desperate act of passion. Samantha ran her fingers up the muscled planes of his back. They each fought for breath: tasting, sucking, wanting.

Luca grabbed her wrists and pulled out of the kiss. With a burning look into Samantha's ice-blue eyes, he regained enough control to direct their play.

"Samantha, on your knees. Take me into your mouth," he quietly commanded.

Seductively, she smiled, and obeyed. Gracefully, she knelt, but not before brushing her rosy peaks against his chest, teasing him. She couldn't wait to taste him, and she planned on tantalizing him like he'd done to her. Thinking this was going to be oh-so-sweet, she provocatively sat back on her heels, pushing out her breasts. Slowly, she unbuckled his belt, and pulled it out of the loops, tossing it aside. After unbuttoning the button, Samantha took her time lowering the zipper. He wanted to draw things out for her, so she planned on taking her time, making him beg in turn. In a quick pull, she removed his boxers and pants until he stood gloriously naked in front of her. Like some Greek god, he stood motionless above her as she admired his steely contours.

Reaching behind him, Samantha languidly glided her hands up his thigh and abs until her hands rested just above his erection. With her lips mere inches from his cock, she darted her tongue out, running it over its smooth wet tip. He tasted wonderfully salty and masculine; she needed more. Unable to hold back, Samantha licked up and down his throbbing shaft, taking his tight sac into her hand. Her other hand reached around so she could dig her fingers into his hard muscular ass.

In a single motion, she parted her lips, relaxed her throat and took him all the way into her mouth. Sucking him, she retracted her lips, releasing his ridged manhood. Grabbing onto the base of him, she slowly repeated pumping him in and out of her warm lips.

Luca rocked himself into her mouth in rhythm with her demand. He hissed in ecstasy, realizing that she knew exactly what she was doing, paying him back for what he'd done to her. Did she comprehend how much power she had over him? He didn't care in the moment; pleasure was all he could feel.

His swollen flesh couldn't take much more without him exploding in her mouth; no, it was much too soon for that. After one more sweet kiss of his shaft, he receded, pulling Samantha onto her feet.

"I need you now, Samantha. I have to be in you. On the bed," he ordered.

Samantha sashayed over to the bed, and fell backwards, giggling. "Come and get me, vampire." She wasn't going to make this easy for him.

Picking up the sash of his robe, he played with the tie, eyeing her from across the room. "Hmm....sassy witch, huh? Perhaps you need to be reminded who's directing the show tonight, darlin'."

Her eyes widened when she saw him fingering the velour belt. Her heart began to race in excitement and her sex grew damp in anticipation.

Luca confidently strode across the room, drinking in the sight of his beautiful red-haired woman, splayed out spread-eagled on his bed. Leaning down, he methodically began to tie a loop around one of her wrists. After securing the knot, he weaved the belt through the slats of the head board and secured her other wrist until her arms were nicely tied above her head.

"Luca," she protested against the bindings.

"Tonight, your pleasure is mine, Samantha. If you really want to get out, your safe word is "cabin"; otherwise, we continue to play. Now what you might not know is that I could hear your heartbeat race as soon as you saw the belt. And since I don't smell fear, I know it's because you are aroused. Am I correct?"

Damn vampire senses. She smiled at him. "Yes, so what are you going to do to me?" She wiggled her hips around on the bed a little, hoping to tempt him into her.

"This." He trailed a finger down her arm, down her side. Goosebumps broke out over her body; she started to beg. "Please, Luca. It's not fair."

He laughed. "This isn't about fair, Samantha. It's about control. Dominance. And your submission." With those words, he left the room, leaving her tied to the bed.

She wondered what he was doing in the other room, hearing a banging noise, and struggled to see what he held in his hand when he returned, literally within seconds.

"No peeking, Samantha. In fact, I think it would be best to remove another one of your senses, don't you agree?"

She simply smiled at him, wondering what he was going to do, and eagerly awaiting his rapturous torment.

Luca straddled Samantha on the bed. He loved seeing her bound, awaiting his pleasure, desiring to make everything special. He smiled down at her, and held up a black scarf. Placing a slow, passionate kiss to her lips, he fastened the scarf over her eyes.

"Luca," Samantha whispered. She felt on fire with want. This man was pushing her to do something she'd never done, and she loved every second of it.

Samantha squealed in surprise as Luca ran an ice cube around her rose-colored areola. The cold sensation was immediately replaced by the warmth of his lips; he sucked the tiny pink bud until it hardened and ached. He gave her other nipple the same attention and she felt herself floating in the absence of her sight. The lips, tongue and teeth on her aching tips sent a jolt of need to her clit, and she found herself writhing, trying to get him to touch her below.

Within minutes, his lips abandoned her breasts. Moaning in delight, she felt his glorious hands caress her delectable pink mounds, while working his way downward to her abdomen with the cool wetness. The icy surface glided for seconds only to be replaced by his warm lips. Her hips rocked up into him; she wanted his frosty heat on her sex, in her.

Moving his hands to the side of her waist, Luca held the almost melted ice cube in his teeth, and slid over and through her wet folds. He could feel her quiver underneath his lips. With nothing left to hold, Luca darted his cool tongue into the crease of her sex, letting it graze over her clit. She writhed under his kiss, but he held her firmly by her hips.

"Luca, I can't take it anymore. It feels so good," she cried.

He didn't answer as he continued to lick and suckle her sex relentlessly. As two fingers entered her without warning, she moaned loudly, bucking her hips into his mouth. He curled his digits upward and stroked the long sensitive spot within her. "Aw darlin', your pussy is so wet and sweet for me." She barely registered him talking dirty, overwhelmed with her impending orgasm.

Luca could feel her squeeze his fingers. She was so close. "Come for me, Samantha, let go," he demanded, sucking hard on her ripe pink nub. He lapped at her sweet cream, so grateful to have her with him.

Samantha saw fireworks as she shattered into a million pieces. It was the most spectacular release she'd ever experienced in her entire life. She screamed Luca's name over and over again, shaking as he untied the scarf over her eyes.

She was panting, trying to catch her breath. She struggled to speak. "Luca. Amazing. Oh my God."

Not giving her any time to recover, Luca roughly grabbed her legs from behind her knees jerking her bottom toward him. Resting her ankles on his shoulders and holding the back of her thighs, his eyes flashed red as he plunged his rock hard cock into her glistening sex.

He grunted in ecstasy; her warm heat tightly fisted around his swollen flesh. She was absolute paradise, accepting all of him into her heat. They locked eyes as he continued to possess every inch of her, pounding into her in a fierce furor.

Samantha tilted her hips upward, craving him deeper still. His eyes burned deep into her soul. In that moment, she knew. She loved Luca. She forced herself to remain silent, afraid she'd cry out the words.

Luca shook her thoughts, as he stopped to release her wrists, catching her attention again. "Samantha, my magnificent, enticing sorceress, from this night forward, we will be together. When I taste of you tonight you will be mine. I will be yours. Do you understand? I need to have your permission. There is no going back."

"Yes, I'm yours," she agreed. "Make love to me, Luca."

He quickly flipped her onto her stomach; sliding his hand under her tummy, he pulled her up so she was on her hands and knees. Reaching his strong hands up her back, he glided them down her spine. With one hand on her waist, his fingers slid down over her bottom. Pressing a finger inside her sex, he teased the wetness up along her puckered rosebud. He felt her tense slightly, but then she rocked back toward him.

"It's okay, pet, relax for me. I want to explore every inch of your lovely body. Have you ever been touched here?" he asked as he ran his fingers over her.

"No," she gasped softly. She enjoyed the feel of his fingers on her anus. A rush of excitement surged through her, knowing what he might do. "But I want to try...with you."

"I'd like to take you with my cock someday, but not today, darlin'. I'm afraid that's something we'd need to ease into. I'll let you think on the sensation of my fingers there for now. Let me know how it feels."

"Um, it feels good. I know I shouldn't like it, but I do," she gasped as he continued to touch her in the place she'd never been touched before, slowly working a finger in her rosebud as his velvety steel shaft pressed into her warm center. Slowly, he eased into her. He didn't want to hurt her. Because of his larger size, he wanted to take his time, and make sure she enjoyed this.

"You're so wet and tight. You feel so good. Ah, Goddess. I need to claim you as my own and I'm afraid I can no longer wait." Within moments, Luca had fully joined his body with hers; she enveloped all of him. As they began to move together, Luca moaned. "Yes, that's it. We fit so well together."

Driven by desire, Samantha pressed her bottom back onto him. She impatiently rocked back and forth, desperately urging him into her sex. "It feels so good, Luca, so full, please don't stop. I need you harder," she demanded.

A primal instinct took Luca over as he began to thrust up into her to meet her need. Keeping one hand on her bottom, he moved the other hand around to rub her soft pink flesh. She was so very close, and he was taking her there again. Over and over, he slammed into her as she begged for more.

"Yes, Luca, I'm coming, Luca, don't stop!" she screamed.

Luca felt the beginning of her spasm around his throbbing shaft. His fangs elongated, and he reached up and fisted his hand into her hair, exposing the creamy skin of her fine neck. In a final glorious moment, Luca thrust one last time against her while sinking his sharp fangs into her sweet silken flesh; he drank her essence, pulsating deep within her.

Samantha was seized by a rush of sensation so intense she could barely breathe. As she came down off the pinnacle of her orgasm, white hot pin-pricks sliced into her shoulder; she shuddered uncontrollably as another strong release claimed her again. Luca held her tight until they both fell over in exhaustion into the sheets.

Perfectly spent, the sated couple fell back into bed. Luca cradled Samantha in his arms, resting her head on his chest. His breathing slowed as he pushed the hair from her face.

"Samantha," he needed to tell her.

"Hmmm," she sleepily responded. She tipped her chin upward to meet his eyes.

"I love you." He smiled down at *his* woman. Luca could not believe that after two hundred years he was, without a doubt, in love with a woman. No longer would he live his life alone, searching for purpose. She was the one; the one he would spend the rest of his days on earth with; the one who he planned to marry; the one who he wanted a family with. *Samantha.*

"Luca," she gasped and then beamed. "I love you too. I never thought. I mean, I've been so caught up in getting my life straightened out, getting everything back to how it was before and now…"

"Now?" he raised a questioning eyebrow at her.

"Now, I don't want it. I only want you."

Samantha kissed his smooth chest as he kissed the top of her head, embracing her in his arms. Luca's heart swelled; he never wanted this moment to end. Watching Samantha drift off to sleep, he was more determined than ever to get the amulet and kill the vampire who was threatening her, whichever came first. He could feel her blood sweep through his entire body. The bond had begun.

CHAPTER ELEVEN

The aroma of coffee wafted under her nose. Samantha's eyes fluttered open; a broad smile spread across her face, seeing Luca holding a cup of coffee. He was already dressed; a casual black t-shirt teased the contours of his chest and his blue jeans hugged his tapered hips. She noticed he was wearing gray alligator boots that suited his personality: sleek and lethal.

"Come on, sleepy head. Time to eat and catch bad guys. It's one o'clock in the afternoon. We've got to get goin'."

She sat up, pulling the sheet up over her breasts, and he handed her the cup of café au lait. He'd placed a beautifully decorated breakfast tray in the middle of the bed.

"Mmmm…this is wonderful. You make this?" she asked.

"Oui Mademoiselle. I've been livin' down here in New Orleans long enough to make a fine cup of chicory and steamed milk. I did not, however, make this delicious spread of eggs and bacon. Kade's cook brought this over; Mandy makes a great southern breakfast," He grabbed a piece of bacon off the plate and bit into it.

"Looks great. Hey, what are you doing stealing my bacon!" she joked as she picked up a piece for herself. "You know, I was wondering. What's the deal with vampires and food anyway? I mean, I've seen you eat food but I know you need blood." She lightly ran her fingers over the small bumps on her shoulder, remembering how he'd bitten her the night before, and then picked up her fork.

"Well, I can eat small amounts of food, but there's no nutrition in it. It's just like a comfort kind of thing, reminds us of our human life. But we don't need it. And some vampires no longer eat human food at all." He smiled slightly. "But they most assuredly do eat humans. The fact is that we need human blood to survive, but not every day and not a lot of it. At least a half cup or so every two to three days keeps us in fightin' shape. If we don't get it, we wither, die. For example, after they attacked us at the coven, the thugs starved me. I was silvered, so I couldn't move, couldn't communicate."

Luca's face hardened, remembering what had happened to him and what Kade and Sydney had done to save him. He hesitated. Luca did not relish telling Samantha the details of his recovery but didn't want secrets between them.

"Listen Samantha, speaking of the attack, I don't want there to be any secrets between us. I know we've just met over the past weeks, but you should know that when that happened - when I was attacked - I didn't recover right away. Kade and Dominique gave me human blood, a donor, but it wasn't enough." Luca turned his head away.

Samantha put her hand on his arm. "Hey, it's okay. I know what it's like to have something happen that you can't explain. You don't need to tell me. What's important is that you're here now."

"No, it's not that. It's just Sydney. Kade." He shouldn't feel guilty. Yet that was exactly how he felt. "Sorry, I'm just not sure how to explain this but Sydney's blood is special. It's because she's human, but not entirely anymore. She's bonded with Kade."

"Like you did with me?" She blushed, recalling their wild lovemaking the night before.

"Well, yes and no. You and I, last night, the bond began. When we made love and I bit you at the same time as we climaxed, it started the bond. So, soon I'll be able to sense where you are, maybe sense your thoughts, but not entirely be able to read them. But we are not fully bonded. That only happens when I give you my blood when we're making love. When that happens, it changes the human slightly. So Sydney, for example, will live as long as Kade. She'll be immune to illness et cetera, but will not become vampire."

"Okay," Samantha was happily eating the last of her eggs, listening intently.

"Okay." Luca laughed at her casual attitude. She was so brave and open to the unknown, quite unpredictably so at times. "What I'm saying is that Sydney's blood is special, more powerful. So when no other human blood would revive me, Kade let me feed from Sydney." Silence blanketed the room.

Samantha thought on it for a minute before commenting. Remembering how it had felt when Luca bit her and what Kat had told her happened at Eden, she was starting to put together what he was trying to tell her. Her stomach clenched in a pang of jealousy. What exactly was he trying to tell her? "So when you say feed, do you mean 'I drank her blood' or do you mean 'I drank and had sex with Sydney'?"

Yes, she was definitely putting it all together.

Luca took her hand in his, craving contact with his lover. "Yes and no. We were all together in Kade's house, his guest bedroom. If you're asking if I had intercourse with Sydney, then no, I did not. But if you're asking if I fed and it was an erotic experience? Yes. I'm not sure how to put this tactfully." He chose his words carefully. "I experienced a release during the process. But it was once, and if they hadn't done it, I could have died. The blood of people like Sydney, the bonded humans, it is rare. I'm sure Kade could have found someone else besides Sydney but it would have taken more time than I had. And besides, they are my friends."

Samantha pondered his words. She wondered exactly what the three of them had done if it wasn't intercourse, but it sounded like they engaged in some kind of a ménage; they all came. Samantha knew he needed the blood but still, what had he done with Sydney?

"Seriously? A release?" She laughed indignantly. "You mean you came? With both of them there?"

"I really don't want to get into the details of the entire session but let's just say it wasn't intercourse and it wasn't oral sex. But yes, the gist of what you are saying is correct. I fed from Sydney. I touched her, and she me. I came." Luca prayed she wouldn't freak out and take off running again. It wasn't as if he'd exactly had a choice in the matter. He would have died without Sydney's blood and was lacking any kind of control during their healing encounter.

"Is this experience something you intend to repeat with them? I mean, I may be experienced sexually, but I'm not that open. I have firm limits, Luca. And sharing is one of them. I won't share you with other women if we are going to be in a relationship. Not an option, Luca." She felt sick thinking that he might have to drink the blood of other women.

"No, no, no. Samantha. I would never ask that of you. It isn't something I wanted. I just needed to be honest with you about how I healed, what happened. There can't be secrets between us, especially when we will be with Kade and Sydney. Believe me, what happened with them, it will never happen again. And you should know that I don't share either. Never," he said through gritted teeth. He'd kill the next man who laid a finger on his woman. "I want you. I love you. And if you will agree, I want to fully bond with you."

Relieved, Samantha jumped up out of bed naked and straddled the clothed Luca. He leaned his head against the back of the headboard, enjoying the view of his beautiful woman, resting his hands on her hips.

"Luca, I love you." It felt strange saying those words yet Samantha couldn't help but tell him how she felt. "Whatever you had to do to stay alive, I get it. But, I'm grateful Kade and Sydney saved you. Okay, I'm not crazy about the three of you in bed, but what's done is done, and today, you're here in bed with me. My vampire."

"My witch." Luca waited patiently as Samantha pressed her lips to his. Their tongues danced, gently tasting and exploring. Samantha began to grind into his hardness, eager to make love with him again.

Luca broke the kiss and threw his head back again. "You are tempting something fierce, darlin', but we've got to go find ourselves an amulet. We can't stay in bed all day."

"Ugh. Hate that you are right." Samantha pouted. "Okay, I'm getting in the shower but you owe me later." She winked at him as she bounced off the bed and padded into the bathroom.

Luca smiled to himself, thinking that the woman was going to be the death of him, and what a sweet death it would be.

After getting dressed in jean shorts and a pink tank top, Samantha walked into the kitchen with a spring in her step. Her cell phone buzzed while she was lacing up her sneakers. She glanced at the message. "Luca! Someone accessed the coven's database. I'm goin' into your laptop," she yelled up the stairs.

Luca ran down the steps, and sat next to Samantha as she opened up her program. She typed furiously.

"Ilsbeth went in this morning. Yes! Gotcha." She brought up the coven's website and quickly entered Ilsbeth's ID and password, pressed enter and waited. "Okay, baby. Here we go. We're in! Now let's see how we can search. Looks like they have things categorized. We've got witchcraft by country. We've got witchcraft by modern types, Wicca, Stregheria...yadda, yadda, yadda. Okay, I see spell casting, ingredients, necromancy. Ew...so not ever doing that. Here's book of shadows, demonology, ceremonial magick, scrying, shamanism. Come on, there's got to be something here." She kept scrolling down, hoping there'd be a category for the *Hematilly Periapt*. "Come to mama! Yes. Talismans. It's an amulet. Does that sound right?" she questioned Luca.

"Yes, that should be it. A talisman usually guards against evil, but considering we've got no idea what it does, let's give it a try."

"There must be thousands of these things, but I'll give it to the sisters, they have each one detailed: what it's made of, purpose, who created it, how to make one. Looks like some of these are blank. They must still be in the process of creating this database. Oh my God, Luca. Here it is, the *Hematilly Periapt*. I can't read this. Is this Latin? What is this?" The description was written in a foreign language:

A potens pythonissam, Maria Voltaire, in septimodecimo saeculo ad certate pestilentia de lamia. Et facta periapt Hematite ex Graeco sanguinem. In actu periapt est proxime duo digitis per unum inch in figura lacrima gutta. Ita dominus periapt oportet esse in magica persuasione potest etiam actiones lamia voluerint. In ordine ad pythonissam ad eu in periapt, requirit gutta intentum lamia. Semel occurrit, in lamia erit sub veneficas imperium vsque mortem. Eam scriptor current location est ignotum.

Luca read the description and translated. "It's Latin. So basically it says that the periapt was created by a powerful witch. Her name was Maria Voltaire. She made it in the seventeenth century to combat vampires, presumably during the great mass hysteria over vampires during that time. Anyway, it says that the periapt is made of the mineral hematite. The word, hematite is derived from the Greek word for blood. Then it describes it; it says the actual periapt is approximately two inches by one inch, in the shape of a tear drop. The owner of such a periapt must be a witch, warlock or mage. Here we go, here's the crux of it. The periapt can control the actions of any vampire. But in order for the witch to activate the stone, it requires a drop of blood from the intended vampire and then the vampire shall be under the witch's control as long as the witch keeps it on her person. It lists its current location as unknown." Running through the scenarios in his head, Luca's eyes narrowed in anger.

"Goddammit, now we know why the hell everyone seems to want it. Imagine if a witch got the amulet and the blood of a vampire. Like my blood, for example. Fuck." He slammed his fist down on the counter, remembering what Kade and Sydney had told him about the needles all over the church where they'd found him. Perhaps someone had taken his blood for a different reason than they thought.

"What's wrong?" Samantha watched Luca pace, visibly agitated.

"What's wrong is that when we were attacked and I was taken, there were needles all over the floor. It's a fairly good guess that someone has my blood. If the same person who took my blood gets the periapt, they could control me, according to what we just read," he said, piqued.

"Okay, maybe it's true, maybe it isn't. We'll get it back. We'll destroy it," Samantha promised. Hoped.

"What I can't figure out is why another vampire would want it? How does he even know about it? According to this notation, only a witch can use it." He dragged his fingers through his hair.

"I don't know, Luca. But we'll get to it first and then we'll get rid of it. If we can't destroy it, we'll take it out into the sea, and dispose of it there. We can do this." She didn't want to admit it to Luca but she was scared too. She prayed that she'd left a clue to its whereabouts.

"Well, thank God you took it from Asgear. And now that we know what it does, we know why someone wants it. We'd better get going to find out what's at the Maid of Orleans. I sure as hell hope this leads us to the amulet. We also now need to find out who took my blood." Luca would be damned before he let anyone control his actions. He knew better than anyone that he was a lethal killing machine when he needed to be. And so did the vampire who was trying to get the periapt. Maybe that vampire was working with a witch? He couldn't focus on the myriad scenarios right now. The only thing that was important was locating the *Hematilly Periapt,* and he hoped the Maid of Orleans would be his savior.

CHAPTER TWELVE

The afternoon sunlight glinted off the shiny golden metal. There stood Joan of Arc with her armor and steed in Orleans. Proudly displayed atop a large stone base, she sat surrounded by landscaping and pavement. Tourists busily shopped on both sides of the wedged streets, oblivious to her history or potential.

"Well, I'm not sure what I was doing over here. It's a couple of blocks from the club. I don't think I could've escaped to this statue on my way there. Maybe I came here on my way out of the club?" Samantha estimated.

"Maybe you did. And maybe Asgear lived around here and that's why you came this way. Maybe you stopped here first before you planted the clue at the club? There's a lot of vegetation in and around the statue. I brought some tools with me. They're in the back seat. I'll grab the clippers and hand shovel just in case we need them. Sydney knows we're coming here today, so the NOLA PD are expecting folks to be digging around it." Luca got out of the SUV, opened the trunk and picked up his toolbox.

Samantha was out of the car and across the street ahead of him. She should have worn jeans, not shorts, she thought to herself. Bushes and bugs. Just great. Stepping into the brush, she began to look for something, anything that would lead them to the location of the periapt.

"I wouldn't have had a lot of time. Whatever I did, it had to be fast. Asgear would've seen me run over here across the street. It's gotta be in or around the brush, maybe over near the cannons." She broke through the branches, searching around near the ornamental artillery that sat in the shrubbery.

Instead of jumping directly into the brush, Luca examined it for evidence of damage such as broken branches or torn off leaves. As he rounded the statue to the front, he noticed the landscaping was not grown as high in one of the corners. Reaching down over the embankment, he pulled off a leaf that had been slightly ripped. Looking up, he silently thanked the saint. With caution, he climbed up into the bushes. Something was off with the ground near the concrete barrier which held the landscaping. Luca stomped his foot down on the dirt. *Hollow?*

"Samantha, over here." Luca knelt down and began pushing aside dirt and rocks until he saw black. He rapped his knuckles on the hard surface. Metal. "Now, what's this? It could be a sewer lid, but I don't know. It looks more like a door of some kind."

Samantha trudged over, reaching the spot Luca was clearing. Something small bounced off her feet, catching her eyes. She knelt down and picked it up. A rock? No, the dark metal covered in dirt was perfectly round.

"Hey Luca, look at this." Rubbing the object, she examined her prize. "What is it? It almost looks like a golf ball." She placed it into Luca's dusty hands.

"It feels smooth, but look at its color; it seems to be made out of pewter." Brushing off the crusted earth, he held it up to the sunlight. "There's an inscription. Something I've never seen before. Maybe an ancient language? Possibly Sanskrit. Now what does this do? That's the question." He rolled the small globe in his hands and pocketed it. He shrugged, continuing to clear the ground. "Well, whatever it does, I have a feeling we're about to find out soon. Ah, what do we have here?"

Luca returned to his original task, fully exposing the black metal trapdoor that had been hidden underneath the boscage. Slipping his fingers around a small loop handle, he pulled up. Dust and dank air bellowed upward. He coughed.

Samantha carefully leaned over, taking a peek at the dingy cavity. She was full of questions, nervously anticipating that they would need to descend into it. "What the hell? There's a ladder on the side here. Where does this go? Hey wait, New Orleans doesn't have tunnels, does it? Don't they have a high water table? Even the cemeteries are built above ground because of it." As she was talking through the feasibility of the tunnel, she remembered the underground prison Asgear had created.

"Magic? Maybe he used magic to keep the water out, but how's it possible it's still here?"

"Not sure. It hasn't rained at all over the past two weeks. Anyhow, no use worrying about how it got here. Here's a flashlight. You ready to go in?" he raised an eyebrow at her; a corner of his mouth lifted in a slight grin. He dug out a stake and a few other items from his tool bag and pocketed them.

"As ready as I'll ever be. But I swear, I'm going to freak out if I see any giant city rats in there. I hear y'all got rats the size of cats down here." She shivered at the thought of running into one of the furry little beasts.

"Darlin', now you know you'll be safe with me. Besides," he joked, "the nutria lives out in the bayou. Come on now, I'll go down first."

Samantha followed Luca down the metal ladder into the tunnel, cursing the day she'd decided to go to a computer conference in the big easy. *Shit. Revolting tunnel. Excrement and other unknown foul smells. Rats. Possible Spiders. Roaches. Ew. Who cares about a vampire trying to kill me for an amulet when I could be eaten by some kind of creepy crawling critter?*

Halfway down the ladder, she heard a splash. Samantha flicked on her flashlight and saw Luca step into a few inches of brown, unidentified liquid. She froze.

"Luca, I don't know if I can do this. What's in that water?"

"Not sure, but you can do this. Come on, I'll carry you. Get on my back," he ordered.

"Are you sure?" she asked, still not moving.

"Yes. We need to go find this damn amulet. Both our lives are on the line. Come on, I'm ready for you."

Samantha released her hands from the rung and put her arms around Luca's neck. Once she had a firm grip, she held tight and wrapped her legs around his waist. The walls of the tunnel looked relatively modern, yet she knew Asgear had probably held it with magic. And now that the magic was atrophied, the walls were leaking. She prayed they would hold, uncertain of their safety. Within one hundred feet, the tunnel abruptly turned left, and they began a long journey into the darkness. The flashlight illuminated barely far enough for Samantha to see where they were going. She assumed Luca had night vision, because he appeared to have no problem walking even when the light flickered.

Samantha glanced over her shoulder; nothing but blackness. Fear blanketed her as she heard a noise behind her. "What's that?" she whispered.

"It's okay. It's just a tiny creature. He won't hurt you. You'll be all right. We probably don't have much further to go," he cajoled.

She rolled her eyes. What was it about men that they didn't mind little beasts with tails? After walking for over fifteen minutes, they finally came upon another metal ladder leading upward.

"A ladder," Luca observed. He sidled up next to it so that Samantha could reach it. "Looks like this is the end of the road. Okay, we're going up. Can you get on? Here, let me get you closer to it so you don't fall."

"Got it, thanks." Samantha easily grasped the metal rungs, and caught a lower one with her feet. She held tight, knowing what lay below her.

"Okay, let me pass. I'll go up first. Looks like there's a different kind of hatch on this one. Look down and protect your eyes. I'm goin' to force it upward. Don't come up until I say it's safe, okay?"

Samantha nodded, curled her head into her shoulder and put a hand over her face. A rush of sunlight and dust beamed onto them both as Luca easily removed the circular cover. He began his ascent and peered over the rim.

A large, spacious courtyard awaited him. Climbing up onto the patio, he scanned his surroundings. Sensing no humans or supernaturals, he called down to Samantha. "You can come on up. All's safe. We're in a courtyard. Well-kept from what I can see."

A decorative three-tiered fountain stood in the center of the courtyard. It was surrounded by several potted impatiens, hibiscus, palm and banana trees. The old red brick patio contrasted with the white clay pottery.

"This is beautiful," Samantha commented. "I love the fountain. Do you think Asgear lived here?"

"Not sure. He could have rented the property. But still, if it belongs to him, then he did it under an assumed name. There's nothing on the records of him owning or staying anywhere else but the warehouse." Luca was not deceived by the immaculately cared for garden. He felt something was off. "Samantha, be careful. Stay close. We'll sweep the courtyard, but I'm guessing that whatever we're looking for isn't out here in the open. Unfortunately, I think we'll find what we seek through that door over there." He pointed to the robin's-egg-blue door that led into the home.

After a thorough but unsuccessful exploration, Luca and Samantha readied themselves to enter the house. As they stood outside, a feeling of consternation swept over Samantha. She stared up at the home, and examined the exterior for any signs of overt destruction. On appearance alone, it held a warm façade, welcoming to all. Looking beyond the surface, a menacing sense of foreboding rained down from above. She might not have been psychic, but she clearly perceived the trickling damnation emanating from this structure. Every cell in her body told her to stay outside.

Anything could be in that house. A trap? A latent spell? It was true that Asgear was dead. But Samantha knew for certain that magic didn't always die with its creator. Magic was a living energy which waxed, waned and only sometimes died. It carried with it the good and evil for which it was intended. She knew it was waiting. What 'it' was remained to be seen. She steeled her nerves, determined to conquer her fear.

Luca guardedly turned the knob and entered. "It's unlocked."

A tidy kitchen located in the back of the home was decorated in red and black tiles with a fifties style chrome and white Formica kitchen set. *Quiet. Cold.* A long, narrow hallway led to the front entrance. As they explored the small home, Samantha couldn't help noticing the lack of furnishing or décor. The hallway led to a small living space which only contained a flat screen TV and a recliner that looked as if it had seen better days. The threadbare tan fabric was frayed, and spots of foam peeked through the tears. Stark white walls gave way to cream roller shades. Yet there was no other evidence of someone living in the home: no remains of food, dishes, glasses or newspapers.

"Whoever lived here sure was a minimalist," Samantha conjectured as she followed Luca upstairs.

"Yeah, that's an understatement. It's got fewer furnishings than a cheap motel. Hate to ask you this, Samantha, but are you sure you don't remember being here? Asgear must have kept you here at some point for you to have left these clues." Luca rounded another chalky-walled hallway.

"I don't remember being here at all. But this doesn't seem right. It doesn't feel right. It's like there's a maleficent presence that's ingrained into every pore of this house. And there are no bedrooms up here, except that one. Look." She pointed to a single brown wooden door. "It's the only one up here? How can that be? This is so strange. I get that this place is small but you'd think there was more than one room."

"Perhaps someone remodeled to combine the rooms?" The oak door was locked with a large nickel padlock. "It's locked, but not for long. Stand back, Samantha. Let's see what's behind door number one," he joked.

"What?"

"Monty Hall. Let's Make a Deal?" He shot her a sly grin. "Okay, here we go."

Samantha stood with her back against the wall, nervously watching Luca. She prayed the periapt was inside this room. She felt anxious, as though she was watching someone open a prank can of mints, waiting for the giant plastic snake to pop out at them.

Luca pulled a thin metal paper clip out of his jeans pocket. He straightened it then bent it back and forth until it snapped into two pieces. Shaping each piece into an "L", they could be used as a pick and tension wrench. He held them up and smiled. "Always prepared. If it were night, I'd just break the damn lock but the sun has me too weak to do it by hand. Here we go."

"By weak, do you mean human? Good thing you are quite the boy scout," she joked.

Luca grasped the lock with both hands, inserted and applied pressure with the wrench and picked at it until he heard it pop. Jerking the lock off in a single movement, he grabbed the antiqued glass knob and turned, pushing the door wide open. He felt around for a light switch but found none. He flicked on his flashlight and shone it into the darkened space. Settling a comforting hand on

Samantha's shoulder, he tried to ease her fear. "It's okay. Nothing living is in here."

Samantha was curious to see what was inside. She pressed up against Luca's back, peering in from behind him. A large, darkened, rectangular room stood before them. Its walls and ceilings were draped in a black velvety fabric. The wooden planks had been painted a lacquered cardinal red. Elaborate candle wall sconces adorned the far wall; burnt candle wax splattered the floor. On the other side of the room, a metal ring was attached to the seam along the wall and the ceiling. Attached to the ring were long steel chains and two metal cuffs. Evidence of a kept captive were scattered across the floor; clothing, a plate, glass, remains of stale bread. On the farthest wall, opposite the entrance, an ornately carved circular wall hanging glowed in the distance.

"What the fuck?" Luca's words trailed off on seeing the entire room, realizing it had been used to shackle and hold a prisoner. *Samantha.*

Samantha turned on her flashlight and ran to the pile of clothing near the chains. "Oh my God, Luca. My clothes. These are mine."

It started to settle in that she had been here. Stripped of her clothes. Enslaved. She didn't want to cry but tears pricked her eyes. Even though she couldn't remember what had happened, she knew he'd done something to her. Gathering the filthy dress into her hands, she fell to her knees and began to sob.

"I was here," she whispered through small cries. "Oh my God. What did he do to me? Why?"

Luca ran over to her. Kneeling down next to Samantha, he put his arm around her, running his hand up and down her arm. "It's okay, he can't hurt you anymore. He's dead. It's just an empty room with memories that are best forgotten. You're safe with me. You'll be all right. Come on, now. Let it go." He took the dress from her hands, and placed it back on the shiny red floor. Pulling Samantha to her feet, Luca lovingly embraced her. "You're okay, now. Remember why we're here?" He kissed the top of her head.

Rubbing the tears from her eyes, Samantha released Luca. "I'm sorry. It's just so hard not remembering. It feels like a dream. A nightmare. Seeing my clothes just makes it real. I hope that son of a bitch rots in hell," she said, regaining her composure. "Okay, I'm fine. Let's do this."

"Over here," he said, pointing to the large circle. "It's carved with ancient markings. And look here in the center. A divot." He ran his fingers into the concave groove.

"Yes, a divot that looks like it might be the exact spot for our little golf ball. Do you have it?"

"Here, hold my flashlight. Shine it over there." He took the rounded pewter ball and held it up to the hanging. "Well, it looks like it might fit but I'm not sure how it would stay in there. It's not deep enough to put the entire ball into."

Yet as Luca placed the ball up into the indentation, there was an audible click. Samantha and Luca stepped back as the ball unfolded; eight pieces of metal pierced out from its internal structure, holding it securely against the carving. As if grabbing onto spider legs, Luca reached up and rotated the orb. A slight whoosh of air escaped as the wooden hanging hinged open, revealing the satin interior of a vault.

Samantha started to jump up and down in excitement, as she caught sight of a smooth, scarlet stone encased within the small repository. The *Hematilly Periapt*. It didn't look nearly as spectacular as she'd expected. A single, brick-red teardrop-shaped rock hung from brown sisal twine. It was exactly as described, yet nothing appeared magical to the eye. Unassuming, yet people were willing to kill for it.

Luca held the highly coveted gem up by its cord, regarding the amulet. "So this little baby is what's causing us all the trouble? I'm relieved to have it, especially knowing there's some freak out there with my blood," he exclaimed. "Would you like to do the honors?"

Samantha gladly took the periapt into her hands; she had no intentions of letting it go. Rubbing it between her fingers, she dreamt of the day she'd be free again.

"Luca, about your blood. We can't risk giving this away to the vampire. What if he decides to give it to a witch? It's too dangerous. No, we can't give this away," she insisted.

Luca raked his fingers through his hair, contemplating their dilemma. "I agree. The vampire who seeks it must be put to death. After that, we will destroy it so that no one can ever get their hands on this heinous object. But know this, Samantha, if it comes down between saving me or saving you, then the vampire gets the amulet. We have to keep it safe. Kade and Sydney can help us." He began sending them a text to explain what had transpired. "I'll send for a car and then we can decide how to proceed from there. The vampire said he'd find you, and believe me, I'll be waiting for him."

Just as Luca went to open the front door, Samantha saw a face peering through the rear kitchen window. "Luca, there's a woman out there." Samantha pointed and started walking toward the back door, inexplicably drawn outside. Intellectually she knew she shouldn't go by herself, but her legs kept walking one in front of another until she found herself at the back door.

"Samantha, no!" Luca yelled.

But Samantha didn't stop. She wanted to listen to Luca, she really did. But something pulled her. Samantha's body hummed with magic, high on power. The magic was beckoning her to keep going. She was drawn to the stranger like a piece of iron being pulled to a magnet. *Compelled.*

Samantha caught a glimpse of straggly black hair in the rain; Rowan stood waiting on the patio, her arms outstretched. What was she doing here at Asgear's home?

Could she have followed her and Luca? How would she have known? Samantha couldn't understand what was happening; it didn't make sense. As Luca repeatedly called to her, she struggled to obey him and failed. No, this wasn't right. She shouldn't go. But the compulsion was too strong. She tried to fight, desperately attempting to shun the entrapment. Failing, she stumbled out into the courtyard, standing mere yards from the raven-haired witch.

Rowan laughed wildly, watching the novice try to fight her command. She knew that Samantha probably had no idea how to stop the compulsion. She almost felt sorry for her, but no, that ungrateful idiot had refused Ilsbeth's training. She was blessed with magic but had abjured both her ability and the graces of the coven. If Samantha had continued to train with Ilsbeth, she would have easily been able to deflect Rowan's will. Instead, she helplessly submitted, like the incompetent she'd always be. No pity for her; Samantha deserved to be overpowered because of her insolence. Rowan was disgusted with the level of disrespect Samantha had shown to her and her sisters by refusing to learn the craft.

She would have given anything to watch Asgear cringe as his puppet floundered. Asgear had always been so pompous in the magical circles, bragging about his new spells and artifacts. In a bar one night, she had learned from another witch that the wily mage was bragging that he had discovered the *Hematilly Periapt* as part of his grand plan to take over New Orleans. Now that he was dead, Rowan would have the last laugh.

After the stir with Samantha returning to the coven and searching her room, Rowan had grown suspicious. When Ilsbeth had told her that Samantha was looking for the periapt, she was thankful for the fortuitous conversation. It was then she knew for sure that she could successfully acquire it. The novice either knew the location of the artifact or with the help of Luca, would surely locate it. All she had to do was wait and watch; she already had the blood of a vampire.

She enjoyed watching Samantha stumble about, not quite sure why her body wouldn't listen to her brain. Enough of the fun. It was time to get down to business and take the amulet for herself.

"Ah, Samantha. You've found the periapt, I see. The rumors were true; it was here in New Orleans. You see, I've been wasting time searching, planning just the right location spell, and now you've helped me find it," she snickered.

"Rowan, what are you talking about? I need this. There's a vampire who's after me. I've got to give this to him," she explained.

Luca walked up behind her slowly, not wanting to make any fast movements lest Rowan might harm Samantha. He held the stake he'd brought firm in his hand.

"I just bet he does want it," she said sarcastically. "I bet all the vampires would like the amulet. Like Luca? Now,

now, don't be shy, Luca. I see you back there. Don't make any fast moves, vampire."

She directed her attention back to Samantha. "You see, my friend, we all have powers. Ilsbeth told me you're an elemental witch, albeit a weak one. Do you want to see my power? No, really, I know you'll enjoy the show. You see, I'm a telekinetic witch, which means I can do this." She held out her arms and raised one palm face up toward Luca and Samantha, immobilizing them with very little effort. She laughed before continuing. "Now, let me help you with the amulet." Rowan's eyes flashed silver. "Dare me in periapt nunc, pythonissam!"

Samantha fought her own muscles as she felt her hand opening against her will. "No!" Samantha cried as the amulet flew across the courtyard, landing at Rowan's feet.

Rowan scooped it up in her hand, and pulled a small vial out of her pocket. "Now, the real fun begins. You know what's in here, don't you?" she asked, wickedly smiling.

Samantha shook her head. "No, please don't do this."

Luca continued his futile attempt at breaking Rowan's spell; he still couldn't move further than an inch. He needed to talk reason into the witch. "Rowan, Ilsbeth will ban you forever for your actions. You will lose all you have. Your coven. Your life. Now, give us the amulet. You can have it once we are done," Luca promised.

"Ha!" Rowan cackled. "Right, like you would simply give it back to me. Since you don't want to guess what's in the vial, should I tell you or keep it a surprise?" She laughed and waved her hand. "Okay, okay, I'll give you a hint. Remember lying in a church chained up? It was such a shame for them to mar your beautiful God-like body with silver, but it simply had to be done."

"My blood," Luca said with a growl.

"Handsome and smart. You vampires are so quick and strong. Very hard to capture, you know. Unless you happen to know when one is coming to your house, it is very difficult, indeed. But when you know one is visiting, well, it turns out it's not very hard at all…just need a little silver." Unscrewing the top of the vial, Rowan poured a drop of the blood onto the already sanguine stone. "So simple, really. It's done. Do you feel it? Come on now, Luca, do you know what this means? You are now my slave, vampire. As long as you are in my presence and I have the periapt, you are mine."

"I'll never be yours, witch. I feel nothing," he insisted.

"Really?" she grinned evilly, itching to play with her new toy. "Let's try it out, shall we? Luca, slave of Rowan, vampire born of Kade, kill Samantha!"

Luca reeled as the command drilled through his brain. The stake fell from his hands as he gripped the sides of his head. Never in his life had he been compelled to do what another told him, yet the desire to wrap his hands around Samantha's neck grew deep within his belly. He roared and shoved her to the ground. Samantha struggled against him, kicking wildly, trying to escape.

"Luca, no," she pleaded. "Don't listen to her!"

Luca fought his own hands as his fingers crept around Samantha's neck. He tried to fight, reeling his hands back. An excruciating convulsion racked through his body in response to his disobedience. He heard Rowan's laughter in the distance.

"Ah, what's that you feel, Luca? That's right; it's slicing agony, isn't it? Get used to it my dear bloodsucker. You no longer have free will. Surely you will fight me, but I will break you over time. Keep ignoring my command, vampire, and you will suffer endlessly. You might even die. What a pity that would be, after all my hard work. Just do it. Kill her."

At Rowan's directions, his fingers wandered up to her neck and squeezed. Samantha pounded Luca's chest with her hands, trying to dislodge him as his hands crept around her throat once more. She could tell from his eyes that he was trying to fight the order, greatly suffering for his refusal to hurt her. But still, his fingers gripped tighter and tighter.

"Grab the stake. It's right there, on the ground. Kill me, Samantha. Don't let her do this," Luca grunted.

Samantha shook her head; the stake was within inches of her reach. "No! I won't. I can't," she protested as she heard a loud whoosh from behind. She lost sight of Luca, as the vise around her throat unlocked. Samantha heaved and sucked in air over and over in an attempt to catch her breath. Pushing up onto the palms of her hands, she sat up and ran her hands through her hair, dizzy from the loss of oxygen.

As she lifted her head, she gazed into the piercing black eyes of the vampire she'd met at Sangre Dulce. He'd rescued her from Luca's grip. For a split second, he caught her gaze, fangs bared. He had Luca in a headlock, threatening to break his neck. Luca struggled against him, unwilling to give into defeat.

Samantha screamed at the vampire to release Luca. "Don't hurt him! Please! I'll give you whatever you want. I promise," she begged. Samantha stumbled as she tried to stand. Pointing at Rowan, she tried to get the attention of the stranger. "Over there! Rowan, that witch right there. She has the periapt. He's under her control."

Luca growled at the other vampire. The clamp on his trachea loosened for a split second, allowing him to maneuver out of the stranglehold. The two magnificent vampires began to roll on the ground, wrestling for control over one another.

Rowan laughed maniacally, "Oh how I love to see the gladiators fight. It's a fine match. But alas, we must be going. Luca, are you ready to come with your new mistress? You really do need better training. I asked you to kill this insignificant excuse for a witch, and here you are playing games with a vampire. Ah, I must admit I am looking forward to making you my slave in every way possible. Oh yes, I plan to discipline you long and hard, night after night," she mused, staring down at Samantha.

"No!" Samantha screamed and lunged for her. Samantha shoved Rowan to the ground, but the witch was strong. She grabbed Samantha by the hair, pulling her downward, refusing to relinquish the amulet.

"You should have worked on your powers, little girl. Maybe if you had, you'd be like me. But, no, you wasted Ilsbeth's lessons. So tell you what, since I'm feeling generous, I'm about to teach you a little trick in transporting." Rowan held her by the hair and slapped Samantha across the face. "Pay attention!"

"Fuck you!" Samantha yelled and hit her back. "Give me the amulet!" She kicked at Rowan as they fought, but she couldn't pin her to the ground.

"Enough!" Rowan waved her hand, sending out a wave of magic; Samantha's body flew across the courtyard and slammed against a brick wall. Rendered unconscious, Samantha drifted into blackness.

Rowan waited for her vampire. After all the work she'd done, she had no intention of leaving without him. Chanting a spell, she opened a swirling gray portal. She turned to the vampires, who'd stopped fighting momentarily to observe the vortex.

"Come Luca, you're mine. You will come with me now," she ordered.

In confusion, Luca started to go for Samantha. He wanted to stay with Samantha and protect her. But as he did, searing pain ripped through his body; he knew he was being forced to go with Rowan. Thrown into an agonizing paroxysm, he doubled over, unable to stand. The periapt was the only key to his survival. If he could get the periapt and destroy it, then his binding to Rowan would be broken.

He looked over to the large vampire with whom he'd been fighting. Luca could tell the vampire was many years older than him, a great warrior. Luca was one of the strongest vampires in the world, yet this vampire was not overcome. More importantly, the vampire had saved Samantha from certain death that would have come at his own hands. He sensed this vampire didn't want him or her dead, but knew he also desired the periapt. *Could he be trying to destroy it too?* He had to make a decision, go with Rowan willingly and destroy the amulet or stay and try to fight against the compulsion.

He tried once again to go to Samantha, and he was blinded afresh as the fiery torture rippled throughout his bones. Falling on his hands and knees, he backed away, and the pain subsided. Through blurry vision, he glared at the devil who'd done this to him.

Rowan crooked a finger at him, giving him no choice. Stumbling toward her, he attempted an attack. With but a flick of her wrist, she threw him into the churning aperture. A rush of energy flooded his senses. Swept inward, he landed with a thud onto a rock-hard concrete floor. Luca hissed as a silver net blanketed his body. The smell of his own burnt flesh drifted into his nose as he prayed for mercy.

CHAPTER THIRTEEN

Samantha dreamt she was floating on a cloud, smiling at a rainbow. As she weaved her fingers into its beams, her eyes fluttered open, and she realized she'd been asleep. *Where am I? Where's Luca?* In a surge of panic, she shot upright. Scanning the room, she didn't recognize her surroundings; an achromatic theme teased her eyes. The room was bright white, with cream crown moldings. The white four-poster bed was covered in a white eyelet duvet with matching bed pillows. A large white dresser and mirror and overstuffed chair were offset by the dark cherry hardwood floor. Despite being devoid of color, the room was tastefully decorated.

Draped in silence, she sat up with her legs crossed. She sighed, relieved that she was still dressed. Her shoes, however, were on the floor next to the bed. Considering she wasn't naked or locked up, she surmised that whoever had taken her wasn't considering hurting her…yet.

Remembering Luca's attack, she carefully touched her neck, grateful she hadn't died. It was slightly bruised but didn't hurt too much. She started to panic again, wondering what had happened to Luca, when she looked up to see the intimidating vampire who'd been stalking her leaning against the door jamb. Coolly, he approached her. Her eyes widened as she systematically ran through feasible escape scenarios.

"Hello, Samantha. I am Léopold Devereoux," he said, with a French accent.

"You!" Samantha backed up against the bed, bending her knees to her chest, wrapping her hands around them. Her heart beat frantically. She looked for a getaway but saw none.

Léopold gracefully glided toward her and sat on the large lounge chair. "Do not be afraid, mon agneau. I will not hurt you," he assured her.

She studied the larger than life vampire who'd threatened her at the club. Remembering the feel of his body against hers, she knew that he had to be at least as tall as Luca. In the darkness of Sangre Dulce, she had barely been able to make out his features, but she'd never forget his midnight-black eyes. Now in the light, she noticed how striking he was. The hard contours of his masculine face accentuated his square jawline. Dark brown, wavy hair was styled into a modern shark fin. Even though his presence exuded power, he looked young, mid-thirties. Sexy. Deadly. Samantha wondered if every vampire had an underpinning of sensuality that kept every woman wondering if he'd bite her. While he was undeniably attractive, she felt nothing but fear toward the vampire standing before her. She realized she was staring, and averting her gaze, she looked away toward the wall.

Sensing her fear, Léopold attempted to soothe the pretty little witch. He didn't mean to scare her, but he needed the amulet. She was nothing more than a means to an end. Looking at her pale skin and full lips, he understood Luca's attraction to the mortal.

"Now, I know you don't trust me. Given my severe actions, I suppose you have reason. But mademoiselle, my intentions this evening are honorable."

"Honorable? You burned down my cabin!" she spat at him. "You could have killed us!"

"Oh yes, well, that was merely a diversion to get you to focus on the task at hand. You see, it was rumored that Asgear had the periapt. After his indiscretion with Kade Issacson's human woman, I searched his properties, or should I say what was left of his properties, but never found it. But I did, however, find you." He smiled wryly. "Convinced of its existence, I simply gave you the encouragement you needed to find it for me. Which you did, quite resourcefully, by the way."

Samantha glared at him in contempt and disbelief. "You risked my life and Luca's for that godforsaken amulet, and now what? Rowan has it. And Luca? Where is he?" she cried. Tears welled in her eyes.

"I'm afraid that is a bit of a problem. Rowan is a devious witch, and she knows exactly why I was so persistent in my search for the *Hematilly Periapt*. She is fully aware that she can control vampires. And now, to my dismay, she has Luca. She'll also have any other vampire whose blood she steals as well. The amulet is very dangerous to our kind. She must be found." He took a deep breath and blew it out. "I called Kade this evening, and he has been detained for several hours, something or other to do with the wolves. We agreed it would be best for me to take Étienne, Xavier and you to extricate Luca from Rowan."

"Me? What could I possibly do? You saw what she did to me." Samantha was embarrassed by what had happened. Rowan had called her and she had come like a dog. She hadn't called on her powers; instead she'd frozen.

Léopold stood, approached the bed and sat next to Samantha. "You are a mere babe in the woods, dear Samantha. But you do have your power. I saw you in the mountains the day you extinguished the fire. You need to concentrate this time. I will need your help to save Luca and acquire the amulet. Of course, Rowan will be expecting us. She very much wants to keep it, so that she can keep Luca. Do you want her to keep Luca?" he taunted.

"No," she whispered, putting her head in her hands. She rubbed her face and met his gaze with pleading eyes. "I can't lose him. We are bonded. What I mean to say is that we started it. He is mine. I am his." The reality of the situation was sinking in, and Samantha hated that Rowan had taken him.

"I would call that a no. And so what you must understand is that he is no longer yours. He doesn't even belong to himself. She is making him a slave as we speak, in every sense of the word. He will not be able to fight her. What she tells him to do, he will do. As long as the amulet exists, she is his."

"No, that can't be. He would never be with someone else. When she told him to attack me, he was fighting it," she protested.

"But it will kill him to continue to fight it…eventually he will give in. In another few days, he will be nothing more than a shell of a man," he calmly explained.

"What are we supposed to do? We don't even know where she is. Ilsbeth…we should call her to help us," she suggested.

"No. That's not going to happen. Any other witch may also be tempted to take it. The periapt is something the witches want in their possession. It must be destroyed."

"So why bring me?" she challenged.

"Because you love him. And only a witch can destroy the *Hematilly Periapt*. He needs you. Hell, I need you," he admitted.

For just a second, Samantha thought she saw a flicker of emotion in his eyes and then just as quickly it was gone.

Léopold continued speaking. "So here's what's going to happen. You're going to get yourself together and meet us downstairs. Étienne and Xavier are coming over to my flat and then we shall go to Rowan's. She bought a home, which she cleverly deeded in a different name, but I am certain she's there nonetheless. She'd never risk taking him to the coven, because if she did, she knows that Ilsbeth would immediately call Kade. To the best of our knowledge, Ilsbeth is not aware of what Rowan's done, but we are not involving her, either. No, this will be done with the four of us. Kade should be here in the morning, should we need to dispose of the witch."

"Dispose? What the hell is that supposed to mean?"

"It means that she will die, Samantha. Kade's the leader in this region and it's fitting that he metes out justice should she survive the night." Léopold walked across the room and opened the door to leave. "And Samantha, you should be aware that Rowan may have created others."

"Others?" she asked wearily.

"Yes, others. Other slaves, vampires. Possibly shifters. We cannot be sure what she has done."

"Who are you anyway? Why would Kade let you rescue Luca?" She couldn't fathom why this stranger cared what happened to Luca.

"I am Kade's maker," he stated with resounding authority. "Now let's not waste time. We have a vampire to save and an amulet to destroy. I need you ready, mentally prepared for what we are about to face. You must be focused. Draw on your power. Remember how it felt at the cabin. Bring whatever elements you need, but help us get Luca." Léopold shut the door behind him, praying that Luca's woman understood what they faced.

Samantha wasn't happy to be in Léopold's home. How could Kade leave her with him? She barely trusted Kade and now she was supposed to trust his maker? She put her face into her hands in grief. Luca was gone, and it was all her fault. If she could have resisted Rowan, she'd never have lost the amulet. If she'd listened to Ilsbeth and tried harder to learn her craft, she would've been able to fight back. Instead, she'd been nothing more than a marionette being played by a master puppeteer.

Wiping the tears away, she attempted to collect her emotions. She may've been useless to Luca in the courtyard, but she'd be damned if she'd give up on him. She couldn't let Rowan wear him down to nothing. Resolving to fight until her last breath, she pushed off the bed. She wasn't a quitter; she was a survivor.

Samantha knew in her heart that she loved Luca with every cell of her being. She wasn't sure that she could trust Léopold, but he'd told her Xavier and Étienne were coming with them. Luca trusted those vampires who'd been at the club. If he could trust them, she would try as well. It was all she had to go on.

Pushing open the bathroom door, Samantha went about her business and then caught a glimpse of herself in the mirror. Her long red mane frizzed out of the rubber band; her face was marred by dirt and a large thin scratch over her right eyebrow remained as evidence of her brawl with Rowan. "Shit," she said to herself, deciding she looked like a hot mess.

She ran the water hot and wet a washcloth. After gently cleaning the wound, she rubbed the cloth up and down her arms, in an attempt to freshen herself up. Wetting her fingers with water, she finger combed her hair, braided a single braid down her back and secured it with the band.

Satisfied that she was ready to face Léopold, she walked out of the bathroom and into her bedroom. Her delicate fingers closed around the brass doorknob. She took a deep cleansing breath; it was time to get Luca back.

Barely conscious, Luca writhed against the burning silver cuffs. Through blurry eyes, he took stock of the sparsely decorated environment. The spacious area held only a single tattered sofa and a dusty area rug, which partially covered the oak planked floor. Intricate antiqued crown moldings around the upper perimeter clued him that it might once have been used as a ballroom. However, not a window revealed his location, as they'd been boarded over.

Footsteps alerted him to the svelte figure watching him from the doorway. Her inky curly tresses spilled over nearly white skin. As his eyes came into focus, he could see she was wearing a scarlet satin corset and matching lace panties; a translucent full-length robe trimmed with feathers, deliberately showed off her assets. Her cherry-red lips began to move as she slithered toward him. A flash of metal in her hands caught his eyes; scissors.

"Luca, darling. So nice that you are finally awake." She knelt beside him, running her long fingers up his chest. Pulling tightly on his shirt with one hand, she began to cut the material until his chest lay naked to her. She ripped the fabric aside until Luca felt the cool hardwood floor against his skin.

"Rowan," Luca hissed. "You've gone mad. You can't keep me here."

"Ah, that's where you're wrong, my vampire." She raked her fingernails down his chest until she felt the button on the top of his jeans. She unbuttoned his pants and unzipped him. "I can and will keep you here. You're my shiny new toy. I do love unwrapping presents."

She smiled wickedly and held the edge of the cold blades flat against his lips. "Keep quiet now, my pet. I'm going to enjoy every minute of this."

Luca jerked his head away in disgust. Rowan laughed as she trailed the scissors down his chest and slid the blade under his jeans, letting it rest against his groin.

"Don't worry, darling. I have no intention of damaging the goods. I have plans for you." She cupped his balls roughly then began to cut his jeans away. Within minutes, she had removed all the denim. Luca lay splayed on the hardwood floor naked save only for his boxers.

"Rowan, don't do this. Ilsbeth will find you. She's the most powerful witch in New Orleans. You're part of her sisterhood."

"Ha! Ilsbeth," she mocked. "All these years, you and Kade have been coming to the coven for her advice, her help. Using her like a whore. She makes me sick the way she panders to all you vampires. She'll never find me anyway. Of course you don't know since you've been out of it, but I'll let you in on a little secret." She straddled him, caging him with her arms placed to either side of his head. Seductively, she leaned over, rubbing her breasts against his chest. Lapping her tongue along the line of his neck, she whispered in his ear, "We're not in New Orleans."

"Are you mad? You know damn well that Ilsbeth can still find you."

"So you think. But you need to accept that I have grown quite powerful too. Even if she managed to locate me by scrying, I've set up wards especially for Ilsbeth."

"I am going to rip your fucking throat out and drain you dry, witch. Release me now and I'd consider showing you mercy," Luca growled, baring his fangs.

"Now, now, Luca dear. You've got to come to terms with what's happened to you. It will be much easier for us all if you simply submit to me. I am your mistress now. And I can do whatever I want with your mind and this fine body of yours." Rowan dug her fingernails into his shoulders and began to grind her pelvis against Luca's.

Luca thrashed against his bindings and tried to buck her off of him. "Bitch, it will be a cold day in hell before you'll ever be with me. You disgust me, you bloody cow. Get off me!"

"Come now, do be a good boy. You are forgetting that I have the periapt. I can make you do anything now, whether you want it or not." She fingered a silver necklace and held up the amulet; a key dangled next to it. Moving her body upward, she pressed the apex of her legs against the cheek of his face as she unlocked the handcuffs above his head.

"You will lie still on this floor, Luca. You will not stand. If you do, you will feel blinding pain. You see, you have no choice but to obey me." Rowan patted his face and got up to attend to his ankle cuffs.

Freed from his bonds, Luca stretched but was weakened from the silver. His arms felt like lead as he pulled them over his chest. Yet the burns from the silver were already beginning to heal. Luca could sense his power returning as the bindings on his feet were released. Remembering the pain in the courtyard, he decided to lie still and formulate an escape plan. If he could somehow get the amulet off her neck, he should be released from its will.

Rowan rubbed Luca's ankles, amazed at how quickly he healed. She congratulated herself for choosing such a fine vampire as her slave. She'd have him in her bed and for her warrior, she decided. Admiring his lean, muscled body, she glided her hands up his legs.

"Ah, you are an exquisite specimen. I can't wait to nuzzle my plaything." Her finger tips slipped into his boxers.

Luca heard a commotion in the hallway. Rowan froze. Five scraggly wolves tramped into the room. An enormous, menacing, auburn wolf growled at the others. Whimpering, the four lesser wolves cowered and scampered out of the room. The gray-eyed wolf approached Luca, sniffing his hair and chest. A piercing howl emanated throughout the room as it transformed into a naked, crouching man.

Rowan jolted upward and scurried off of Luca. Coming up behind the man, she placed her bony fingers on his shoulders. "Sköll, please forgive me, I was just amusing myself with my lovely prize while you were out. He's very pleasing, don't you think?"

Sköll stretched upward and hoisted Rowan into his burly arms. His fully bearded lips crushed Rowan's; a gruff hand fondled her breast. Wrenching away from her for a minute, he regarded Luca.

"You've done well, Rowan. He'll help us greatly in our cause."

"Your woman isn't very faithful, wolf. She was about to touch my dangly bits; sometimes only a vampire can satisfy a woman," Luca goaded. He was slowly gaining strength but continued to bide his time on the floor.

Sköll padded up to Luca and knelt beside him, grabbing his face with grubby strong fingers. "Brave you are, for a man whose balls are owned by a witch. You, my friend, will do as I say. The witch and I are business partners, nothing more. If she wants to fuck you when we're done, she's welcome to your sorry ass. Hell, I may join her." Sköll roamed his hands over Luca's chest, admiring the slave. "But first, you will go to war."

Disgusted by the wolf's touch, Luca batted his hand away. "War?"

"Marcel will pay for refusing my brother his bitch. Now, I'm gonna take his pack. And you will help me."

"Kat? What in hell makes you think I'll do that? Besides, you'll never win. Marcel knows this land blind. There's no way an outside pack could take over."

"I have an insider who's going to help me, vamp. As far as fighting for me, with this amulet," he fingered her silver chain, "you'll have no choice. Rowan here, is going to train you real good to obey her. By the time she's done you'll be as compliant as a little lamb. Not only will you fight for me, you'll lick my balls if she tells you to." Sköll clutched Luca's cheeks in his hands and forced his closed lips against Luca's. Laughing out loud, he walked across the room to Rowan.

Luca bared his fangs at the wolf, disgusted by the thought. "Fucking never, wolf. I will never help you or that bitch."

He watched as Sköll took Rowan in a rough embrace. She writhed and purred against him like a cat in heat, then ripped off her clothes, decidedly aroused by the wolf. Falling to the floor, growling and mewling, they began to have sex. Luca watched in abhorrence and planned his attack.

Sufficiently engrossed in their coupling, Rowan and Sköll had inadvertently exposed their vulnerability. Luca patiently waited for the perfect moment. He needed to rip the amulet from Rowan's neck. She needed it on her person to control him. If he could get the amulet away from Rowan, even for a second, he could escape.

CHAPTER FOURTEEN

When Samantha entered the foyer, she immediately recognized the extraordinarily good-looking vampire, Xavier. She felt relieved to see him, even though she'd only met him once in the dimly lit club. Sculpted, mocha-skinned muscles bulged from his black spandex tank top. Black jeans hugged every firm curve of his glutes; he looked like a Greek God.

He smiled at her as if he'd been expecting her. Extending his hand, he bowed. "Xavier Daigre, at your service, ma cher." He took her hand in his, brushing his lips across it. "I understand mon ami, Luca, was taken earlier today."

"I'm Samantha," she replied, noting his old world charm. "I know we didn't get a chance to talk at the club, but Luca mentioned you and Étienne. As for your question, yes, Rowan, from Ilsbeth's coven, took both Luca and the *Hematilly Periapt*. It's an amulet of sorts. It controls vampires but only someone of magic can use it and also only if they have the blood of the vampire they wish to control." She lowered her head and shook it. "It's my fault that she has him. I should've resisted her. She took it from me. Then she took Luca. You should have seen him."

Xavier placed a firm hand on her shoulder. "We will find him, Samantha."

Étienne walked in to see Xavier with his hands on the petite human woman who Luca cherished. Although he wouldn't admit it to them, they'd both known Luca had been entranced by the witch as they'd watched him dance with her at Sangre Dulce.

"Hello Samantha," Étienne nodded. "I'm Étienne. We met at the club but weren't formally introduced. Léopold told us what happened. Xavier is correct. Luca is very old and strong."

Samantha looked to Étienne who she sensed was a younger vampire. His dark-blonde hair was tied at his neck. Like Xavier, he was attractive and well-built. Wearing black jeans and a white polo shirt, he was casually cool and looked like he could have been in a GAP commercial. Samantha looked around to see if Léopold was nearby before whispering to them both. "What about him? Léopold. Can he be trusted?"

Xavier and Étienne passed a silent look between them. Xavier spoke first. "We are loyal to Kade. He sent us here because there is very serious trouble with Marcel's pack that he must attend to. All I can tell you is that Kade would never have left Luca in such a predicament if he didn't trust Léopold. Luca is his best friend and confidant.

Kade explained Léopold's role and said he's more than capable of helping Luca. Being that Léopold is Kade's maker, he is much more powerful and can help us retrieve our friend."

Étienne nodded in agreement. "It's true, Samantha. Léopold knows of the *Hematilly Periapt*. And he'll be much stronger when we need the power of another vampire, but in the end, it's you who is needed to destroy it."

"But how?"

"When the time comes, I shall help you, Samantha." Léopold strolled into the room. "Consider it on a 'need to know' basis." A corner of his mouth lifted in a slight smile.

He was so smug, she thought. Dressed head to toe in black leather, he shook hands with Étienne and Xavier and began to discuss their plan on what vehicle and route they'd take to the location. Samantha tried to concentrate on his words but soon found herself lost in his aura. Léopold emanated authority and command; energy had reverberated throughout the room on his arrival. Samantha's own magic started to hum in response, and she rubbed her arms up and down in an effort to ease the sensation. She was not only unsure of her magic, she was afraid. What if she accidently lit the place on fire?

Léopold stopped speaking to observe the small woman. She'd gone quiet, acutely aware of his vitality. He strode over to her and placed a calming hand on Samantha's shoulder. "You're okay, mon agneau. Breathe. Take deep breaths. You sense me, no?"

"I...I'm sorry. It's just your power. My skin. I feel like I'm on fire. I'm new to my own abilities. For a minute there, I thought I might set something ablaze. It's like I can't contain it once the magic surfaces."

"Save it for Rowan. You're going to need every last bit of energy you've got. Okay, now?"

She nodded. Something about the vampire excited her nerves, but his hand calmed her. She hated being out of control and was anxious to get Luca back. She'd never been a violent person but knew in that moment, she could kill. Rowan was destroying her life. Luca was her future, and she was ready to unleash her fury to save them all.

They'd been riding in the car for an hour. Marshes, fields and bayou sprinkled the landscape along the way. At night, she couldn't see much, but sensed they were in the country. "Léopold, how much further do we have to go? How do you know they'll be there?" she asked.

"Rowan's place is near Houma; we're almost there. She's got nowhere else to go. She inherited the antebellum several years ago, according to the records. What she plans to do with Luca is the big mystery, however. Ilsbeth and the other witches would have had the assistance of the vampires if they'd needed it. But then again, power is quite the aphrodisiac," he surmised.

Aggravated and confused, Samantha rested her head against the window, staring out into the darkness. She didn't care about why Rowan wanted the periapt; she only wanted Luca. Her stomach knotted as the SUV's tires turned into a narrow driveway lined with Spanish moss-covered elm trees. An eerie feeling blanketed Samantha's entire body. Quiet fog weighed onto the graveled road; the headlights pushed through the pale mist.

Léopold, in the front passenger seat, directed Xavier to park out of sight of the house. The thrum of the engine cut to silence. Samantha took a deep breath, knowing their battle was about to begin.

"Xavier, Étienne. Take the back of the house. Samantha. We're going to enter the front door together. Now listen up, everyone. We can't be sure who or what Rowan's got in there. She could have wards. It's even possible that she could have another vampire besides Luca. Not likely, but possible." He caught Samantha's eyes. "Samantha, I'll try to take Rowan, but as she demonstrated, her gift of telekinesis is strong. If she spots me, she can shake me off with a hand. You need to go after her with your gift in kind. Call on the elements. Show no mercy, for she will not show it to you. Understand?"

"Yes," she lied. Samantha nervously bit her lip. She wasn't sure if she could take out Rowan, but she'd die trying.

As they got out of the car, a humid breeze blew hard against them. Lightning flashed in the distance. Within seconds, thunder roared and Samantha reacted by wrapping an arm around Léopold's. She barely knew the lethal vampire, yet here she was holding onto him for dear life. She rolled her eyes silently in embarrassment but she held firm. *Better the devil you know.*

Léopold smelled Samantha's trepidation. He'd gone to war many times over his lifetime, accepting that battles seldom came without loss. But one thing he'd never done was knowingly go into a situation attached to a fragile mortal woman. If he'd had any other choice, he would have left her at home. But he knew damn well that he needed her to dispose of the amulet, for only a witch could demolish the diabolical object.

If Luca didn't survive the attack, he'd pursue the beautiful girl, he thought to himself. He knew he shouldn't think such things while on the brink of combat. He blamed it on the adrenaline coursing through his veins. Every sense was heightened, including his need for sex. He enjoyed the feel of her body tight against his and wondered what it would be like to bring her to climax.

Before climbing the staircase, Léopold shoved Samantha behind a tree. Her back pressed tight against the bark, the evidence of his arousal grazing her belly.

"What are you doing?" she whispered loudly, quite annoyed by his state.

"Patience, my dear Samantha. I'm listening." He smiled ruefully, aware of his surroundings.

"Do you hear anything?" She tried to ignore the fact that a large, sexy vampire had her pinned to an elm tree, not to mention the inappropriate hardness in his pants.

"Lovemaking." A broad smile broke across his handsome face. He leaned down to smell her hair.

"Excuse me?" It was obvious the man had sex on his mind. But Samantha couldn't for the life of her fathom how he could talk about it when they were about to go on the offensive.

"Lovemaking. Sex. That is what I hear. Someone is getting it on, as Al Green would say. A perfect time for a party, don't you think?"

Samantha's stomach lurched. She'd die if Rowan made Luca do something sexual against his will. She'd seen firsthand the power the amulet had had over Luca back in the courtyard.

"Don't worry, my sweet. We're about to go in now. You ready?" he asked.

"As ready as I'll ever be. Let's do this," she replied.

Stepping out from behind the tree, Samantha took in the sight of Rowan's home. The once magnificent antebellum stood dilapidated before them. The gabled roof peaked with an uneven slope and paint peeled from majestic Grecian pillars. Fig ivy had nearly taken over the sides of the home and was creeping onto the porch.

Léopold placed a silencing finger to his lips and pointed at the stairs. Slowly they climbed up toward the door. Aside from the cicadas singing, she could only hear her own heartbeat in the darkness. She trusted that

Léopold was correct about the sex; yet as they approached the door, she heard nothing.

Silently, Léopold traced a finger down her cheek, seeking her attention. It was time. He held up a finger. On the count of three, he'd enter. One. Two. Three.

CHAPTER FIFTEEN

Luca watched as Sköll lifted Rowan to position her over the sofa. The sight of Rowan's pale ass in the air pointing toward him repulsed Luca. Sköll growled and looked over at Luca to make sure he was watching as he roughly entered her from behind. She screamed in delight and soon Sköll lost himself in his actions, ignoring his unwilling audience.

Luca breathed deeply as he steeled himself for attack. *Remove the amulet*; the words reverberated through his head. It was his only chance of breaking the spell. Lunging forward, burning agony tore through Luca's spine. He had disobeyed Rowan's command to lie still on the floor. His blatant insubordination was met with blinding torment. A thousand invisible knives pierced his skin; his head screamed for alleviation. Sucking in a breath, Luca charged onward into swift propulsion.

Immersed in passion, Sköll barely registered the danger before Luca sank his fangs into his shoulder. Energizing shifter blood rushed into Luca's mouth as he held Sköll in place. Plowing his hand madly toward Rowan's neck, his fingers felt for the periapt and slipped under the silver chain. A pop sounded as it snapped.

Luca saw the crimson amulet rattle across the floor. Instantly, the ghostly knives receded. Twisting herself round to look up at Sköll's attacker, Rowan met Luca's eyes with a clear understanding that the spell was shattered. Refusing to retract his fangs, he bit deeper into Sköll. Raging, the shifter jerked Luca upward, wildly attempting to dislodge his attacker. Sköll began to transform into a wolf, successfully bucking Luca onto the ground. Within seconds, the man turned wolf, and Luca renewed his assault, giving the beast little time to assume an offensive position. In the midst of the struggle, a loud crash sounded, distracting Luca. The vampire from the courtyard had erupted through the barricade, and his beautiful Samantha rushed directly into the skirmish.

Running through the foyer, Samantha chased Léopold as he shouldered his way through a double set of locked wooden doors. In the melee, she could have sworn she heard dogs growling, but didn't turn around to investigate the noise. Samantha froze upon entering. Rowan, nude, was scrambling around on her hands and knees. Luca, barely dressed, held the throat of a red wolf. Its jaws snapped at Luca's neck as they fought for dominance. Léopold, baring his fangs, turned toward her and roared. She ducked as he flew over her head. Crouching down, she peeked to see him wrestling two brown wolves. The crisp pattering of feet could be heard from the hallway; more wolves approached.

Spying the periapt in the corner, Samantha tore across the room. Out of the corner of her eye, she caught a glimpse of Xavier tearing the fur from a gray wolf. Blood sprayed across the room. Focusing on the amulet, Rowan and Samantha raced to get to it first. Rowan, deciding to use her magic, stilled and blasted Samantha, effectively smashing the back of her skull against the wall. Samantha gritted her teeth, staving off the pain. Touching the back of her head, blood trickled onto her fingertips.

Rowan grabbed the amulet and sneered in victory. "Stupid Samantha, did you really think you could come in here and take what's mine?"

Samantha stumbled to her feet. Instead of feeling lightheaded, strength and loathing rushed through the whole of her body. Samantha closed her eyes, concentrating on the element she wished to call. She'd had enough of death, fighting, torture. It was time for it all to end and she'd be the one to end it. The room started to slightly vibrate at first. The vampires and wolves barely noticed the buzz as they bit and tussled. Within seconds the house came into a full tremble. Dust cascaded from above as the ceiling threatened to collapse. Floor boards creaked and snapped as the foundations began to heave and rock. As the room began to shake violently, the vampires and werewolves steadied themselves against the barrage of tremors.

Rowan attempted to telekinetically bombard Samantha with magic, but was thwarted by her reflective palm. Rowan looked around as the planks beneath her feet began to split open and crack. Screaming out for help, she collapsed into the crawl space. Holding onto the sides of the flooring, her upper torso supported her weight. Rowan's face turned stark white in fear, unsure of how Samantha was causing the quakes.

Samantha's eyes flew open as she called upon the elements. "Care dea aperuerit mihi thesaurum terrae. Hoc malum pythonissam in sinu. Quia non est de hoc mundo. Adhaerere. Tolle eam nunc!" *Open the Earth.*

Rowan screamed Sköll's name as the earth began to cleave open at Samantha's command. Luca bit deeply into Sköll's shoulder, rendering him immobile. Helplessly he watched as his lover, Rowan, flailed her arms, shrieking as she plunged helplessly into the crevice.

Samantha walked over to the gaping chasm, and knelt down to Rowan.

"Save me, sister," Rowan pleaded. "I swear to you. I will share it with you. Please, grab my hand."

Samantha considered her plea but knew in her heart, that evil was speaking. "Dear sister," she chided. "You are no sister of mine. Back to the earth you go. May the Goddess grant you peace." Peeling open Rowan's fingers, Samantha took the periapt and shoved it into her pocket.

Rowan cursed her. "You little bitch. This will never be over. There are others who will want the periapt. They know of its existence. They will find you! This will not end!"

"That's where you're wrong, Rowan. This! Ends! Now!" Samantha yelled.

A seism rocked the entire house as the fissure grew wider and deeper. Samantha closed her eyes and called once again on the elements. "Lorem benedictionem, dea. Accipere, Rowan, soror Ilsbeth, in calore et munda eius eius malum."

Rowan clawed at the crumbling dirt in an effort to save herself as Samantha's words took effect. A loud shriek emanated from Rowan as she plummeted deep into the fiery core of the earth.

Samantha breathed deeply, willing the brown terra together again. Within seconds, the gaping crevice consolidated, leaving nothing but disturbed dirt in its place. As exhaustion racked Samantha's mind and body, she crumbled to the floor, and sobbed.

As the shaking subsided, Sköll sliced into Luca's arm. Not lethally, but it was enough to make Luca release his hold. Sköll transformed into his human form and scurried toward Samantha. "What have you done, witch? I needed Rowan. Now that you have taken her, I will take you." He wrapped his arm around Samantha's neck.

Xavier, Étienne and Léopold stood still, acknowledging her capture. They had killed all the wolves except one or two who'd retreated out to the woods. Luca stalked cautiously toward Sköll.

"Don't hurt her. You need me for your war. Take me," he ordered.

"Now you want to come willingly? Hmmm....this one smells good," Sköll growled and licked the back of Samantha's neck. She hung like a ragdoll helpless in his grip. "Ah, she'll do nicely. A fertile witch who can serve all my needs. And she's got the periapt." He reached around with his free hand to grope her breast and smirked. "Go now, and she'll live. I'll find another vampire to do my work."

"Get off her. She's mine, wolf," Luca snarled; his bared fangs dripped with the blood of his enemy. He was going to kill the wolf for touching his woman. But he resisted the urge to attack, knowing that Sköll could easily snap her neck. Cornered, Sköll was running out of options, and that made him particularly deadly and unpredictable. Luca was certain he'd kill Samantha just to make his point.

Samantha felt dazed as the wolf held his arm tightly around her, crushing her trachea. She barely felt his grubby hand touching her. All of the energy she'd exhausted on Rowan had left her weak. She peered up at Luca through teary eyes. Sucking in a quick breath, she tried to speak but couldn't.

"Wolf, you're making a mistake. I'm warning you, let her go or you die within minutes. Your choice," Luca growled at him. There was no way he was taking Samantha alive.

Sköll laughed violently and flashed his canines.

Samantha trembled under his touch and sought a means of escape. Closing her eyes, she intensified her thoughts, praying that she had enough energy to call an element. Unable to speak, she silently chanted to herself, "Adducam ignis ad manus... Adducam ignis ad manus... Adducam ignis ad manus..." *Bring fire to my hands.*

At first she simply felt a tingling. Soon, the smell of burnt flesh and hair wafted into her nostrils. Sköll hollered as the searing heat scorched his arm. Reacting to the scalding pain, he threw Samantha aside. Red handprints were branded into his bubbling flesh.

"What the fuck did you do?" he screamed at her.

Léopold rushed to gather Samantha from the floor as Luca charged Sköll. Wrapping his hands around the wolf's throat, Luca tore his fangs into Sköll's shoulder, tearing and spitting the raw flesh onto the ground. In a struggle for dominance, the two men lurched onto the floor. Sköll pinned Luca down, and landed a punch to his face. From the corner of his eye, Luca saw Xavier and Étienne rushing to help him. He held up his hand to them. "Back off. He's mine."

The pain of the strike only served to fuel Luca's anger. Adrenaline surged. Reaching up with both hands, he wrapped his fingers around Sköll's neck, digging his thumbs into his windpipe. Sköll coughed and faltered as his oxygen was depleted. Luca wrapped his legs around the man's waist and flipped him over. He straddled Sköll's chest. Sköll clasped his hands around Luca's wrists, but could not shake him off. For a second, he thought Luca was releasing his hold. Luca quickly grabbed the back of Sköll's head and palmed his chin. In a fluid, accelerated motion, Luca shoved upward and down, twisting Sköll's neck until he heard a loud pop. Bereft of life, death bled out of Sköll's eyes. Discarding his prey, Luca roared in domination, wild with fury. Rising, he scanned the room for Samantha.

Like a ferocious animal, Luca searched for his mate; he was dangerous, primal. Léopold carefully watched Luca approach him. Restraining Samantha had been the only way that he could keep her from attempting to enter the fray, in what would have been a treacherous and unnecessary effort to stop Sköll from killing Luca. Luca hadn't needed help; this kill was his and his alone. Cautiously, Léopold released Samantha's arms, facing his palms upward toward Luca, gesturing that he had not hurt her. Léopold was unsure if the already enraged Luca understood that he was friend, not foe, and did not want to agitate him further.

As Samantha broke free, she ran into Luca's arms. "Luca," she cried.

Possessively taking her into his embrace, he cupped her face, and pressed a punishing kiss to her lips. She was his woman. "Samantha mine," he said, his lips against hers.

"Yes, I'm yours. It's okay now," she said softly, reassuring him.

"It's over." Luca wasn't quite sure if he was trying to convince Samantha or himself. He only cared that she was safe.

"Luca, oh my God. Are you okay?" she reluctantly pulled away, inspecting his face and body, noting the bruises and cuts that were already beginning to heal.

He laughed, wincing slightly as she touched a gash on his face. "Am I okay? I'm better than okay now that I've got you in my arms."

"But he bit you," she protested, continuing to inspect his body.

"Don't worry darlin'. I've had my rabies shots. Now come on, let's get the hell out of here."

"Not so fast, Luca. We must discuss the periapt." Léopold stepped up to introduce himself. "Mon ami, I'm Léopold. Léopold Devereoux. I am Kade's maker and you are descended from my blood."

Luca was shocked. Kade had never spoken of his maker, and Luca had never asked. He was loyal to Kade only. Despite Léopold's claims, he did not fully trust the vampire.

"You kept Samantha safe?"

"Oui."

"Pardon me if I sound ungrateful, but why the hell would you bring her here? And where the hell is Kade?" Luca asked.

"Ah, there is trouble with the wolves. Kade entrusted me with your safety while he provided them with assistance. I don't know the details, but I suspect these dead wolves here have something to do with the problem." He perused the room, counting six dead men. "There were others who escaped. They planned to use you?" He raised a questioning eyebrow at Luca.

"Yes, they're going after Marcel's pack. But why would you bring Samantha? She located the amulet. Wasn't that enough for you?" he demanded.

"We need her. The *Hematilly Periapt* must be destroyed and only a witch can do it. In addition, we needed her help in subduing Rowan. As you can see, she was more than capable."

Luca recalled Samantha's display. Her command of the elements was extraordinary. "You were amazing, my little witch." He kissed her again, hugging her against his bare chest.

"Hmmm…." was all Samantha could manage. She was exhausted from the ordeal; her legs felt weak.

"We must destroy the periapt now," Léopold informed him. "We can't risk it getting into the wrong hands. The wolf was correct about one thing. Others may know of its existence. The temptation will be too great for any witch who toys with black magic. To have a vampire as a slave is quite the coup. He could be used in war, to harm others, for all sorts of purposes. Do you have the amulet, Samantha?"

Samantha twisted around in Luca's arms enough so that she faced Léopold. Luca's strong arms remained secure around her belly. She leaned into him. "Yes, I've got it here." She dug into her pocket and held up the teardrop-shaped rock. Eyeing the amulet, she affirmed her commitment to its destruction. "So, how do we destroy this thing?"

CHAPTER SIXTEEN

Back at Léopold's townhome, Samantha waited in his study for the vampires to join her. She ran her fingers over the volumes of antiqued books on the bookshelves that ran top to bottom on the wall around the entire perimeter of the room. He had quite the library, all alphabetically categorized. She wondered what it would be like to live so long. Would you miss those humans who died when your own youth stood still? Would you try a thousand different hobbies to keep boredom at bay? Her thoughts drifted to Luca and how he'd lived for centuries. *Centuries. What must that be like?*

Watching Luca kill Sköll had reminded her that Luca was more than a man. Vampire. He was immortal. In contrast, she was very much mortal. If she honed her witchcraft, she could extend her life considerably. But she considered what Luca had told her about Sydney. If she fully bonded with Luca, then she'd live as long as he did.

She knew deep in her heart that she loved him, but the human part of her still wanted normal everyday things: a home, a family, children. She and Luca hadn't discussed the future. Would Luca want children? Could she even have children with a vampire? After what had happened today, she reasoned that perhaps she had no right to bring children into the paranormal world where evil lurked and waited for weakness. All she'd known of the supernatural world was chaos and violence.

She herself had killed tonight. Rowan was dead by her hand. Samantha had never gone hunting before, let alone killed a person. She wasn't sure what she felt yet. Realistically, she'd been given no choice. Rowan would have killed her in a minute, given the chance. But still, she felt pangs of guilt knowing she'd taken a life. Conflicted, she threw herself into an overstuffed, brown leather couch; well worn, the soft grain caressed her skin. She closed her eyes, praying for forgiveness and also thanked her lucky stars that her magic had saved her and Luca from certain death.

Sighing aloud, she grew irritated and impatient. The only thing she wanted was to go home, take a shower and sleep. *Home?* She laughed. Samantha truly had begun to think of Luca's home as her own. She wondered if she should start making plans to return to Philadelphia. Tristan had promised he'd help her get a new job within the paranormal community. Should she try to start a fresh life so far from Luca?

Maybe Luca would ask her to stay. She certainly wasn't crazy about managing a long distance relationship. He'd told her he loved her. But declaring love wasn't the same as a commitment. It wasn't asking someone to move to where they lived, nor was it asking them to move in with you. It was a feeling. People threw around the word 'love' all the time, only to choke when it came to marriage. She knew plenty of friends who thought they were in love only to end up being dumped a week later. Then she knew some of her guy friends who, despicably so, used the 'love' word to get a woman in bed. People weren't always the way they seemed.

But deep in her heart, she knew Luca was honorable. He wasn't a user or the type of man who needed to trick women into bed. No, a man like that could have his choice of women at the snap of his fingers. She resolved to discuss her future plans with Luca at another time, considering they still had work to do.

Samantha pulled the amulet out of her pocket and rolled it between her fingers. Impatiently humming to herself, relief hit her as Luca opened the door. Showered, he was wearing sweatpants and a snug t-shirt that Léopold had lent him. She smiled up at him, admiring his fine physique. Almost all of his wounds were healed.

"Samantha," he said as he reached for her hands. He pulled her into his arms, waiting on Léopold to begin.

"Will this take long? I really want to go home," she said wearily.

"It should be quick, but we'll need to take a quick trip to dispose of it. Léopold will explain."

Léopold entered the room, commanding their attention. He walked around to his desk, opened a drawer and retrieved a black velvet pouch. He'd brought a marble cutting board from the kitchen and laid it on his desk pad. Looking up at Samantha, he explained what needed to be done.

"Samantha, as I've told you, only a witch can crush this particular amulet to mere particles. While it is essentially a mineral at its core, it's enchanted. You must be the one to destroy it, to dispel its magic. Once it is done, you and Luca will scatter the dust so that it can never be reconstituted, understood?"

"Yes, but how are we going to break it up? A hammer?" she quipped.

Léopold smiled, "You, my dear, are much stronger than any man made tool. This amulet is of the earth. And to the earth it shall return. You must manipulate it, break it down with your mind. After your demonstration earlier, this should be child's play."

"I'll try. But I don't know if I can do it. I mean, it seems to just kind of fire off when I get upset. I don't have much control, yet," she explained.

"You must try. Now," Léopold ordered.

The tension in the room became palpable. Xavier and Étienne entered and remained behind Luca and Samantha, who stood in front of Léopold's desk. Léopold watched with great intensity as Samantha placed the amulet on the marble platter. Closing her eyes, she tried to concentrate but felt no magic hum. Thoughts of the amulet before her formulated in her mind's eye, yet nothing stirred.

Sensing no magic, Léopold silently warned Luca with his eyes. He intended to agitate the witch into destruction. Luca had known this might have to happen, but still hated seeing Samantha brought to her knees.

"Samantha, we must try a different approach. Close your eyes, and hear only my voice," Léopold ordered. His accented voice was smooth as silk yet iron willed. "Picture the amulet. And Rowan. She took Luca. She took your vampire. She silvered him. Stripped him. She ran her fingers up his legs, felt his chest, felt his body in her own hands."

Her eyes snapped to attention, glaring at Léopold. *Why the hell was he saying all these awful things?*

"Close your eyes! Concentrate. You must destroy this object," he demanded. "That's right Samantha, she touched your mate. How does that make you feel? Are you angry enough yet? Think of what she did to Luca. She burned him. Used him. Think of what she did to you. She wrecked your life, laughing while you searched for the amulet. Think of Sköll. He helped Rowan. He was going to break your neck...he felt your breasts in front of your vampire. I sense your anger, Samantha, now focus it. Focus it into your magic."

Samantha let Léopold's words feed the angry beast within. He'd done nothing but repeat the truth. Rowan had silvered Luca, had touched him intimately, something that was hers. Sköll had groped her. She could still smell his foul breath against her neck. And for what? For an amulet that made slaves. A diabolic object that was utilized to propagate evil, wars. No, that damnable amulet must be annihilated so that no one could ever use it again. Fire built within Samantha's belly. The object began to glow into a red bright ball. She held her hands over the amulet, letting the magic flow as the destructive words spilled from her lips; "Natus ex inferno, cineri moriemini. Frangere ut revertatur in pulverem terrae." Willing the periapt to dust, it burst into flames and soon all that remained was a pile of ash.

Samantha opened her eyes and smiled. The vampires in the room all stared at her in amazement and fear. "What? Tell me it's gone. I felt it. It's gone, isn't it?" she asked innocently.

They burst into laughter at her words. Luca hugged her; she truly had no idea of the sheer magnitude of her abilities. Nor did she realize how frightening she could be when working her magic.

Léopold brushed the ashes into the bag and handed it to Luca. "Now go. The remains of the stone shall return to the earth as it should be. Xavier, Étienne. I shall see you again someday, perhaps." He nodded, curtly dismissing the two. "Luca, Samantha, it has been a pleasure meeting you albeit under the most unfortunate circumstances."

Taking Samantha's hand in his, Léopold drew her to him. Luca tensed, distrustful of the older vampire. Léopold met Luca's fiery eyes and proceeded cautiously. With a smile, he turned to Samantha and looked deep into her blue eyes. "My dear witch, while I'm certain you are glad to have Luca home, I admit there was the smallest part of me who wished he would not return. For I would have kept you as my own."

Gently, he leaned in and kissed her forehead. "I am sure your blood is as sweet as you are beautiful, but alas, it is Luca to whom you belong. Again, I do apologize for burning the cabin. Sometimes we all need a small incentive to do our best work."

His sexy voice warmed her although she stiffened at his confession. This man, smoothly and coolly, had just admitted he wanted her in front of Luca. Samantha wasn't sure what to think of Léopold. He was sensual and alluring, but powerful. Intimidating. Protective. And oddly caring. Giving into her desire to say goodbye to him, she briefly hugged Léopold and then quickly returned to Luca's embrace.

"Léopold, thank you for helping me save Luca. I do forgive you for the cabin. But next time you need my help, please just ask," she joked.

Luca and Samantha exchanged looks as they walked out of the office. As she went to steal a last look at Léopold, Samantha glanced over her shoulder to see only an empty office. Once again, he'd vanished.

CHAPTER SEVENTEEN

The waves splashed against the side of the boat as the sun crested the horizon. Turquoise waters sparkled in the morning sun, while dolphins danced in a celebration of life. Samantha sighed in relief, knowing she was finally safe. She was looking forward to a new, hopefully calm, life. She silently reminisced about how much her life had changed. Once she'd spent hours in a cubicle, her only excitement driven by catching errors and breaking codes with co-workers.

It wasn't just that she felt different; she was different. She could no longer deny the magic within her. No longer a desk jockey, she needed to find a new calling. Or perhaps the calling had found her. A newfound witch, she resolved to do something positive with her powers. While she longed to have better control, she knew that would come with practice. She wanted to train with Ilsbeth but knew for certain that she wouldn't live in the coven.

She could not deny what she was any more than she could deny Luca was vampire. It was time to face the music. Either she'd have to accept Tristan's offer or move to New Orleans. Given that she didn't know the witches in Philadelphia, and she had a perfectly good mentor ready and willing here in New Orleans, in that moment, she decided to stay and learn her craft. She hoped that Luca would ask her to stay with him at his home, but wasn't going to pressure him.

No matter what he'd said about bonding and love, she knew men didn't always mean what they said in the heat of the moment. Since they'd left Léopold's, Luca had seemed distant, quiet. Samantha was utterly exhausted and didn't press him to talk. Now wasn't the time.

She glanced over at the deck clock, and realized they'd been on the boat for at least seven hours. Léopold's captain sailed the vessel down the Mississippi to the open Gulf of Mexico. Within minutes of boarding, she'd passed out in bed as soon as her head hit the pillow. After taking a hot shower, she made her way up to the back deck. The boat slowly bobbed and swayed to the rhythm of the ocean; she surmised they'd anchored. Peering out to sea, she wondered where Luca had gone.

When she'd woken to a cold bed, she'd missed the warmth of him. She hoped he wasn't having second thoughts about their relationship. She wasn't the clingy type, but was somewhat insecure about where they stood.

Love. Samantha had thought she'd known love before Luca. But she realized now that it had only been a shadow of love. Maybe infatuation? Maybe just her need to be close to a man? Regardless, Luca had shown her time and time again, through his actions, what real love was. He'd shown her what a real man was.

He'd cared enough to fly across the country and find her, to save her from her own foolishness. He'd let go of his inhibitions to earn her trust, swimming with her in the lake and sharing his past. He'd showed her the bliss of tender lovemaking and then pushed her limits to explore her sexuality. He'd fearlessly opened up to her emotionally and declared his love. He'd helped her discover what the amulet was and had fought with his life to protect her. And even though she'd seen him ferociously attack the wolf and kill, she didn't fear him. Respect for his courageous act swelled in her heart. Captured and tortured twice over the past weeks, the man seemed indestructible and had an unbreakable spirit.

Reaching in the pocket of her robe, she fingered the small sack Léopold had given her. The older vampire was somewhat of an enigma. Dominant and sexual, she felt drawn to him. Deadly as he was, she trusted him like an older brother. She knew he wanted her, but he didn't take what wasn't his. Nor was he the type to take women against their will. Given his dark and mysterious good looks, she knew someone like Léopold could have any woman, and had probably already had hundreds of lovers over the years. Even though he'd made attempts to put her at ease, she also knew he could be cold and calculating, remembering how he'd burned the cabin to get her to do his bidding. Encouragement, he'd called it. She smiled. Only in the paranormal world would someone call torching a cabin an 'incentive'. After watching Rowan bring Luca to his knees, she was certain Léopold had done what was necessary to protect his kind.

She looked down at the satchel with anticipation. Samantha couldn't wait to dump the dreaded contents, so she could finally be free. Looking around the spacious wooden deck, she hoped Luca would return soon. She wanted to tell him about her decision to stay. Butterflies danced in her stomach. She prayed he felt the same way about her as she felt about him. In the heat of passion, he'd said he loved her, but she longed to hear him say it again. She wanted a life with Luca and could not imagine loving anyone else. She was his.

Luca briefly spoke to the captain, explaining how they'd make a brief stop and then return to New Orleans. As much as he'd like to take a Caribbean cruise with Samantha, trouble was brewing with the wolves. Earlier, he'd slipped out of Samantha's arms to go call Kade. Both Kade and Sydney were at the pack house strategizing with Marcel. Apparently, Jax Chandler, the New York Alpha, had not taken kindly to Marcel's message refusing him access to Kat. Although it may have been typical in some packs for an Alpha to pick a mate of his choice, Tristan and Marcel, both unmated, refused to take a mate who wasn't in agreement. Once mated, wolves could seldom separate without physical repercussions. The brothers fiercely protected their sister. Although she had a wild side, she was deeply loyal to their packs.

Ever since Luca had rescued Kat, he'd kept tabs on her over the years; 'friends with benefits,' but friends nonetheless. He was concerned for her safety, knowing how independent she could be. She often went missing for periods of time only for them to find out later she'd been on holiday with friends somewhere on the other side of the world. She lived life to the fullest, but now someone wanted her to be his. Someone, an Alpha, like Jax, who wouldn't take no for an answer.

He regretted that the wolves at Rowan's mansion had escaped them. Interrogation would have yielded critical information about their true purpose in causing a war. Sköll had insinuated that he was there because of Kat, but it could have been a ruse. He wasn't even certain Sköll knew Jax or was in his pack. He could have been lying to protect another wolf.

His thoughts turned to Samantha as he dug into the ice box and located a bottle of champagne. She was a feisty little witch, and actually a little scary now that he'd seen her powers. Petite and fair, she'd stolen his heart. He rolled his eyes in disbelief and laughed to himself. All these years he'd been so insistent that he'd never fall in love again, let alone with a human. When he reflected on his young love for Eliza, he realized that he'd never been in love with someone as deeply as he loved Samantha.

Fearless when faced with the unknown, she stood her ground. And she was smart as a whip, amazing him with her knowledge of cryptic code breaking and how she reveled in the challenge. Samantha had never backed down to Léopold either. When he was captured, she'd risked her life with the ancient vampire just so she could find Luca. Strong-willed. Beautiful. Intelligent. *His.*

Luca's thoughts drifted to their lovemaking and how passionately she had embraced the experience. He loved watching her climax, letting go of her inhibitions. He grew long and firm thinking of how she'd taken him into her mouth, teasing him endlessly. She trusted him, a vampire, to take her to places she'd never gone before. Remembering the sight of her tied to his bed sweetly moaning and writhing in pleasure, he smiled. Lascivious and loving, she brought him to a new level of felicity that he'd never known in his long life. He couldn't imagine what life would be like without her. It wasn't just the bonding. It was everything about her. He loved her more than life itself. He wanted her here, building a life together. Forever.

A broad smile broke across Samantha's face as she felt Luca's strong arms encircle her waist and a kiss to her ear. She turned in his arms to face him and smiled. God, she loved this man. The sight of the gorgeous male took her breath away. Shirtless, he wore white cotton drawstring pajama pants and padded around barefoot. He was confident and comfortable no matter his surroundings. Over her shoulder, she noticed the champagne and glasses he'd set on the glass end table.

"Hmmm…champagne? So early in the morning?"

"Yes, darlin'. This is New Orleans," he drawled. "Think of it like mimosas without the orange juice."

"Well, when you put it that way, how can a girl refuse?" She gave him a flirty smile.

"That's what I'm counting on. But before we toast, let's get rid of the remains, shall we?" he suggested. "Would you care to do the honors?"

"Nothing would make me happier." She carefully opened the packet, and turned it upside down. Red, gray and black ashes floated downward, falling gently into the sea.

When the pouch was fully emptied, Luca raised a knowing eyebrow at her and held up a lighter. "Just to be on the safe side."

"Just to be on the safe side," she agreed as she watched him light the bag on fire.

Tossing the lighter aside, he pinched the end of the sack and held it up to the air to burn. Devoured by flames, he cast it into the waves.

"I can't tell you how relieved I am to see that thing gone," she sighed.

"You and me both," he concurred. "Now for something really important, a toast and a proposition."

"A toast sounds wonderful. But a proposition? Sounds cryptic, but then again, I do love a good mystery."

"Ah, but you are good with puzzles. First, the toast." He held his flute to hers. "To finding more than just an amulet. To finding you, Samantha...the love of my life."

"And to finding you. To us," she countered.

Clinking glasses and then taking a sip, Luca took her slender hand in his and led her over to the open-air deck bed. He pulled her onto his lap and held her.

Samantha's cheek rested on his bare chest. The masculine scent of him piqued her desire. She wanted to make love to him again over and over. Sensing he wanted to talk, she resisted the urge to slide her hands down into his pants. Instead she caressed his chest and played innocently with his flat nipple.

"You are making me lose my train of thought, you naughty girl," he groaned at her touch. His arousal grew, but first, they needed to talk.

"Samantha, look at me." He placed a finger under her chin, tilting her head toward his.

"Yes," she said lazily.

"I told you about Eliza. She was my first love...long before I was turned. I was only a young man when I met her. When we were attacked that night and she died, I was devastated, just filled with rage. I swore never to love again. And for all these years, it's been fairly easy to do. In truth, I never met anyone who could make me feel. Sure, lust is something that comes and goes like the wind. But finding someone, someone like you; it is rare." He absentmindedly rubbed her palm with his thumb.

"What I'm trying to say is that I want you here with me. Not just now, but forever. I know this must seem sudden, but I can tell you that I am certain of my feelings for you. I want you as my wife. I want a family. I want a real home, not just a museum full of antiquities. Please. Stay here with me," he whispered as his words trailed off.

Samantha regarded him for a minute, stunned by his proposal. Her heart bloomed at the prospect of spending her life with Luca. She placed her hand on his cheek and looked into his eyes. "Yes, I'd love to stay with you. I know we haven't known each other very long, but over the past few weeks we've been through more than most people have been through in a lifetime. And now, I can't imagine my life without you. I don't think I ever really knew what love was until I met you. And I never knew what it meant to have a man love me back. There is only you. I am yours."

Luca gathered her red locks in his fingers and drew her soft, pink lips to his. He gently kissed her, slowly, deliberately. Savoring the sweetness of her mouth, his tongue found hers. She opened willingly, intoxicated as he sought to send her into ecstasy.

Samantha's blood raced in anticipation of his touch. She wanted all of him now, and couldn't hold back the urge to strip him naked and take what was hers. Sensually releasing his lips, she rose off his lap and straddled his legs. Leisurely, she untied the belt to her robe. As the panels revealed her skin, she seductively peeled the fabric down her shoulders and let it pool at her feet. Standing bare before him, she smiled as he tried to reach for her hips.

Luca marveled at the way her ivory skin glowed. She was a magnificent creature. The blonde highlights in her curls reflected off the sunlight and flowed over the soft, ripe swell of her breasts.

Flipping her hair aside, she exposed her pebbled pink tips. Flush with arousal, she held his hands firmly to her hips, teasing him, driving him mad with desire.

"Luca, I'm in control this morning," she purred. "Will you let me take care of you?"

"Darlin', you'd better do something soon. You know, I can't resist you for one minute longer," he said, hanging onto a thread of control. His rock hard erection was straining to be released.

"As you wish." Samantha agilely dropped to her knees, letting her fingernails graze his chest all the way to the fine trail of hair that led into his pants. Gripping the sides of his pajamas, she yanked hard until she tore the pants down off his body. Animalistic, she planned to take him in every way she could. She wanted to possess him, to be possessed.

Luca's breath startled as his cock sprang free. Samantha was rough, wanton. He'd never seen her so aggressive and loved every minute of it. He extended his arms backward, laying his palms flat to support his weight. Completely nude to her, he patiently waited as he watched her graze a path with her nails to the apex between his legs.

Excited by the sight of his exquisite musculature, Samantha grew wet, yearning to have him inside of her. Meeting his eyes, she leaned forward and attentively licked the tip of his firm flesh. She delighted in the spicy taste of him. He hissed in delight as she swirled her tongue around it, lavishing the head with long, wet brushes. Wrapping her fingers around him, she parted her lips and devoured the full length of his aroused manhood.

Luca thought he'd explode; her warm moist tongue caused his shaft to bob in eagerness. Unable to restrain himself any longer, Luca sat up and plowed his hands through her hair.

She mercilessly plunged him in and out of her hot mouth. She felt him grow close to climax and backed off. Still stroking his hard male heat, she lifted him up with one hand as she felt for his scrotum. Opening widely she sucked him into her mouth rolling them one at a time, licking and teasing.

Luca moaned out loud at the intrusion. The vixen was going to make him insane. "Aw fuck, that feels so good. Please," he begged for release.

Hearing his plea, she grinned and once again began to suckle his hot swollen flesh. Slightly twisting her grip, she built the sensation within him. He was so very close and bucked his hips upward into her warm sweetness. In and out, her head rose and fell, sucking him harder and harder.

"Samantha, I'm gonna come." He didn't want to release in her mouth without her permission.

Ignoring his pleas, she held onto him tight and increased her pace. "Mmmm, come for me." She resumed her assault, sucking him deeply.

Luca groaned as he lost control, stiffening as he exploded into her.

Greedily, she took all of him, milking his essence until he collapsed backward onto the bed. Licking her swollen lips, she stalked over him. Her naked body straddled his belly.

"Samantha," he panted. "You'll be the death of me, woman. My God. That was unbelievable." She quietly smiled down on him as he caught his breath.

"Tired, vampire?" she challenged.

"Not on your life, witch. It's my turn to feast!" With preternatural speed, he flipped Samantha on her back.

She giggled uncontrollably. "Not fair! Not fair!" she feigned a protest.

Luca captured a rosy taut nipple in his mouth and sucked it. "Mmmm....it's more than fair. You taste delicious. I love your breasts, so soft and so very ready to be plucked." He pinched a firm peak while laving the other with his tongue. "I plan to kiss and worship every inch of your lovely body."

"Um...Yes. That feels so good. I love you so much. I've never felt like this in my entire life. No one has ever..." Her words trailed off as she felt his lips kiss down her stomach. Her sex ached in need, awaiting his mouth on her core. She yearned to feel him on her, in her.

As he dipped into her sex with his tongue, she lost track of all thoughts. Biting down on her lip, she resisted the urge to scream, knowing the captain was somewhere on the boat. Not one for public sex, she almost forgot they weren't entirely alone. Yet she was too far gone to stop now.

As he parted her folds with his fingers, she sucked in a breath. Tendrils of magic wisped over her naked body; he swept around her most sensitive point. She pushed her hips up into his mouth, seeking what she needed. But he continued to tease her, licking, tasting but not directly licking her clit. She felt like she was almost there…almost. But she needed more. "Please," she begged.

Luca laughed a little as she wove her fingers into his hair, attempting to guide him to where she wanted. He planned to make love to her slowly. Her honeyed essence tasted so delicious on his lips. Feeling her quiver, he knew how close she was to going over the edge. Sensing this, Luca halted and began to leisurely kiss her pink mound. He wanted to bring her up to the precipice and back down, over and over until she was ripe with need. Teasing and tantalizing.

"Luca, please, don't stop. I need…I need…" She couldn't finish, feeling as if she was riding a roller coaster of passion, up and down.

"Mmmm….what do you need? Do you know how delectable you are? I could stay here all day," he joked as he began to create a crescendo of sensation once again.

She smiled, realizing he was purposefully driving her crazy. "Luca, please…please lick me," she pleaded.

"You mean here?" He playfully sampled her clitoris and started to build speed and pressure with his tongue.

"Yes, there. Oh my God!" She realized she was starting to scream. *Oh well. Fuck the captain.* She gave up on worrying about being seen or heard.

"Or do you mean here?" Luca inserted a thick, long finger into the heat of her sex, quickly followed by two. He pumped in and out of her core, sweeping his broad flat tongue over and over her clit.

"Yes!" She screamed again. Samantha was starting to shake. She fought for breath; her head rolled backwards as her body tightened like a spring.

"Or did you mean here?" Luca put his soft, firm lips around her swollen pink bead, sucking. At the same time, he stimulated the stretch of skin inside her by slightly crooking his fingers upward toward him. He loved hearing her scream in pleasure, loved making her feel good. It was music to his ears. Unrelenting, he kept up the torturous delightful invasion, bringing her into a rapturous state of frenzy.

"I'm coming! Yes! Luca! Luca!" The crest of an incredible climax broke over her. Samantha felt as if she was floating out of her body as a zenith of pleasure rocked throughout every cell of her being. She grabbed tightly on his hair, holding him to her. Quaking under his touch, she gasped for breath.

Relishing the sweet taste of Samantha and the sound of her climax, Luca was hardened in arousal. He climbed over her, resting his forearms next to her head. The tip of his erection pressed against her wet entrance. Belly to belly, he reveled in the feel of their flesh as one. He smiled down on her as she slowly opened her eyes.

Every inch of her skin was hypersensitive after the amazing orgasm Luca had given her. Feeling his weight above her, she gazed at him through heavy-lidded eyes, and smiled back. "Did you enjoy teasing me? Because I sure enjoyed it. That was unreal."

She couldn't get over how incredible he made her feel. She'd gone years never being able to come during intercourse, yet this man knew exactly what to do to make her body sing. It was as if he'd known her forever.

"I love you, Samantha," he affirmed. "You have no idea what you do to me."

"I love hearing you tell me that. I love you. I want to be your wife, to be with you, forever. I guess I just want to keep saying it and hearing it to make sure this is real."

"Oh, this is real, all right. So is this." Luca dipped his head and passionately kissed her. Their tongues danced together as he drove his velvety steel shaft into her hot center. Samantha was slick with need and ready to take all of him as he sheathed himself in a single, smooth stroke.

Luca stopped kissing Samantha so he could look into her eyes as he possessed her. She was so responsive to his every move, and he could not seem to get enough of her. Unhurriedly, he rocked in and out of her, enjoying her tight heat. Rolling over onto his back, he brought her with him so she was on top.

"That's it, baby. Ride me, good and slow," he directed. He placed his hands on her waist, letting her set the pace.

Samantha hadn't been on top very often, but it was something she had yearned to do. Writhing on Luca, she closed her eyes and let the sensation take over her body. Arching her hips, her breath hitched as her clit brushed against his pubic bone. She pressed down to meet his every primal thrust stimulating her sensitive nub.

Luca was lost in her rhythm. His heart beat for this woman. She was resplendent and sensual, so open to discovery. He took his time, provocatively surging into her again and again. Luca splayed his hands across Samantha's ass: massaging her, guiding her. The sight of her perky breasts mere inches from his face teased him. His tongue darted out to capture one. She accommodated his silent request, leaning toward him so that he could suckle her tightly beaded point. Taking it between his teeth, he bit down slightly, then sucked it once more.

Samantha moaned in blissful pain; his bite tingled down to her aching sex. She could feel the rise of her orgasm evolving. So close, but she needed more of him. As if he could read her thoughts, his fingertips approached the crevice of her bottom. The feel of his hands on her so close to her ass, where she'd learned to experiment, thrilled her. She couldn't explain her urge; it felt like a driving primal pulse within her. Encouraging him, she pushed herself further into his hands.

Luca sensed that she craved the touch of him inside her. Reaching around her mound, he glided his forefinger over her wet folds. Lubricating his hand, he moved around her back again. Softly, he feathered his moist digit around her rosebud. He felt her shudder under his touch, yet she pushed back again, seeking more.

"Is this what you need?" He continued to circle her bottom.

She shook her head, not wanting to voice her desire.

"Come on, Samantha. Let go. It's okay to let go. Tell me and I'll give you want you need."

"Inside me. Please," she panted. As the pace and tension increased, her heart raced. She wanted it, needed it.

"Yes, so nice. I love how you open for me," he whispered. Slowly and gently he slid a digit into her untouched need. Feeling her clench, he guided her. "That's it baby, let me in. Relax, feel me and push back a little. Ah yeah, you're taking me." He felt his finger slip all the way into her tight hole. Her core began to quiver and clench down around his cock. She was going over the edge.

A thrilling awareness ripped through Samantha upon Luca's dark invasion. She felt deliciously full. As soon as she'd felt his finger enter her from behind in conjunction with his engorged masculinity, a mind-shattering orgasm slammed into her. Rocking feverishly, she thrashed above him, riding the glorious climax. He was thrusting up into her hard; the sound of flesh meeting flesh rang through her ears. Her senses had never felt so abundantly bombarded. She screamed Luca's name wildly as she came. "Yes, Luca, fuck me, please," she cried.

Luca thrust up into her over and over, possessing her, taking her. Hearing his name, he reveled in how easily she submitted to the throes of passion. As soon as he'd filled her, she fisted his swollen shaft in a tingly hold, pulsating around him.

Seeking to bond with her further, he extended a claw, slicing his own wrist. He held the beaded blood to her pink lips, and she instinctively captured it, sucking greedily. Shocking her into another climax, his powerful blood filled her mouth. She came fast and hard and took him with her. Losing every last shred of control, Luca jarred and spilled his hot seed deep within her.

Lying still beneath Samantha, Luca's body celebrated the simultaneous wild release they'd experienced. Their bodies mingled as one as they drifted into a relaxed state of euphoria. Samantha rolled off Luca onto her back. He wrapped an arm around her, pulling her close to him. She lazily draped her leg over his and placed a palm on his chest. An awareness of calm settled between them. Having sated both their physical and emotional selves, they silently touched and luxuriated in their newly blossomed love.

Samantha immediately felt Luca's blood whirr through her veins. She loved everything about Luca and realized that after weeks of turmoil, she simply was at peace. She loved him more than she'd ever thought was possible.

He'd helped her transform from mere mortal to witch and soon she was to be his wife.

Tracing a finger on his chest, she looked up to meet his eyes. "I want you to know that in this moment, I've never been happier in my entire life. These past few weeks have been life-changing for me. I felt horrible about what happened, not knowing. I was scared about being a witch…actually I hated being turned into a witch. And maybe my gifts still do scare me a little bit," she admitted. "But I don't care if I never remember what happened to me. I am who I am now. There's nothing but the future ahead of us, and I can't wait to marry you, to start our life."

He kissed the top of her head. "Me too. It's strange. I've been living for hundreds of years, but ever since I met you, I've realized that I haven't really been living. Or loving. Don't laugh, but I feel kind of reborn, so to speak. I need you in my home, my bed. You're already in my heart."

Samantha and Luca lay naked in each other's arms for over an hour on the deck, talking and planning for their future together. A lazy ride back up the muddy Mississippi eventually brought them back to their port. The sounds of street players ripping jazz tunes along the waterfront welcomed them home.

CHAPTER EIGHTEEN

Two weeks had passed since Luca had asked Samantha to marry him. As if she was living in a dream, they had fallen into a comfortable rhythm. Samantha spent her days planning and training with Ilsbeth. She'd nearly forgotten the chaos of her tribulations with Asgear and the amulet. The stray wolves that had escaped had never been found. Pack troubles temporarily calmed, Kade and Sydney had returned to their mansion.

Having them as neighbors was great company for Samantha. She didn't know anyone else in New Orleans yet, except Luca's friends and Ilsbeth. She'd grown closer to Sydney, happy there was another human woman around to talk to on occasion. Sydney and she had lunched a few times, discussing wedding plans. Sydney and Kade planned to elope since Sydney had no family, while she and Luca were still deciding what to do.

She'd called her sister, Jess, and told her about the engagement. Jess was thrilled and making plans to visit within the month. She also filled her in on how she'd become a witch, and explained Luca's vampirism. Her older sister seemed to take it in her stride, wishing she'd been the one who'd been turned into a witch. Jess had always been a bit more adventurous than her. Samantha felt like she'd had all the adventure she'd ever wanted and then some. Passionate sex with Luca was all the excitement she needed to keep her blissfully content.

Samantha hadn't told her parents about her vampire lover or her newly-acquired magic. Her parents could be quite reserved and she thought it best to tell them in person. Ringing her mother, she simply told her that she'd fallen in love with a wonderful man, they were engaged and she was moving to New Orleans. Happy for Samantha, they'd congratulated her and told her they were anxious to meet him. She laughed when she hung up the phone, thinking about how that get together would go. *Hi Mom and Dad. Meet Luca, my fiancé. He's a vampire. And oh by the way, I'm a witch now. Yeah, I've given up computers and can make fire with my hands.*

She hadn't really given up computers. Kade had offered her a job working in Issacson Securities in the technology division. She agreed to do it part time, given her new responsibilities and training at the coven. Xavier, Chief Information Officer and fellow geek, would be her new boss. They got along really well, and she was looking forward to starting her new career once she moved. Having already given notice at her old job, she arranged for movers to pack and bring her belongings to her new home.

Her home. Luca's home. Their home. At first, she'd thought it would be strange moving into his lovely Garden District mansion, already furnished. But Luca insisted they redesign the interior together. He desperately wanted, not just a menagerie of precious collectibles, but a warm loving space. A home they'd built together with love.

Sometimes Samantha was amazed at her gentle giant. There was no doubt that Luca could be a dominant, impressive man, especially in the bedroom. Yet time and time again, he'd shown Samantha his tender heart, caring for her like no other man had ever done. She loved him back with every ounce of her being.

That morning, she'd made plans for a dinner party with Luca's close friends and a few of her sisters from the coven, to celebrate their engagement. Samantha had even coaxed a reluctant Dominique into coming over, promising she'd find a willing human donor who'd be interested in taking care of her specific nutritional needs. Acquiescing to Luca's demand for peace, Dominique had agreed to call a truce, especially after hearing of their engagement and that they'd be co-workers. Samantha apologized for what she'd done to her even though she still had no memories of silvering her.

Even though Luca insisted she hire a caterer for the event, Samantha planned on making a few of the dishes herself. She'd always loved to cook, but had never had the time or anyone to cook for when she was single. She knew vampires didn't eat much, but planned on donating any leftover food to a local shelter immediately afterwards. Her aunt had given her the recipe for homemade bread, so she was busy kneading the dough when Luca walked up behind her and kissed her neck.

"Hey there, home early today?" she asked, enjoying the feel of his chest against her back.

"Yeah. Now that I've gotten things under control again at the office, I can work from home like I usually do. Besides, I thought I'd see if you needed any help today," he offered. "I can't tell you how delightfully strange it is to see a hot woman in my kitchen rolling dough in her hands. Once upon a time, I thought I'd be alone forever. Now here I am, wishing I was that dough."

"You're sweet. Let me wash my hands, and I'll see what I can do. I'd much rather be running my hands over your body than playing with bread." She winked. "Besides, there's not much I really have to do to get ready."

"I'm gonna go downstairs, take a shower and wait for you. Don't want to interrupt you, or I won't get to taste that secret recipe you've been hiding. Did I ever tell you how much I love hot buns?"

His double entendre wasn't lost on her. "Well I have some hot ones with your name on them. Just give me a minute, and I'll be down to join you," she promised.

Luca turned to look at her and noticed her cheeks were dreadfully pale. "Hey, you okay? You look as white as a ghost. I wish you'd let the caterers do everything. Come rest with me before the party," he pleaded.

"I promise I'm fine. I'm just a little tired from all our non-stop, mind-blowing sex. Now go on. Shoo. I'll be down soon. I promise."

Reluctantly, Luca went downstairs, but something was bothering him about the way she looked. She hadn't seemed tired but then again, he'd been gone all morning. Maybe she'd been out in the garden earlier and the late summer heat had gotten to her.

Samantha watched him go downstairs. The truth was that she hadn't been feeling well, but her optimistic spirit kept her going. She was so excited about the party that she wasn't about to let a little lightheadedness ruin it. A few times during the morning she'd needed to sit down from the dizziness. Normally not one to feel faint, she chalked it up to the intense sessions she'd been having with Ilsbeth.

Every day, Samantha spent several hours training and testing her powers. She'd learned how to better control her call on the elements, no longer afraid that she'd mistakenly set fire to something. Instead of spouting in tongues with little understanding, she had started studying Latin and other foreign languages used in the spells. Ilsbeth had given her the responsibility of shoring up the coven's digital library and website after she'd been able to breach its security. Reorganizing the database gave Samantha the opportunity to sift through and learn everything important to being a sister within the coven. She'd committed to learning the craft and actually found herself having fun every time she mastered a new skill.

Patting the dough one last time with oil, she covered the bowl to give it time to rise. After washing her hands, she dried them and decided to join Luca. Maybe he was right. Maybe she just needed a nap before the party.

Halfway down the stairs, her vision started to blur slightly as a wave of nausea rolled over her. Grabbing the railing, she steadied herself. A few more steps and she reasoned that she could make it over to the sofa. By the time she reached the landing, she could no longer stand. A tunnel of black enclosed her as she fell to the ground.

Luca took a hot leisurely shower, hoping Samantha would take it easy. He knew she was looking forward to celebrating their engagement, as was he. But he was worried she'd been overdoing it with all her training at the coven and then insisting that she had to cook at least one dish for the party. He would have been happy with just champagne, but had given in to her desire to create a more human-like affair that would allow her to meet his friends. It was also an opportunity to do something wonderfully normal, given all the nasty supernatural events that had preceded tonight's festivities.

But Luca worried that Samantha's usually fair skin looked a lighter shade of pale. Despite her best attempts to hide it from him, he could sense she was suffering from malaise. It didn't make sense. He was very careful with their blood exchanges, ensuring that he never drank too much from her and that she'd always drank his in return. Energizing and virile, his blood should have had her blushing pink with vitality.

Deciding to surprise her he lit the candles in their room, turned on soft music and lay naked on the bed, awaiting her presence. Fifteen minutes went by before he lost all patience. Annoyed, his worry rose yet again. *Stubborn woman, must still be cooking when she doesn't need to do that. What she needs to do is rest.*

Sliding on a robe, he exited the bedroom and spotted Samantha lying still on the floor. He felt a surge of an emotion he'd long forgotten, terror. Had she fallen down the stairs? Was she alive? He breathed a sigh of relief after hearing her normal heartbeat. Rushing to her side, he scooped her up into his arms. "Samantha, darlin'. Come on baby. Please wake up," he begged.

Slowly Samantha's eyes fluttered open. "Ummm....what happened? How'd I get here?"

"Dear Goddess, I'm so glad you're awake. What happened? Are you in pain? I'm calling a doctor." He knew doctors existed who served supernaturals. Kade had called for one who'd checked him out after he'd been kidnapped. He reached for his phone and frantically flipped through his contacts list looking for the number.

"No, Luca. I don't need a doctor. Please just call Ilsbeth; she can look at my aura. I think it must be the magic. Something's wrong. I've been using a lot of energy when I've been training. I told you it was exhausting. I just need to close my eyes and rest," she insisted.

There was no way in hell he was letting a witch diagnose his wife-to-be. Sure, he'd call her, but he was also calling the doctor. "Okay, stay here. I'm going to go get your robe, a glass of water and make the call. Don't move," he ordered.

After calling both the doctor and Ilsbeth, he phoned Sydney and Kade to ask them to come over. They waited outside his front door for the doctor to arrive. Within thirty minutes, Kade escorted the doctor downstairs. Luca was surprised to see how young the woman doctor was, given that he had no recollection of her from when he'd been ill.

She extended her hand. "Good day, I'm Dr. Sweeney. Do you think we could move the patient into the bedroom so I could take a closer look at her?"

"Certainly." Luca gently cradled a sleeping Samantha in his arms and carried her into the bedroom. He laid her on the bed and pulled a sheet up over her.

Ilsbeth poked her head into the bedroom, having come in late. "May I stay, Luca?" she asked quietly.

Luca shot her a look of irritation, blaming her 'training' for Samantha's health issues. "Come in, but let the doctor work," he growled.

Luca and Ilsbeth watched patiently as the doctor took blood and pulled out her small lab kit. "Exactly how long has she been dizzy?" the doctor asked.

"This is the first time she's passed out. She never even told me she felt sick. I noticed she was pale upstairs, and I insisted she rest. Right before you got here, she said she'd been exhausted from her training with Ilsbeth," he sneered. "Did you have to work her so hard?"

"Magic would never do this, Luca. If anything, she should be getting stronger, healthier. She's been taking your blood. I can see it in the brightness of her aura. In fact, her aura is the healthiest I've ever seen it. Quite extraordinary, really. It's almost iridescent. It's almost as if she's..." Ilsbeth shook her head, not wanting to speak without the doctor's consent. It was not her place to tell Luca what she suspected. Deciding to leave the room, she left him and the doctor to work alone.

Samantha slowly woke up, hearing voices in the room, and was surprised to find herself a specimen under several pairs of peering eyes. "What's going on?" she said with a hint of annoyance. "Oh my God. Did you call a doctor? I told you that I'm fine. I just need rest. You took blood?" She looked down at the band aid on her arm. Irritated with the unnecessary attention, she pushed with her hands and sat straight up in bed, much to Luca's dismay.

Dr. Sweeney sat on the edge of the bed and held Samantha's hand. "How are you feeling? Can you please follow my finger with your eyes?" she requested, shining a light into her pupils. Flipping off the light, the doctor glanced down at the blood results. While most doctors sent out for results, Dr. Sweeney carried a basic lab kit with her, since most of her clients were supernatural in nature. She ran a full lab out of her office.

"I'm fine. I can't believe Luca called you. I'm afraid my fiancé overreacted. Really, I'm just a little lightheaded. This is so embarrassing," Samantha said, trying to convince everyone she was fine.

"Well, it's good to know you plan on getting married," Dr. Sweeney commented nonchalantly and began to efficiently pack away her supplies.

"What the hell's that supposed to mean?" Luca was pissed. The doctor was supposed to be diagnosing Samantha and she was talking about marriage? He had a mind to call Ilsbeth back into the room.

"What I should say is congratulations, you're pregnant." She smiled ruefully and walked over to the door. "Now of course, this is quite a special event. It is rare that a vampire can breed, but I'm certain that as a witch, you knew it was a possibility."

Samantha couldn't have been more shocked if the doctor had told her she was going to the moon. It couldn't be. No, Sydney had said vampires don't have babies; they'd discussed it at length during one of their lunch dates. She wanted children but that didn't mean it could actually happen. And while Luca said that he also wanted children, she'd assumed he meant they'd adopt, not literally create one of their own.

Luca was sure his heart had stopped beating. A baby. He couldn't believe it. He'd queried Ilsbeth weeks ago, but hadn't given a thought to birth control, considering how seldom it happened. He couldn't help the broad, proud smile that broke across his face. He jumped into bed with Samantha, needing to be closer to the mother of his child.

As the shock wore off, Samantha held a protective hand to her belly. "A baby?" she whispered, and beamed at Luca.

"A baby," he repeated. "My precious Samantha, we're going to have a child. I love you so much." Luca embraced her on the bed, not caring that Kade, Sydney and Ilsbeth had come into the room. Despite having spectators, Samantha and Luca kissed each other gently.

"A girl to be exact," Ilsbeth noted. "Babies who are born of vampires and witches are girls. And your little girl will bring her own special magic into this world. She will be quite exceptional, of that I am certain."

"Well, of course she will be. Just like her mother. Beautiful and magical!" Luca could not stop smiling. *A baby. A family. A home.*

Sydney and Kade wrapped their arms around each other, happy for Luca and Samantha. It was unbelievable how this little witch had transformed Luca. Once cold and serious, he now was truly enjoying life, exuberant about the future.

"Okay, everyone, as much as I enjoy sharing this phenomenal news, I really need a bit of privacy. It's time to get ready for the party," Samantha stated as if she hadn't just fainted.

"No, no, no," Luca asserted.

"Doctor?" Samantha looked up at her with puppy eyes hoping she'd get the correct response.

"You're okay for the party, but you are to remain seated for the rest of this evening. Also, you should expect to be taking daily naps from now on. Don't wait until you feel dizzy to lie down. As soon as you are tired, rest. While the fatigue and nausea are perfectly normal, you need to go easy. Usually women don't faint but it can happen, as you just found out. As far as your training, no more than one hour per day. In another month, you'll be feeling much better. Luckily for you, your pregnancy will be only six months. One of the benefits of being supernatural," she quipped. "Okay now, I expect to see you in my office next week, Samantha. Luca's got my number."

After thanking everyone for their assistance, Luca and Samantha lay quietly in bed. She cuddled into him, resting her cheek on his broad chest. They were both thrilled to be having a baby together; neither thought it could really be happening. Unassumingly, Luca took her hands in his.

"Samantha."

"Yes, daddy-to-be?"

"I was going to wait for tonight, to surprise you. But now, this news. I'm so happy. I never thought. Damn, I sound incoherent. Okay, just close your eyes."

She closed her eyes and added, "I'm not sure if I can take any more surprises today."

"I think you'll like this one." Slipping an engagement ring on her finger, he smiled down at her. "Since I'm not so good with words right now, I'll simply say, 'I love you.'".

Samantha opened her eyes and glanced at the stunning ring he'd given her. "I love it! Thank you, it's beautiful."

His head dipped down as he captured her lips. Deliberately seeking her sweetness, he swept his tongue over hers. They kissed lightly, unable to stop smiling; altogether exhilarated from learning they were expecting.

Samantha laughed. "You know, this is crazy, don't you? A month ago, I was down here for a conference, and now I'm a witch who's getting married to a vampire. And we're having a baby who's going to be a witch."

Luca laughed. "How are we gonna explain this one to your parents?"

"Guess we'd better get married soon, huh?"

"The sooner the better. I can't wait to hear her little feet running around this house," he said excitedly.

"Hey, speaking of running, is Kat going to make it tonight? I invited her you know, but she hasn't called me back. I left a message on her cell phone. I sure hope everything's okay. And Tristan, it's a shame he couldn't be here tonight either. Told me had some sort of pack thing going on."

"I'm sure Kat is fine and we'll celebrate with Tristan when he comes down here again next month. No worries, my little witch. Tonight is for celebration, and I want to spend every minute showing off my new fiancée and sharing our good news."

Luca held Samantha as she drifted off to sleep. He did wonder why Kat hadn't replied to their invitation, but he didn't want Samantha to have concerns tonight over the wolves. In the morning, he'd phone Tristan to tell him about the baby and make sure he and Kat were all right. Regardless of wolf problems, he now had a family to care for; it was not his responsibility to monitor pack concerns. As requested, they had flown Kat down to New Orleans. He knew both Tristan and Marcel would have her back. As far as Luca knew, their pack was still actively patrolling the area in search of the two escaped wolves. He guessed they would have made their way back to New York by now anyway.

Kissing Samantha's soft hair, he gingerly touched her belly, knowing his daughter was growing inside. Peace. In all his life, he'd never felt it. Today, lying here with his mate, Luca had finally found it within her magic embrace.

~·❀· *EPILOGUE* ·❀·~

Tristan burned down the open highway on his Harley. Aside from going wolf, there was nothing like the freedom of tearing it up on his steel horse. Returning from a week of running his wolves had brought a much needed peaceful vibe to both him and his pack. After helping out with the mess down in New Orleans with Kade and Sydney and trying to keep Kat out of trouble, his own wolves needed his attention.

He smiled, considering the she-wolves who had vied for his attention over the holiday. Preferring to keep jealousy and discourse to a minimum during their run in the wild, he'd rebuffed their advances. Sure, he'd danced with a few and flirted shamelessly, in his usual style, but he'd decidedly stayed celibate. Tristan wanted to keep his head clear and focused, and women certainly had a way of blurring the lines. At the very least, they took up a lot of his time, and time was a commodity when it came to pack activities. Instead of self-indulging, he'd given of himself, concentrating on the needs of all the wolves.

It was no secret that the pack elders yearned for him to mate, but Tristan knew it wasn't going to happen anytime soon. Leading the pack was an earned honor that he enjoyed doing alone. After all, he was by no means lonely; the ladies were drawn to him like bees to honey. Everyone knew that the Alpha happily played the field as long as no commitment was required.

Tristan had made up his mind a long time ago, that he wasn't willing to settle for any woman just for the sake of mating. Yes, there'd been women he liked a lot over the years, but no one female was a true mate to his wolf. The only serious relationship Tristan had had in recent years was his friendship with Sydney. While she was well and truly an Alpha female, she was human, not wolf. So while they'd made love on occasion, and he'd even asked her to move in with him, he knew she wasn't his mate.

He admitted to himself that watching his good friends find love struck a chord in his heart. Kade and Luca were at peace and truly seemed happy. At times, it made him wonder if perhaps he was missing out on something in life. Regardless, it wasn't as if he had even a hope of finding his true mate within his own pack. While many of the she-wolves appeared quite lovely on the outside, he knew that most only wanted him for his Alpha status. And the human women he'd met were mostly interested in his bank account.

Despite the pressures to create a breeding pair for the pack, which would greatly increase the number of cubs born to all wolves in the pack, Tristan had no intention of giving into an arranged mating. No, he'd grown up seeing many an Alpha pair irrevocably tied through a forced mating, hating each other, yet shackled together for eternity for the sake of their wolves. Even though the archaic custom was still practiced in a few regions, Tristan and his brothers had long ago begun the tide of change from old world to modern pack laws. As a result, all of the Livingston brothers lived unmated, but were contentedly and successfully leading their packs. Adhering to the law of the natural selection of mates, they frowned upon imposing an artificial Alpha mating. The new tradition bred strength and happiness into his pack members. Tristan felt strongly about the law; he would not be forced into a pairing nor would he force others in his pack to submit to it either.

The shit storm that New York Alpha, Jax Chandler, had caused was brought about by his perverse belief that a male Alpha could simply pick his wolf as his mate, indifferent to her agreement. Tristan had always felt strongly that not only would his woman submit to him of her own volition, she'd also choose him as a mate. So when Jax decided he wanted Kat for his mate, there was no way Tristan was letting that asshole simply take his baby sister. From what Marcel had relayed to him, things had settled with Jax. Marcel had spoken to him over the phone, explaining clearly that Kat was in no way interested in becoming his mate. Jax was understandably irritated by her brush off but told Marcel that he'd back off if that's what she wanted.

However, Tristan didn't trust that Jax would give Kat up without at least a face-to-face meeting. It seemed too easy that with one call from Marcel, Jax would give up his claim. After Marcel had told him that Luca had been attacked and had killed Sköll, who claimed to be a New York wolf, how could he trust that Jax would back down? It had been reported that at least seven wolves had been killed outright, and two were missing. Over the past two weeks no one had spotted them, despite large sweeps of Marcel's territory. Despite Jax's insistence that Sköll and his wolves were not from his pack, Tristan and Marcel weren't convinced either way.

When he got home, Tristan planned to call Kat to tell her to stay down in New Orleans for a few more days, to take some more time off before returning to Philadelphia. It had only been a few weeks since Luca's attack and Tristan wanted to make sure things were nice and calm at home before she returned. Being down in New Orleans would make it harder for Jax to abduct her if he didn't keep his promise. By the time Tristan reached the city, the Sunday traffic had died down. Taking the direct route into town, he figured he'd stop off at Eden. While away, he'd left his longtime manager and friend, Zach, in charge of running the club. After a quick inspection to make sure there were no problems, he'd go home and call Luca to congratulate him. *Damn bastard was getting married, too. His friends were dropping like flies.*

He smiled, thinking of the petite sorcière that had captured Luca's heart. Now, she was a lesson in perseverance, he'd thought to himself. She'd been through hell and back and now was making great gains as an elemental witch. Before he'd left on his pack run, Luca had called, and spoke about her like she literally walked on water. Tristan had teased him about being whipped, but he honestly was happy for his old friend.

Rounding the corner, Tristan's tires came to a screeching halt as he pulled into the parking lot. Police cars and fire trucks flashed their angry lights as spectators watched the melee. Tristan jumped off his bike, and ran up to the front entrance. Grey smoke billowed upward as the firefighters put out the last of the flames. Zach held up his hands, begging Tristan to step back.

"What the fuck is going on here?" Tristan demanded.

"I had to run an errand. I was only gone for thirty minutes, man. I swear."

"I don't give a shit if you had to leave. I am only going to ask you one more time, what the hell happened to my club?"

"Police say someone broke in and set off a Molotov cocktail in the main room near the long bar."

"Security cameras?"

"Not sure, 'cause they won't let me in. I've been trying to tell them about the cameras. I don't know the extent of the damage yet. And Eve, she's still in there."

Eve was a fifteen foot yellow boa constrictor, who was on display behind the bar. She wasn't exactly cuddly but Tristan had raised her from a baby. He needed to get in the building to see if she was alive.

"Fuck!" Tristan raged. Someone had deliberately set fire to Eden; not enough to burn the whole building down, but enough to send a message. Sensing that the trouble with the New York Alpha was far from over, he pulled out his cell and called Marcel. His suspicions were confirmed; Kat was on the run from a couple of rouge wolves. Her car had been carjacked and they'd killed her driver. She'd managed to make it into the marshlands and had led them on a chase, narrowly escaping capture. Marcel was on his way to pick her up and was setting a trap for her attackers. Tristan cursed Jax Chandler as he ended the call.

Ignoring Zach's pleas to stay out of the building, he charged forward. As much as he wanted to interrogate Zach about witnesses or what else the police had said happened, he knew that he could find the kind of evidence that only a wolf could identify. A hair. A nail. Body fluid. A scent. The perpetrators might have left an identifier behind. This had just become personal, and he vowed to go on the offensive.

Firemen and policemen shouted at him as he tore into the building. Tristan trod carefully as he entered the main room, near the dance floor. The entire area was charred; a fine black soot covered every surface in the room. A barrage of chemicals from the extinguishers along with kerosene permeated the scene. Normally, the club would have been thoroughly bleached in the morning hours; there shouldn't have been any odors remaining except the jarring whiff of Clorox.

Foam and water made walking slippery, but he was thankful it was now clear of smoke. Approaching Eve's vivarium, he noticed someone had broken the glass. She was missing. Maybe one of the firefighters or policemen broke the glass and took her? It was also possible that the perpetrators had done it and that she'd escaped on her own. Tristan walked behind the bar inspecting the area for evidence of his snake, but saw no trails in the soot or foam. Someone had carried her.

Sniffing the air, Tristan lifted a board that had fallen off the wall. Underneath it was a small pool of blood; he dipped a few fingers into it and held it to his nose. Female blood. The scent was heady, but he couldn't place it as a shifter, witch or vampire. Yet it wasn't exactly human either. If she wasn't a wolf, then that meant Jax might not be involved in this stunt. With no other identifiable scent besides Zach's, she was most definitely a person of interest. He'd tear up the city to find the woman who'd torched his bar.

Tristan wiped the blood on his jeans and scanned the room, surveying the vast damage. He predicted they'd need to tear the entire structure down and rebuild. Releasing a sigh, he resolved to find the arsonist and put an end to Jax's nonsense, especially given the ambush on his sister. The two events had to be connected.

Leaving the bar, Tristan heard screaming mere seconds before he registered the sickening sound of creaking. As if appearing in slow motion, flecks of ash floated gracefully from above. Tristan only had time to look up before the charred ceiling came crashing down upon him, crushing him into the rubble.

The Immortals of New Orleans

Kade's Dark Embrace
(Immortals of New Orleans, Book 1)

Luca's Magic Embrace
(Immortals of New Orleans, Book 2)

Tristan's Lyceum Wolves
(Immortals of New Orleans, Book 3)

Logan's Acadian Wolves
(Immortals of New Orleans, Book 4)

Léopold's Wicked Embrace
(Immortals of New Orleans, Book 5)

Dimitri
(Immortals of New Orleans, Book 6)

Jax's Story
(Immortals of New Orleans, Book 7)
Coming Spring 2015

About the Author

Kym Grosso is the award winning and bestselling author of the erotic paranormal romance series, The Immortals of New Orleans. The series currently includes *Kade's Dark Embrace* (Immortals of New Orleans, Book 1), *Luca's Magic Embrace* (Immortals of New Orleans, Book 2), *Tristan's Lyceum Wolves* (Immortals of New Orleans, Book 3), *Logan's Acadian Wolves* (Immortals of New Orleans, Book 4), *Léopold's Wicked Embrace* (Immortals of New Orleans, Book 5) and *Dimitri* (Immortals of New Orleans, Book 6).

In addition to romance, Kym has written and published several articles about autism, and is passionate about autism advocacy. She also is a contributing essay author in *Chicken Soup for the Soul: Raising Kids on the Spectrum*.

Kym lives with her husband, two children, dog and cat. Her hobbies include autism advocacy, reading, tennis, zumba, traveling and spending time with her husband and children. New Orleans, with its rich culture, history and unique cuisine, is one of her favorite places to visit. Also, she loves traveling just about anywhere that has a beach or snow-covered mountains. On any given night, when not writing her own books, Kym can be found reading her Kindle, which is filled with hundreds of romances.

• • • •

Social Media/Links:

Website: http://www.KymGrosso.com
Facebook: http://www.facebook.com/KymGrossoBooks
Twitter: https://twitter.com/KymGrosso
Pinterest: http://www.pinterest.com/kymgrosso/

Want to get the latest release information? Sign up for Kym's newsletter — http://www.kymgrosso.com/members-only

CPSIA information can be obtained
at www.ICGtesting.com
Printed in the USA
BVOW06s0122210217
476738BV00009B/119/P

9 781480 199262